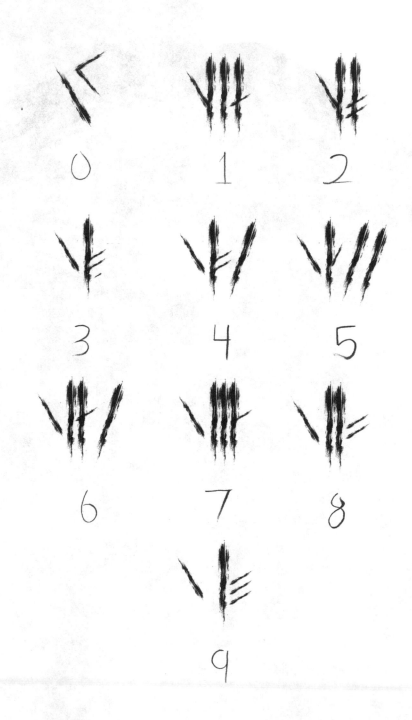

This is the story of Jacob,

Our leader

Every event in this sacred document has been gathered up from recorders of the people that were near him. His people. Close friends, family, and a personal journal of his.

I always knew I was meant to do something in my life and I would never give up in what I believe. Which is this...

To reach for what it is that it is meant for me to do, and to protect the ones I love. To make sure nothing will harm them.

My name is Jacob, and if you are reading this you are allowed to read, for you are special people of mine. But, if you are not allowed know that we will be watching you.

I was about ten years old in the year of 1849, being born on the fifth day of May in 1839. I am the second to the youngest of four children born to my parents, Mary and John. I had two sisters, Kate and Mary Ann, and a brother Joshua. My sisters were the oldest, Kate being the eldest, and Joshua was the youngest. We lived in California in Santa Clara County. My father migrated from the East Coast of New England and my Mother was a native of California, she was petite and had Native American traits. My father was very tall and husky, he came here for a better life. Word had spread east that the state and town were booming with mills, especially mining.

Our family was considered a middle-class to lower-class family. My father was a very hard worker and worked at a nearby wood sawmill. My mother took care of us when my father worked. This was for most of the day as we only saw my father at night. He would come home and we would all have dinner together. Thinking about it now, these were the only times I remember talking with him, laughing and sharing the day.

My first memory occurs around this time. Just an ordinary night when my father came home from work. Before this I have, no recollection...

"Kate get your brothers at the lake and tell them supper's ready."

"Yes, Mother." Kate hollered out to us, "Jacob! Joshua! Come back, supper is ready!"

I sat by the lake in a daze feeling as though I was in a dream.

To this day I can still dream it vividly.

I close my eyes and I can hear everything that nature has to offer to me. The sound of birds, the wind blowing through the trees, fish splashing in the water, and every time I feel this dream my head moves up and I see a particular mountain.

"Jacob! Let's go! Ma, wants us back." Kate beckoned.

"Huh?" Shook from my dream, "oh, ok come on Joshua." Collecting my brother I headed toward the house.

"Pa!"

"Hey Son. Where is your brother, Joshua?"

"He's outside, Pa."

"Kate, go get your sister from the room and I will go get Jacob."

"Yes, Ma."

"Jacob come in supper, is ready." Pausing Pa looked at me with a trace of concern. "What's wrong Son?"

Those days I would spend as much time as I could outside. Whenever I was called back into the house, especially if I had been out for quite some time, I just had this sad feeling inside. I would look at the other houses around us and watch the people walking, talking amongst each other. Always, I had a lot of worried feelings about heading in.

When my mom pulled me towards her I was in a daze.

"What's wrong?"

"Nothing, Ma."

"Come on, supper is ready and your Pa is here."

I hardly knew my father since he was constantly working to keep us alive and together. Often I would try to say something to him, but never knew what. The hard fact of it was I hardly had any special moments with him. No recollection of any if I had. I was very saddened by this and it was the main reason why I was so shy growing up. I wasn't ever the talking type.

"How are you, Son?"

"Good," I replied out of habit.

"Jacob, look at your Pa when he is talking to you," said mother.

I could not look at him. For a long time he was a stranger to me.

Our food was scarce and we ate every bit of it. We could not let it go to waste.

"Eat all your food kids," Mom would tell us.

"Yes Ma," everyone replied but me. I rarely responded to that comment.

"How was your work, John?"

"Too much of it Mary," Pa sighed looking tired. "A lot of people are working to the bone and there is talk that more people will be migrating here. The word is spreading, from what I have heard at work and around town, that this land is promising. Seems everyone wants a part of it."

"Well, at least there will be more help coming and enough work around here," Ma kept optimistic.

"That's what I'm afraid of, Mary. I put us here to be away from the other people. We can't have very many people knowing."

"Knowing what, Pa?" My sister Mary Ann was sharp and always curious.

"Nothing Mary Ann." Pa was fast to silence her questions.

Every time the "knowing talk" would go on I would see my mother react in a worried or concerned look. Again, I would be silent. Silent, yet observant.

"Everything will be ok. Yes Mary Ann, more people will be coming over to this small town of ours soon." He continued.

"More kids Pa?" asked Mary Ann.

"Yes, I am sure kids will be coming also."

After dinner it was time for bed. We did not have the luxury of single rooms to ourselves. There were only two rooms in our small house and the bathroom was outside, an outhouse. My sleeping arrangements were unpleasant, but I remember that it was where I spent the most time with my brother and sisters. We would pretend together at night and play, making our own little stories and adventures. I was a listener and never really spoke much. Out of all of us my oldest sister Kate was the best storyteller. I always asked her questions during each story. I was always able to talk with Kate, no matter what we might be talking about, we both had a special understanding of each other. Kate heard me talk more than anyone else in the family, actually. I guess I looked up to her.

During the mornings we would wake up and get ready for school. This year I was already into my second year, because school started at age eight. Joshua was the lucky one of us since he was too young to go to school and didn't have to go. Both my sisters enjoyed school, however I did not. Before I started school I never had a problem with other people. Our school was at Saint Anthony's Church, it was located in the town of Almaden. To get there we would ride our horses. When I got a little older I remember going into town and seeing people looking at us and vividly recall how they would stare. My sisters however, did not seem to notice like I did. I almost always saw things they did not.

In class I was about the same, mainly a listener. The other kids would say things to me or talk amongst their friends. Still, I did have a few friends and their names were Matt, Brian, and Jack.

Matt was very active, well, more like hyper. He was a good kid and we talked a lot. He would come over to my house more often than the others and we would play. Brian was the athletic, competitive type. He never liked to lose in games or any challenges for that matter. Jack was more like me. He was very shy and not very talkative with anyone else, besides me.

We all lived in the same small neighborhood and sometimes, usually on the days when I didn't take my horse to school, I would walk with my friends. It was a long walk but we did not mind at all.

I have to be honest, I did love to learn in school, even though some of the kids and environment made me uncomfortable. I remember school being like this.

Brian would say, "hurry you guys, before we're late! Miss Ross will ring our necks!"

We ran into the classroom before the bell stopped ringing. I always sat in front and my friends would be in the middle towards the end of the classroom.

In school we had these writing boards. We would use them in class for English and we couldn't forget them or else Miss Ross would hit us on the hand with a ruler, as a punishment.

"Good morning class."

We would answer together, "Good morning Miss Ross".

I loved Miss Ross. She was a very good teacher to me and worked closely with me to make sure that I understood what was being taught. Honestly, I learned my best reading and writing lessons from Miss Ross.

"Class let's begin with spelling," she said.

I would always hope she wouldn't call me to spell out in front of class. I was a little afraid to do so, but luckily for me she did not call my name first. However, the second student she called was me.

"Jacob, can you come up and spell out a word for us please?"

I stood up and walked to the front of the class.

"Can you spell out Apple for us?"

"Ahh-A-ppp-P," I could hear the other students giggle in the back of the room as I spelled.

"Pp-P...L-E."

"Very good, Jacob." Miss Ross was sure to make me feel good about my spelling.

Returning to my seat I looked around the hall and could see a group of kids snickering at me. For the rest of class we practiced the alphabet.

Most days after school I would go home with my sisters, but occasionally I would walk back with Matt, Brian, and Jake. It was always great to talk with my friends outside of class. We would tell jokes and re-tell things that happened in school. It was one of the only times I could let my worries go and just have fun. One afternoon in particular however, things were much different.

That day, when school was over, I went outside and met my friends Matt, Brian, and Jake. Whenever I planned on walking home with the other boys I would let my sisters know my plans and make sure they went home on the horse. Kate found me while I searched for her and she had Mary Ann by her side.

"Jacob, we are leaving to go home." Kate checked in with me. "Are you walking home with your friends?"

"Yes, Kate."

"Ok see you at home. Be sure to get back before supper or else Ma will fret." Our mother always wanted to know where we were.

When my sisters left I started walking with my friends, and as we left the school grounds, away from our class, I could hear that the same kids from earlier were giggling at us. We just ignored them and kept on walking.
We made it just down to the main road before a group of those boys stopped us.

One boy called out, "your ma is a red skin and your pa is white skin, what does that make you Jacob?"

In that moment I realized that all the snickering I had heard that day was directed towards me. I was surprised and didn't know what to say back.

"Huh?"

The other boys giggled liked it was the funniest response they ever heard.

"He doesn't know what he is!" The gang began to walk away, laughing.

This was the first time I had ever heard someone say something like this to me, but my friends didn't seem to care less about what that other boy said. After they left we picked up the pace. My friends walked on either side of me and we continued on a path we would never forget.

During the rest of our walk home we talked about what we were going to do the days after we left school. Along the way I would always find a walking stick, so I picked one up. I wasn't sure why I would do this. I guess it was one of those things that was a habit of mine. Jake would always find rocks and throw them around. Matt would hum or whistle and sometimes make jokes. We each had our own traits during our walk.

Matt joked. "Boy, Miss Ross' breath smelled today, huh?"

We laughed at Matt's joke as we neared the lake. We would often stop at this spot just to hang out and spend some extra time together. Sometimes we would play in the water or fish. We would grab sticks and stab the ends of them into the lake, trying to catch crawdads or bugs like grasshoppers or dragonflies, which we used as bait. Mostly though, we talked together.

Matt asked, "what are you guys going to do when you're about your Pa's age?"

Brian answered first, "I wanna have a farm with a lot of horses."

Jake said, "I don't know."

When it came to me everything passed through my mind, thinking of the things I wanted to do and things I didn't even know about yet. I was searching for words and about to answer when we heard something. We froze.

There were noises being made directly behind us. As the rustling grew louder we tensed. We knew that whatever was making the noise was heading out of the woods and straight for us. We stood up and faced the direction of the racket head on.

Just then six older and taller kids came out of the forest, right before us.

"Hey you!"

One pointed right at me and yelled.

"Yeah, you!" He looked like he was the oldest out of the bunch with blond hair, blue eyes, and facial features that were very elongated. He had a mole on the right side of his chin.

"Me?"

I responded, even though I knew it was me all along he wanted.

That tallest boy with the mole stepped closer. "Yeah, what are you boys doing here with him?"

Matt took a step towards him and yelled back.

"What do you mean?"

"He is not like you, why are you with him?" Mole Boy walked closer.

"Because he is our friend!" Matt and the taller boy were nearly nose and nose now.

"You boys better leave here now!"

Brian stepped up next and hollered, "we are not leaving our friend."

The boy with the mole looked grim.

"I am giving you boys one last chance to leave," he said very deeply and slowly, raised a fist.

There was a long pause. We all knew deep inside they were older and taller than us, but we didn't care. For me, I wasn't even sure why those other boys were acting like this. I was more curious than nervous as to why they approached us and called me out.

We didn't move.

"Ok then," the boy led the others, "y'all get them!"

The group of boys came quickly in on us. We turned and started to scatter.

Brian broke out first and one boy went after him. He was one step ahead of the boy and managed to get away. The boy let him go.

Jake next. Even though Jake was shy he was very sneaky and quiet. He knew the lake area better than me or the rest of us. He succeeded in hiding from one of the boys.

Matt was grabbed by one of the group and was struggling to break loose and did, though only for a moment. Just as he was about to get away one of the boys snuck up behind him and grabbed him. The gang brought Matt back towards the edge of the lake.

As for me, I broke away and was running, always looking behind me every time I had a chance. For a split second I turned back. In another split second I was down.

I tripped on a fallen tree and tumbled to the ground. My leg felt like someone had punched it. I was down in pain and couldn't move when I saw three of the gang surround me. Another boy came towards me, then the one with the mole stared back to me. It was clear by then what they were after. I knew they intended to capture just me.

"Get him up," the mole boy yelled. Two of the boys grabbed me.

"Bring him back over here!" He pointed to where my friends and I had been sitting last, at the edge of the lake where Matt was.

When they brought me back to the spot I looked up and saw Matt being held by one of the boys. The boy started smiling then the others followed and started to laugh.

"Listen here boy," it was Mole Boy. He was talking directly to Matt.

"This friend of yours is bad, you shouldn't be around him or things will happened to you! He is not like the rest of us, ya hear?"

Matt didn't believe a word of it.

"Let me go!" He yelled at the boy, trying to move around and fight back. Another boy grabbed his other arm, pinning Matt in place.

Mole Boy got closer to Matt and spoke very low.

"Do you know where this boy is from?"

Matt struggled and said nothing.

"His Ma is Indian and his Pa is white, like us. His Pa is like the rest of them for doing this."
My mind began piecing the mole boy's story together. At first I hadn't quite understood what he meant.

So what does it matter that I'm different, I thought. Just because my Ma is Indian.

Now though, I knew what he was saying.

Suddenly, Mole Boy turned to the two boys holding me and yelled his next order.

"Dip him in the lake!"

My eyes glanced at Matt and I could see the fright in his face.

I tried to get out. I struggled to break loose of the boys. Suddenly one of the other boys came towards me, right up close, and punched me in the stomach. My air was gone from by body. Then the boys turned me around and dragged me to the lake. As we got closer I was still trying to catch my breath, I was in such a daze. They had me in their arms and I tried so hard to break free. Gasping, they slid me into the water as Mole Boy came beside them. Outstretching his hand he grabbed my head hard, yanking at the hair. He was furious.

"I don't want you around our boys or your friends anymore, ya hear me Red!"

I did not know what to say and couldn't really talk at all. I was confused and the blow to my stomach made me speechless.

The boys smiled sternly in return.

"As you'll have it, Red."

In one movement the boy dug his fingers tight against my scalp and pushed my head under.

My vision was blurring and all sounds were lost. At that moment I couldn't breathe, couldn't cough, and couldn't think. I struggled against the strength of the boys pinning me under. The hand at my head held me still as I twitched and yearned to break the surface for air. Every fiber of me fought to break loose but with every attempt I was lost more and more to the water.

The rest of the memory is foggy. At one point the boys let their grip loose and my head breached the surface. Gasping for air I looked at the boy with the mole who in turn looked behind him. Matt had broken from the hands of the other boys.

Just when I thought it was about to end Mole Boy called out to his gang, "let him go boys! We got what we want here!"

He had been talking about me. Turning back, he drowned me some more. Only this time, the water didn't hide the cruel pleasure of his laugh while he did it.

The last thing I can remember was seeing flashes of images in my head. There were many that appeared before me. Images of my family, my sisters, my parents. Memories of my school friends and better times at the lake. Only one image burns fresh in my mind today.

A circle. Clear and cut, surrounded by an arching circle made of feathers.

To my understanding, after what others have told me of this event, Matt ran home to get his father and mother. He told them what was happening at the lake and led them back to help. They didn't live far and as they ran closer Matt's father hollered at the boys to let me go. The boys holding my body ran quickly but Mole Boy stayed an extra moment to push me under. It was only when Matt's father got to the edge of the lake did he finally let go.

Fainting in and out of consciousness I saw Matt on my left side and his parents on the right. They started to talk to me, but I only heard muffled noises. It was very hard to hear what they said. I fell back to unconsciousness.

When I awoke I saw Matt's family and then my father approaching me from a distance.

"Son are you ok?" It was Pa.

"I, I think so Pa." My stomach and head pounded in pain.

"Don't worry Son, you'll be ok. You stay put and don't move, ok?"

"Yes Pa."

I watched my father walk outside with Matt's father. From the bedroom I listened to them talk.

"Thank you for taking care of my son, Mr. Eaton."

"No problem, John."

"I'm much obliged,"

My father paused, "So Paul, what happened to my son?"

"Some older boys tried to drown him at the lake, John."

"Why would they do such a thing?"

"I don't know, maybe just a bunch of juvenile boys I guess. Well John it's a good thing he's ok now, could of been a lot worse".

"Yeah, thank you again Paul."

"No problem John."

"I will get my boy now and head on home."

Right when father was about to come back inside Matt camc out to them crying.

"Mr. Smith! The boys said bad things to him."
 "What's that Son?"

Paul, quickly grabbed his son. "Matt it's ok, he knows already. Be quiet now ok?"

Matt cried out again, "but Pa!"

"Son." The voice was firm and final.

Matt's father must have held a firm gaze because Matt came back into the bedroom. He did not talk after that.

After some time Pa came in too and picked me up. Mr. Eaton followed.

"Thank you all again for taking care of my son, Paul."

The Eaton family nodded and father took me home.

———————————

I remember my father carrying me and seeing the sky full of stars. It felt like they were moving while my Pa was walking.

I looked towards him, "P-Pa."

My father looked down, "yes Son."

"I am hurting everywhere."

"I know Son, you're going to be ok. We are almost home."

I turned my head back to the stars and closed my eyes.

The next day I woke up to the daylight beaming through the window. I got up and looked around; I was in my room. I heard my mother and father talking outside in the yard and my mother sounded very worried.

"John, I thought we were away from all of this?"

"Mary, it's going to be around everywhere we go. It's going to stay with us and our kids even when they get older. They have to be strong and understand that someday."

"Our boy almost got killed yesterday!"

I could hear Ma stifle a cry.

"We don't know if they were going to do that or just bully him. I don't know what happened."

"Well I do not want my boy to get hurt every time he goes out, he should just stay at home for a while and help out with the chores for a bit." I could hear Ma click her heel to the ground and imagined a plume of dust rise from her boots.

"I will find out who the boy's parents are and see what's going on."

I visualized Pa holding Mother's arms.

"The neighborhood is a small one, so it won't be a problem finding who they are."

My mother must have nodded because next I heard Father begin to walk towards the house. Coming through the front door and peeking into the bedroom he looked at me.

"How are you doing, Son?"

"I am feeling ok, Pa."

"Good." He started to collect tools. "I want you to stay home from school today and help your Ma with the chores. I also want you to clean the chicken pen for me too, ok?"

"Yes Pa."

My father left and I looked out the window again. I saw my mother hugging my sisters. It looked like more of an assuring hug. She held them for a long time before letting them leave for school on horseback. After they had gone I walked outside and saw my mom begin to tear up. She turned her head away from me.

"Ma? Are you ok?"

"Yes Jacob, I am ok." She hugged me. "I am so glad you're ok."

I smiled and hugged her back.

"Come on Ma, let's go. I need you to help me with some chores."

Sometime during that morning my father was on horseback when he saw Matt walking to school. The meeting was described to me years later, by my father.

"Mr. Smith!"

My father turned around and came back to him. "Yes Son."

"How is Jacob?"

"He is doing better Son, he is staying home for a few days to help around the house."

"Oh, that is good." Matt paused, "Mr. Smith I also have something else to say."

"Yes, Matthew?"

"I know some of the boys that tried to drown Jacob."

"What's that, Son?"

"Yeah. I seen a couple of them that live around here."

Matt pointed to the houses that they lived in.

"Do you know what some of them look like Son?"

"Yes Sir," Matt replied. "Some are very tall and some a little taller than me. A couple have brown hair and one had some freckles. The one that tried to drown Jacob, he grabbed Jacob's hair and put his head in the water, he has a mole on his chin. I don't know where that boy lives, but I'm sure it's near, Sir."

"Thank you Matt, I will talk to their parents soon."

"Oh Sir, I want to tell you that they really frightened us and they were shouting bad things to Jacob like, 'Red' or something like that."

Father was surprised by this last comment and thanked Matt.

"You better be getting to school Matthew. Thank you for letting me know."

As Matt left Father stared out of disbelief, thinking of the conversation, he was not sure he should tell Mother about what the boys were saying to me.

They called him, Red. Was all Father could think of.

The days following the incident at the lake I did not sense Ma was the same. For days to come my Pa kept me home and I didn't attend school. Pa wouldn't even let me go to the lake, my special spot. Every day I would just help Ma around the house with the daily chores. Things had changed not just for me, but for everyone.

For my Pa, well he didn't talk as much as usual. When he would leave and come back from work the only thing he would say to me, before he left again, was a reminder. He would say, "summer is almost over Son." Or something like, "get ready to start pulling out the corn and the rest of the vegetable plants."
My sisters were going to school and I was constantly wondering why they were going and not me. I would see other kids in the neighborhood walking or riding their horses to school and wanted to join them. My parents kept me home though.

Usually I think of my mother as being very spirited and happy nearly always, but not during this time. I remember one day, while I was fighting with the chickens, I looked at my mother through the chicken pen wire. I could see her washing clothes and hanging them outside. She was not smiling as much as she used to though.

After finishing in the chicken pen I went inside, where my mom and brother Joshua were. Once in the front door my mom immediately looked down at my shoes. They were worn from the chores and chicken pecks.

"Jacob I'm sorry, but your shoes need to last you for a while. They're not too bad, and you know we can't afford new shoes for you. Try to keep them chickens off you, alright."

I looked down shameful.

"Oh," I said. "I hadn't noticed, Ma. They're fine with me."

I was trying real hard to try to put a smile on my mother's face.

"Ma?"

"Yes Jacob." "

"What's for supper today?"

Without glancing up she replied. "Left overs, Jacob. I am going to add some more vegetables into them too."

"Well...Ca- Can I help you?"

She glanced to my tattered shoes then looked directly into my eyes, smiling. From that evening onward I helped her every night to prepare dinner. It was our special moment we made each day together.

One evening during these months, when my father was coming home from work, he stopped by a small township close to the lake. Within this grouping of houses was the home Matt had pointed out to him. The house where the gang of boys lived, who had tried to drown me. I didn't learn of this meeting until many years later, however.

My father recalls passing by the first house, because there were no lights on, so he went to the second that was alight. Father approached the door and knocked. No one answered the door. He knocked one more time and waited.

Someone began to come, he heard footsteps.

While he waited something caught his eye. To the left of the door was a window and someone had rustled the drawn curtain. A boy appeared in the window.

"Hello Son, is your father home?"

"No he is not," said the boy.

"Is your mother home?"

"No, but she will be back soon."

My father looked around and thanked him. After the boy closed the curtains my father headed on foot towards the other homes. Particularly to the one Matt had pointed out to him.

He knocked at another house and a woman answered the door.

"Hello Ma'am, my name is John Smith. Is your husband here?"

"No he is not Mister Smith, he would be back in a little while I assume."

Father nodded. To the side of the woman a young boy appeared. Pa describes the boy to be just as Matt had said. Taller than me, darker hair, and had a mole on his chin.

"Do you mind if I talk to you in private, Ma'am? I promise it won't take very much of your time."

"Not a problem Mister Smith. Wait inside Son," she turned to the boy. She closed the door behind her and she stepped out to speak with my father.

"My name is Janet Hill, Mister Smith."

"Nice to meet you Mrs. Hill," my father shook Janet's hand. "Mrs. Hill, I have some questions about your son."

"What about my son Mister Smith?"

"Well, apparently he was involved in a situation by the lake with some other children. They put a pretty good beating on a few other boys in the area and one of them happen to be my son."

"What makes you think my son was involved, Mister Smith."

"Mrs. Hill, my boy's friend describe him to me and he pointed to your house."

"What? What is the boy's name?"

"Matthew. Now Ma'am, please listen to me. I am not looking to punish the boy, he is your son and I am sure you will take care of it. What I want is to talk to your husband, so this will not happen again."

"I don't believe you, Mister Smith! My son is a good boy. A very good boy!"

"I am sure he is, Ma'am. I am just asking you this because I found my son beaten and nearly drowned. I am just looking for answers, that's all." My father's eyes scanned to the right and saw the boy looking through the window.

"I am sorry Mister Smith, but I can't help you. Good bye."

Mrs. Hill abruptly turned her back on my father, returned into the house, and locked the door. My father looked at the house with disbelief then walked to his horse and rode back home.

By this time in our life Father had been working at the mill that year and he knew just about everyone in town. So later that week he was surprised that when someone new came up to him. Someone he didn't know.

"Are you John? John Smith."

"Yes, who's speaking?"

"I am the husband of Janet Hill." My Pa immediately recalled his search in the township for the gang of boys. " I am the father of the boy who you were looking for a week back."

"Oh, nice to meet you sir, I-"

"Can we talk outside for a minute?" The man cut him off.

They both walked outside of the mill and the other workers stared out of curiosity.

"Listen John, I don't want you near our house again or something is going to happen."

"What do you mean?"

"Just stay away from us! You hear?"
"Well Sir, I was looking to speak to you that evening. I didn't mean any harm. Your wife said you weren't there. I explained what was going on and what happened to my son."

The man looked eye to eye to my father out of surprise. He pointed at him and said again, "listen...stay away or else."

The man started to walk back in the mill. My father, frozen in disbelief, followed behind while everyone looked on. There was rarely any tension around my Pa at the mill, everyone there liked him and knew him to be a good man. It was no surprise to my father that his fellow workmen looked alarmed that day. Still, my father finished his day at work like he would any other as if nothing had ever happened.

That night I was helping my mother prepare the table for supper when I saw my father on his horse through the window. I walked to the front door and opened it to greet him.

"Hi Pa."

"Hello Son."

I noticed the sudden sadness and frustration in his face.

"Pa, are you ok?"

He got off his horse and came up to me, putting his hand on my shoulder he smiled.

"Yes Son, is you mother inside getting supper ready?"

"Yes, she is Pa."

"Can you call her over here, please?"

I nodded then walked inside. Mother was in the kitchen.

"Pa wants to talk to you outside."

I could see curiosity in her eye.

"Ok Jacob, watch your brother for me. Ok?"

"Yes Ma."

Mother tidied up supper before leaving the kitchen. She called back to me and my brother before leaving the house.

"Jacob, tell your sisters we will be back. We are going on a little walk."

"Ok Ma."

My mother closed the door and I wondered what was going on.

————————

In later years my mother told me what happened that night.

On the other side of the door my mother met with my father. His face was full of sadness, but also anger. My mother walked closer to him and asked what was going on. My father looked to the ground and then grabbed my mother's hand and they started to walk.

He didn't say anything.

While they were walking my father took deep breaths, to try to calm himself down. Mother suddenly pulled his arm to stop him. She couldn't take the silence anymore.

"John, what's wrong? Tell me what's wrong!"

"Mary, what I tell you is not a good thing." He breathed deeply again. "It's going to anger you very much."

She needed to know, "John, tell me what it is. Now."

"Mary, 'member how I told you we are going to be ok? And how I always promised you that we will always be ok? That we can live here without any fear?"

"Yes John, you promised that."

He continued, "and that our kids wouldn't have to fear either, when they grow up?"

"Yes."

My father grabbed my mother closer to her and said, "they are knowing now."

My mother didn't understand, "knowing what John?"

"They know about our kids, Mary. The townspeople, they know about Jacob. That is why those boys went up to Jacob and his friends. They only wanted Jacob. I know this because I went to one of the boy's houses a week ago and tried to talk to their father. He was not there, so I talked to the boy's mother. She didn't want to believe what her son had done."

Father gripped Mother closer, drawing deep breaths as he continued. Ma said he was nearly shaking he was so tense.

"Mary, today the boy's father come up to me at work, by surprise. He warned me not to go near them, or where they live, ever again. Their son told his parents Mary, and the parents know. They are not going to do anything about it. I think it is time for us to be more cautious and keep a closer eye on our kids, Mary."

I didn't know it at the time, but that same night a letter arrived on our porch addressed to me. Pa had found it, but waited until the right time to tell me.

"Sorry J, Pa said Wwwe cant be freeinds any mo." At the bottom it was signed by Matt.

After that night everything changed.

Before my father moved us here in 1849 the United States had just won the Mexican-American War against the Spanish, winning control of California. When my parents settled in our town, called Almaden, it was only recently taken from the Spanish so most of the population was comprised of American white men and a couple Hispanics who were moving out. Few Native Americans stayed past this point, but more immigrants fled in from the American West, Europe, and Asia. It was only during the Gold Rush did I see the shade of humanity.

Since the Gold Rush was in full swing people from other states were noticing the excitement and migrating here, to California, to strike it rich. In no time our quaint hometown became very crowded. All across California, north to south, more homes and villages were being built to house the migrants. In our town they even built a hotel called the Casa Grande.

Before all this began, in 1824 a native of "Californio," by the name of Secundino Robles, discovered cinnabar deposits on vermillion rocks high in the hills above Los Alamos creek. Searching for gold he and his colleagues found nothing, their efforts all for not, and they abandoned the venture.

Then in 1845 a man by the name of Andres Castillero, a Spanish native, became interested in the red rock. Formally trained in geology and chemistry, Castillero experimented on the rock. After numerous attempts of heating, roasting, and frying the stones he made an astonishing discovery—mercury. Word flooded throughout the neighborhoods and nearby towns that there was mercury here and they called it, "our gold." People would walk around and say, "we have our own gold here!" It was fun to see this and wonderful to see people having parties and dancing throughout the night.

I was about fifteen years old by 1854 and a lot of things had happened over the course of the past five years. My skin drastically got lighter as I aged and I took this as somewhat of a blessing, but I was cautious since I had a lot of troubles growing up about my skin color. Still, now older I was not afraid of people looking at me anymore. I also wasn't the small, tiny boy anymore. I had seen a growth spurt and was almost about six feet tall by this time. I definitely received my father's height. I was also free to go out and walk around those days, to look at the town that was building so rapidly.

Before the influx of migrants I thought growing up that the majority of people were white. Here in my town that was the truth, but that wasn't true everywhere or for me, with my dark skin. My father put us here in this area to "mix in." Obviously, that did not work for us. It is of my belief that father did not want to live in an area populated by Mexicans, because well, of his skin and the fact that he was married to a native.

This year though, as I had grown quite older and taller, my parents knew that I could take care of myself. At last, they let me wander around the greater area and I saw other people and other cultures. Of course, I had to do my chores before anything, and since I was a young man now my chores became more intensive.

My father lost his mill job that year. I personally think it was not him losing a job, but more of him just walking away from it and not dealing with certain people there. However, he never wanted to talk about it around us. Still, I know it was something else by his expression. I believe he knew he was not going to be jobless long. Father knew about the recent mining spike and the Gold Rush here in the state so he got a job mining. It was owned and operated by The Barron, a Forbes Company. This was the first job Father had with a mixed-race of workers. Among his fellow miners Father was one of a handful of light-skinned men, but he suddenly felt okay, comfortable, to work there.

Although he never said this I remember the look on his face well. Whenever he got home from work he seemed satisfied. I think at that time he opened up a little more. I remember him coming home happy, always very dirty because he was working in a mine, but content. My family was too. I even remember my mother pleasantly washing his clothes, day after day with a smile. I recall my mother continuously washing his clothes, actually. The job, the people, the excitement of the year, and also it paid more than the mill - we were finally striking our own little gold mine.

That year my older sister Kate finished her schooling and helped my mother with the daily chores. Kate and my sister Mary Ann would go to the market to buy food for my mother. Mary Ann was still going to school, but was almost done. By now Joshua was about seven and he wanted to go to school, but my mom insisted he stay home and do chores. He would help me out from time to time and I would help him by going to get supplies for the barn and feed for the animals.

Before I would start to work I would go back to my retreat, the lake. I would just sit there and look around, closing my eyes from time to time. Even though I nearly drowned at that lake I was never frightened to go back. I was not afraid and I knew things were changing. I knew other races were coming into the neighborhood. Sometimes I would think of the intolerance and it was sad for me to see people act the way they did when I was a kid. It was almost as if all of a sudden, when there was a boom with work, everyone was getting rich and they seemingly brushed you off because of how you may look. They were happy, but why weren't they happy from the beginning? I would always remember that feeling growing up.

Sitting by the lake peacefully enjoying the breeze over the still water, I heard a noise behind me and I quickly turned around.

"Hey Jacob."

It was my brother, Joshua.

"Did you follow me here?"

"No I did not, I goin' fishing. See my pole?" My brother held up a branch with a line attached.

I smiled at him, "oh ok, don't fish too long then. We have to get back for supper."

"I won't, Brother," and Joshua dunked his line in the lake.

While Joshua was fishing I began thinking about my day tomorrow. I wanted to walk around the other towns, it was like a venture for myself. I had to figure when I could go. I was going to do my chores before sunrise then leave for the town. Deep in thought, planning what to do, I hardly realized after an hour had passed and I noticed the sun going down.

"Joshua let's go, Ma will get mad at us if we don't come home before supper."

Right when I said that I looked at the corner of the lake, near Joshua, and I saw them. Dark figures in the distance. I squinted to get a fix on it and shook my head, looking there again and the black figure vanished.

"Are we going?" Joshua yelled back.

I hesitated to respond. Looking back at Joshua I stammered, "yeah, let's go home."

When we got home my sisters started preparing the table. Joshua and I walked in and Mother asked us how our trip was.

"We didn't catch anything," I replied.

"Nothing Ma, but I'll get them tomorrow," Joshua finished, "I promise."

She smiled at us and continued to prepare supper.

I really felt bad for my mother. She did not want to mix with other people because she was afraid of what the others might say or do. I always asked my mother if she wanted to go with me to town and she would always say no. One day though I knew something would change for her. Something would come and make her happier.

It happened that night when my father came home with a surprise.

I remember it well. That night we had our favorite for dinner, leftover stew. We heard my father coming in, first the sound of his horse then his boots on the stoop. Coming in the house my father didn't act like anything out of the ordinary was about to happen or anything. He just came in and took off his jacket and shoes then sat down and started eating. I remember those days, when he worked at the mine, he ate a lot. He ate more than any other man could, but still stayed slim. This night was no exception and my mom began to worry when he didn't talk. Me, my brother and sisters just stared at my father.

My mother asked, "how was your day, John?"

He muffled from the food in his mouth, "gooood." Then he stopped to take a breather. "Sorry Mary, it went well, they are working us very hard. The work is never ending so that is good."

"I see," said my mother. After we all ate and my father stood up and looked at us then he fixed his eyes directly on my mother.

"Mary, I have good news." Pausing, he looked around at us all again.

With a look of wonder my mom waited for him to finish.

He looked at us all slowly then exclaimed, "we are moving out of here and getting a bigger house and farm!"

My sisters cheered and jumped. My little brother yelled out of joy and my eyes went wide open on that night. The room felt very positive and happy.

The next day after I was done feeding the animals I let my mother know I was going to ride into town for the first time and look around. She and my brother and sisters were getting everything in the house ready for the move. The move was not very far, a few miles at that. However, with a total of six people living in a house there were a lot of things to move out, not including the tools and equipment outside for the live stock. Needless to say, there was still much work to be done before leaving. We were all feeling the pressure and me in particular as I was dreading moving the livestock.

That day I left on my horse to go into town. Skip, my horse was a medium sized horse, but when I was a small kid he seemed very large to me. He was a dark brown horse and his name was Skip because he used to do this skip trot before he really started going.

When I got to town I saw a large amount of people within the town center. This was not a surprise though. With the booming Gold Rush and quicksilver mines crowds were common inside our town. As I rode in I saw a very exquisite stagecoach coming into town. Moving deeper among the homes I saw a very beautiful Spanish-style church on my left and to my right there was a small row of shops still being built. One looked like a tool and feed place and down the road I saw a much bigger grocery store, a newly built bank, and a couple buildings that read, "Jail" another "Sheriff." Of course there were also a few saloons, scattered here and there. Looking closer I saw an even bigger building being built. The sign said "County Courtroom and Town Hall" I stopped near this building and tied up my horse so I could wander around a little bit.

As I was walking through town I noticed people being much friendlier than they were before. I noticed how the people were dressed too. Some were very elegant for the era, but even though I was wearing my dusty farm clothes I did not worry about my appearance.

While I was walking a few men came toward me.

In passing they said, "howdy" and tipped their hats. This was common to our town so I did the same and tipped my hat, just as my father taught me as a kid. I started walking again looking around, looking at all the interesting people. Usually, I would say hello to my sisters when they were at school, but now that we were moving they were at home, so I merely walked by the school.

After I passed by school I noticed what appeared to be books stacked in a nearby store window. I walked towards the store, took my hat off, and walked inside.

Walking through the entryway there was a large amount of books on the right side of the shop sitting on a self that lined the entire wall of the building. I looked around a bit and headed towards the books. I saw a lot of people in this area, picking up different books by the spines and walking between the tight shelves. It was difficult to dodge their movements, but eventually I managed to get to the shelf I wanted.

I was amazed how many books were there. Pulling one out I read the title out loud quietly, "The Pit And The Pendulum, by Edgar Allan Poe." The book seemed very interesting to me, even though I still needed to learn to read and speak much better. I held on to the book and browsed around some more. I found more books that I liked, so I grabbed those as well.

By the time I was done I had gathered a heaping pile by

my side; then I noticed another section in the shop that displayed paper clipping of current news. After browsing through the articles I put them back and after I did so a woman came towards me.

"Afternoon Sir."

No one ever called me Sir in my entire life.

I thought to myself, maybe she thinks I am of adult age now. It was a different feeling to me and surely my expression was more of dazed and confused. Paused in thought, the woman spoke again.

"Sir?"

"Ahh yes... Hello ma'am. How much?" I pointed at my pile of books.

She looked at the pile, then me. Firmly she said, "they are two cents each sir."

My father would give me some money from time to time, but it was not much. I only had about 5 cents in my pocket. I asked the lady, "can I buy this one book ma'am?"

She glared at me with a frustrated look, maybe because I took all those books off the shelf and left them on the floor, only to purchase one. I pulled out my money and gave her two cents. She thanked me and I nodded as I left, grabbing my hat and book. That was a feeling and experience I will never forget. It was the first time I ever bought something just for myself.

As I walked towards my horse I went across the road to look at the sheriff's office. I never saw one before so I was a little curious to see what it looked like, especially while it was being built. Some of the men that were working on the building looked at me and stared for a bit. I just thought of tipping my hat since those guys did the same to me before. I tipped my hat and they acknowledge that, tipping their hats back.

During my time I spent in town I got used to the fact that if you passed people, or if they looked at you, all you needed to do was tip your hat. It was simply out of common practice, a gesture. Before this happened I did not believe what my father told me until I saw it with my own eyes. I started to smile too, tipping my hat to people that went by. I even tipped to the ladies who would smile after me. It was a good feeling for being the young man that I was.

The rest of that day I felt pretty good walking through town. I enjoyed the sights that I saw and felt comfortable there for the first time. It was also very exciting to see our small town changing so much.

As the day wore on the sun was getting closer to the mountains. This signaled that it was about that time to go back home and finish the rest of my chores. When I turned and looked at the sun I could see the tall mountain peak above me. I would always look at it when I rode with Skip. I was amazed how beautiful the mountain looked from the town.

I turned back and walked towards my horse and as I was walking I passed by one of the saloons. There was a clatter coming from within, loud sounds of laughter and music. I saw people go in and out from the swinging doors. Some of the men looked drunk while they were walking away from the saloon.

I continued to look in while walking. In the back of the saloon, in a far corner tucked away within the building, I noticed a figure of a man. I stopped to get a better

look of him, even though people were walking past me.
It was a man with tan skin wearing a taut and wrinkled
elongated face. He looked about my height and he was
just staring at me. I couldn't picture what he was
wearing, it was quite possibly the same attire just like
everyone else here in town. I paused for a moment then
started to walk away.

While I was walking away I noticed him move from the
corner and begin to leave the saloon. Going through
town some more he stayed behind me. He was following
me. As I walked on I saw him hide behind every
building, tailing me. I started to feel a little worried, but
I knew people were around so if anything happened
other people would see it. I tried to look less worried
than I actually was, toughening my face, and walking a
little faster to my horse.

When I got to Skip I saddled up and loaded myself onto
him. Riding onto the street I turned my horse to the
direction back home and as I did I saw the man again.
He was leaning into the shadows of a nearby building,
his hat was low and his eyes were covered by the shade
of its brim, but I knew it was him. It was an eerie
feeling, just him standing there and the area around me
got quiet. The sound around me felt muffled and
cloudy. I shook my head a few times to get my
composure back and everything came back. The sound
was normal again and Skip galloped out of town.

The sun was starting to go down and when I got home I
put Skip in the barn right away because I still had to
wrangle up the livestock from their pens. Joshua was
playing what was called hoop rolling in the back while
my mother and sisters were getting things out of the
house. I finished corralling the animals and walked to

the house to ask my mother if she needed help with anything.

"Yes Jacob, I do. Some of these tables and chairs need to come out and the drawers in our rooms need to come out also. They are too heavy for me and your sisters."

My older sister yelled out from a distance, "I can carry it all by myself Ma!"

My mother looked back, then looked at me, "try to get that done before dark Jacob, if you can. If you can't finish it your Pa will help you when he gets home."

Stepping in the house to get the drawers I was met by a scene of complete chaos. All of our belongings were everywhere, as if someone had ransacked our home. It was hard maneuvering the furniture out of the house to the backyard through all the mess. I think I ran into my sister Mary Ann a few times during the process. Joshua was just sitting around while we all moved items so I called out to him.

"Hey Joshua, wanna help me?"

My brother smiled and said, "sure."

Since I was the big brother he looked up to me a lot. Whatever I was doing he would quickly respond to help out, even with the chores. I can say he learned a lot from me and I would think I was a father figure to him since my father would work the whole day.

"Joshua, be careful when we pull this drawer out, ok? It's gonna wanna slide down, just let it slide down. Don't fight it or push the drawer."

My brother did not listen to me and he fell right on his rear. I had to grab the drawer so it wouldn't smash my little brother.

"Ok, hold on to it and I'll come around the front to help you out ok?"

When I went around I could see his knees were buckling from the weight of the drawer. I ran to my brother and grabbed the drawer.

"Ok, I got it Joshua. Why don't you go inside and grab some chairs from in the house and bring them out here?"

"Ok Jacob."

I continued to pull the drawers out and put them against the wall of the house. Joshua assisted with the rest of the furniture too, which was much easier and lighter. After not too long I had gotten the heavy pieces out and returned to my mom

"Ok Ma, the furniture is out, Joshua helped me out."

"Oh he did?"

My brother looked at my Mom and nodded, smiling sweetly.

My mom hugged him and said, "I am very proud of you, Joshua. You're becoming a very strong man, now wash up for supper."

"Yes Ma," and he ran off.

I looked at my mother and she winked at me. Together we headed into the kitchen to prepare dinner.

While we were cooking I told Ma about my experience going in town. I shared the way the town was changing and how everyone was smiling at each other. I told her about the men tipping their hats to me and how I did the same. As I spoke her face expressed looks of happiness and spirit. She knew I was comfortable and welcomed at last. I told her more and her face continued to glow, growing excited when I mentioned the buildings under construction.

"There was also a store Ma that had books."

"Oh yeah?"

"Yes. I went in a bought a book for the first time. It was only 2 cents, Ma. See, here's the book."

With delight my mother grabbed the book and said, "wow Jacob, that is wonderful! You better read that book, ok?"

"Oh, I will Ma."

She put the book down then asked, "so the folks there, they were nice to you?"

"They treated me respect and I treated them the same. I like going to town now."

My mother smiled, "that's good Jacob, very good."

I smiled then told her something I did not intend to. I spoke about the man that I saw, who was staring at me.

"He kept following me and looking at me"

She listened and asked what he looked like.
"Well, he was dressed like normal people do and he had a hat."

"And what else, Jacob?"

"What else?"

She nodded and I continued, thinking back about the man. "His face was very narrow, long, and he had wrinkles on his face."

I watched my mother's eyes get bigger every time I described a certain feature of the man.

"What color was this man's skin?"

I thought about it for a bit then I said, "he was the color of the trees, Ma."

My mother looked surprised and shocked, she suddenly grabbed me.

"What did he do to you, Jacob?" she was alarmed.

"I..I.."

"Tell me Jacob, what did he do to you? Did he harm you?"

"No. No, Ma he did not. I got on Skip and rode off."

She let go of me and then walked away from me, combing her hair with her fingers out of frustration. She walked back to me.

"Jacob, do not talk to him. You hear?"

Before I was about to say anything my mother said, "don't speak to him. Stay away from him. He is up to no good."
I paused and looked around.

"You hear me, Jacob?"

"I won't talk to him Ma, but I couldn't see him good. He had his hat on."

"Jacob, if you feel inside that it's him next time you go into town don't talk to him, ok? Stay away from him. He will cause trouble and harm our family."

"I..I won't talk to him, Ma."

Even though my mother forbid me to talk to the man I was still curious as to why he was looking at me. I was older now and not that boy who was beat up at the lake. I was not afraid of anyone, a brave young man at that. But my mother could see that in my eyes. She knew that I would find a way to learn more about the man.

"Jacob, do not talk to him. He will go after us, and your brother and sisters. He is very bad."

"I understand Ma, and don't you worry."

My mother left it at that and her eyes got a little watery. She smiled then turned around and started supper.

Over her shoulder she reminded me, "make sure Joshua washed up for supper and tell your sisters to help set up the table outside."

Since we moved all the furniture we had to eat outside at night. "Ok Ma, I will tell them."

This wasn't our first time eating outside. When I was a very young child my parents would camp outside, even before we had the house we basically lived in a tent for while. This evening was a very warm typical summer night. My mother put some candles out on the table as we all gathered around it. My little brother was excited and he was looking up at the stars.

"Look," he said pointing.

He hardly was able to go outside at night since he was young, so it was a very nice surprise for him. My sisters however, didn't seem very amused by it at all.

Suddenly, we heard the unmistakable sound of many horses galloping in the distance. Like a stampede of some sorts. We all looked towards the front of our house and saw my father round the corner, appearing with a huge carriage and six horses. We all stood up promptly, in amazement. My little brother ran to my father looking at the carriage. My father stopped and came down from the carriage and picked up my littler brother and smiled.

I said to him, "Pa, where did you get this?"

"I bought it, Son. It will help us with the move, make it easier and faster. So, y'all better eat up and go to bed early, we have much to do tomorrow. Alright?"

"Yes, Pa." My mother walked toward him and hugged my father. Smiling, she whispered something into his ear.

My father looked at us and said, "kids you all have supper then. I am going to talk to your mother in the front."

Father set Joshua down and he ran back to me. Ma took father's hand and they walked to the front of the house.

I knew the outcome of what was happening even before they talked. I knew because my mother had her worried look on her face. This was a telltale sign of hers. It was a look that we learned early on as kids, if we had done something wrong that Father needed to know about. Ma was going to tell Pa what I shared with her.

The next day would be interesting.

The next morning my father stayed home to move everything to our new house. It took a while to put the furniture on the huge carriage, but we did it. It was very grueling work. My mother and sisters put all the little things in wooden boxes as we loaded up the heavier items.

My father said, "this ain't nothin' Son. Wait until we have to move the livestock."

He got on the carriage, "Ok Son let's go. Joshua, you wanna come?"

Joshua ran to the carriage and yelled, "yeehaw!"

He jumped right up next to me.

My father called out to my sisters.

"Ok girls, we will be back."

My mother and sister called out and waved. My father let out a loud holler and the enormous power of the horses started us on our way. We were off and headed towards our new home.

After a couple of hours, a great distance away through uneven meadows and scattered oak trees, we got to the last turn of the road before our new home. I remember after that last turn on the trail that the valley just opened up. I could see the house from the distance. It was huge. Big for us or anyone else at the time. It sat in a large expansive part of the valley, surrounded by oak trees. Even from this view I knew it was twice the size of our old home.

I looked at my little brother and remember his reaction to seeing the house for the first time.

"Wow Pa!"

Beaming, I looked at my father and he was smiling proudly. My father rode towards the house and it looked bigger and bigger the closer we got. When we got to the front he turned the carriage adjacent to the front door and called the horses to a stop.

"Ok boys, let's get the furniture in and surprise your mother when she opens the door."

Pa never wasted time.

"Ok Pa," my brother and me said together and leapt off the carriage.
While we were taking the furniture down I noticed a deer in the woods behind our house. Even from the far distance I saw it looking at me. He paused, and so did I.

"Jacob."

I was still looking at the deer.

"Jacob!" My father called.

I finally shook my gaze from the deer and looked at my father.

"Come on Son, let's get this table in. Joshua, open the door for us."

My brother opened the door and went in first. We followed and as soon as we entered we were welcomed by an expanse of space. There was an entryway, apart from the main room. The house had many bedrooms. There were enough rooms for all of us. One for me and Joshua, one for my sisters, and one for my parents. Off of the entryway was a large room with a fireplace. This was where I knew we would all be spending a lot of our time, our family room. Behind the family room, apart from everything else was a kitchen that my mother would love. The walls were crafted of wood and the ceilings were higher than our old house, making way for a lofty attic in the rafters. It was home in an instant. My brother started to run around the house.

"Wow, are these stairs?"

He started to run up the stairs, "be careful Son, walk don't run."

Joshua still ran up the stairs with excitement.

Still carrying furniture, my father kept to his agenda.

"Ok, let's put the table right here near the window."

We placed it down and standing up I realized just how many windows were in the house. Light was streaming through and filling the home, bringing with it a very tranquil feeling.

My father went outside towards the carriage again, I followed him. He turned around, patted me on the shoulder, and smiled.

"Son, your mother told me what happened yesterday. I want you to promise me you will never to speak to that man. I do not want any trouble brewing. Now that we have a new home, I don't want anything bad to happen. Ok Jacob?"

I was getting tired of my parents telling me these things. I quickly said, "yes, ok Pa."
He looked at me for a bit and nodded.

"I know you're a grown man now and I can trust you. I know you can take care of yourself, Son. Mothers will always know their children as infants. Your mother will have it in her mind that you are still her little boy. You know she worries about you and your brother and sisters. That is just how it is, Son."

"I know, Pa." Even though he was telling me this tenderly Father did not scare me off.

"Pa, he just stood there and just followed me to my horse."

His brow dropped at this statement. "You have to be careful Son, even a stare can be trouble. Just watch everything around you and if you sense trouble always stay around a group of common people. Then they will leave you alone. Be careful, Son. You never know if he will pull a gun out and shoot you." He firmed his gaze as he said this. "Now that there is money to be made here people will be carrying guns."

I looked down and asked, "is that why you carry a gun, Pa?"

He looked at me quickly, as if he was surprised that I knew.

"Yes Son, you have to protect yourself. Especially when you have a family."

Even though he told me this, to look out for the bad people in town, I had already known people had guns for protection. Still, I knew nothing was going to happen to me because I was not the troublemaker.

"Pa, is that why there is going to be a sh-shieriff? A sheriff?"

"Yes Son. The sheriff will take care of the town and make sure no one is breaking the law. The sheriff will protect the people also."

"And the building next to the sheriff?"

"That is a jail. That's where they will put all the troublemakers when they break the law."

"I see."

"Just promise me Son, don't talk to that man. I don't know why he followed you. Stay away, ok?"

"I will, Pa."

My father patted my shoulder again. "Come on, let's get the rest of the furniture in."

"Hey Pa," I said to my father. He turned back to me and I continued. "I bought a book at the store in town yesterday. It is a storybook, Pa."

At the time I didn't know the difference between history, storybooks, and literature. My reading proficiency was still not up to par, however, I was captivated by this book for some reason.

"Oh yeah, Son?"

"Yeah, I am gonna read it tomorrow."

"That's good, Son. You didn't spend all your money on it, did you?"

"No Sir, it was only two cents."

"Good Son, you need to save as much money as you can. You will never know when you will need it."

"Pa, I want to get more books after."

"I will help you out, ok? I do not want you to spend your money. Save it."

"Thank you, Pa."

My brother suddenly ran down the stairs.

"Jacob, come look up here!"

"I will Joshua, let me finish helping Pa put the furniture in, ok?"

Father cut in. "Joshua, go grab the chairs and stools for me, ok?"

"Yes Pa."

My father turned back to me after Joshua had left. "Remember when I told you people will be leaving you when you get older, and you have to make decisions on your own?"

I was hesitant but answered, "yes, I remember Pa."

"Well, very soon you will have to start thinking about decisions for your life. What you want to do. You'll need to start thinking about things like work and having a family."

Even though hearing this at my age was common I still was confused and felt very young, but I did learn very quickly.

"I know Pa. I wanna make you proud."

My father smiled, "you're already making me proud, Son. You will be a good father when you're older."

———————————

Once all the furniture was in Joshua grabbed my arm and took me upstairs. As soon as we climbed the stairs my eyes widened with wonder. I stared and looked around this new space, it was so large in the loft.

"Look Jacob how far the window is," Joshua ran to the window and his voice echoed a little. "See Jacob?"

My father suddenly came up behind me with a smile and said, "boys, this is going to be your mother's room. So she can work on her yarn, but don't tell your mom. Let's surprise here when we bring her up. Ok?"

"Ok Pa," we said, eager to surprise our mother.

"Well boys, let's get going and help Ma and your sisters with the rest of the things." As we walked out my father locked the door with a key.

"What's that, Pa?" said Joshua.

"It's a key Son. It locks the door just like it does at our old house, but instead of locking it from inside, with the wood, you can lock it from the outside. See? When you're inside you turn this and it will lock the door Son."

"Oh," my brother said.

"Ok boys, let's go back and help out your mother and sisters."

By the time we got back my mother and sisters had finished packing. There were wooden boxes everywhere around the sides of the house. My father stopped the carriage in front of our old home and my mom came out.

"You boys want to start putting the boxes in the carriage now?"

Me and my brother started to put the boxes in the carriage and my father went around the back, to make sure everything was clear.

Kate came up to me while I was loading the boxes.

"How does the new house look, Jacob?"

"It's beautiful," I replied. My sister smiled and right when she started to walk away I whispered, "don't tell anyone yet about it, but Pa wants to surprise Ma."

"Oh ok, I won't say anything Jacob."

We pulled everything onto the carriage and rode to our new home. My father rode on the carriage while me and my brother rode our horses beside the caravan.

When we arrived my mother was very happy. Beaming, she jumped up from her seat and hugged my father and sisters. My father jumped out of the carriage and picked up my mother, bringing her gently down to the valley floor of our new home. She walked to the house with my father as we followed behind them. With so much delight my mother was speechless. Father kept holding her and hugging her as she walked through the house. My sisters were just like my mother, their eyes reflecting such joy as they saw our new home.

My father directed my mother up the stairs and she let out a cheerful cry. She was thrilled with the space.

"Mary, this is where you can work on your yarn. All this space is yours."

My mother cried and hugged my father.

_____

Later on, while everyone continued unpacking and exploring I walked out to the backyard and sat on top of the fence. This was where we would put one of the animal pens. It was very peaceful here. There were even birds singing. As I rested on the fence something caught my eye.

I looked to my left and saw the same deer as earlier in the day. He was just looking at me for a while and I looked back, holding his gaze. I started to smile at him and he looked toward the meadow and started to walk away.

I stood still and was silent for a long time after, for who knows how long. I let my mind drift away with the land and the deer and it's peace.

My father's footsteps broke the silence. He came up beside me and together we watched my brother running around the huge backyard.

"Let's go inside Son and have some lemonade before we start with the livestock. I wanna get them here before the sun goes down."

As we walked into the house I saw that my mother was already setting our cookware in the kitchen. My sisters were helping to unpack and they were all giggling together.

Our home was quickly filled by our happiness, as a family, and it flowed from every inch of our property.

———————————————

Wherever Father was taking me he was in a hurry. He was walking fast through the house quickly and grabbed his pack. He told my mother that we would return soon. I think he was in a hurry because he had to work early in the morning. Once we were outside again my father called my brother to help us wrangle up the livestock. Together we followed my father on our horses and headed towards our old home.

When we got there the cattle were very agitated, probably because no one was there and they hadn't been fed. Father told me and Joshua to feed the livestock before we tied them up to transport. Still on his horse my father instructed us on how to tie up the cattle. We were to work together to control them, one of us in the front and another behind to bring up the rear. All was to be done on horses. To add to the difficulty of the task at hand we had to add the donkey, which carried the chickens in a small carriage. As expected, my younger brother served as lookout as my Pa and I prepared all the animals for transport. With Joshua as a set of eyes he could let us know if any trouble came our way. This allowed for Pa and me to freely guide the stock.

Father seemed hopeful in this plan.

"If this works out we can get all our cattle to the new house in one trip."

Father moved swiftly and loaded himself on his horse. Tonight I noticed my father's gun was visible on his person, whereas every other day it was concealed. This was a sign to anyone who might want to make trouble with us. What I hadn't known about before was a second weapon. He had also uncovered a rifle from the side of his horse.

We began the slow journey back to our new home with the livestock. The sun was settling close behind the mountains in the background. I looked around, inspecting our progress, and everything seemed good. I started to look from my right to left and I saw Joshua on his horse, moving up to my father. While I continued to survey the land, keeping an eye on our animals, something odd happened. My horse's ears suddenly began to move around, repeatedly.

If I was ever worried about anything I always relied on my horse Skip. If something was going on, something out of the ordinary, he would react. I put my full trust in him because of this.

I knew then, when his ears were twitching, that something was going to happen.

"Pa! Skip's hearing something out there," I yelled.

My father was somewhat skeptical to the horse's reactions, and my theory of trust, and at times he wouldn't believe my suspicions.

"It's probably an animal out there Son, don't worry. Whatever it is won't come close."

I felt a tinge of doubt, but Father knew best. We continued to move on.

The sun was now half down and the light was starting to fade. When we came upon an open expanse of the valley my father wanted to stop and give the animals some water by the nearby steam. Waiting for them to drink I continued my lookout, thinking of Skip's alert state. Concerned, I went up to my father on my horse and talked to him.

"Pa, it's getting dark soon. Should we head out and get them to the house?"

"Don't worry Son, we will be ok. The moon was full last night and it should be full again tonight so that will be our light. We will head out soon." My father then started to drink his water and I went to go check the cattle to make sure they were drinking.

"Are you doing ok, Joshua?" I asked my brother from a distance.

"I am ok, Jacob."

"How's your horse doing?"

"Good," he said and continued to watch the sun setting.

My father then said, "ok boys, let's get going now. We're halfway there."

Even though the distance from our old home to our new home was about six miles it felt like it had doubled or even tripled that night. Mainly because we had to go in walking strides to keep pace with the cattle. Joshua helped my father wrangle up the animals while I drank some water then we headed out.

It was now night and the moon was full, its light glaring through the forest trees we had to get through. Up ahead the moon's shine illuminated our path, long and far ahead of us, as my father led the way.

Suddenly, my horse Skip stopped and pulled me back.

"Whoa! Whoa Skip! What's wrong boy?"

I could tell my horse was very agitated. Ahead of me, without calling out, I watched my father continue riding.

"What's wrong boy?"

Skip continued to breath heavily. His ears and head had begun to move at a not so normal pace, looking around. Joshua noticed me and stopped in his tracks. This halted my father as well.

My father looked back with a frustrated look.

"Whoa! Whoa!" My father said to his horse.

"Son, stay up front here. I am going the stop the animals so they don't run all over you."

My father rode past our livestock on his way to me, whispering words to soothe the horses and cattle. As he did this they began to slow.

I put my head on my horse's neck and I could hear his heart beating fast.

"Skip, what's wrong boy? What do you see?"

I looked up and I saw my father galloping towards me. Pa yelled, "what's going on Son?"

"It's Skip, Pa. He stopped and his hearts beating fast. Faster than normal for the pace we've been at. He's also looking around, like something it out there."

My father looked around the valley. As he did his own horse started to turn his head like Skip had, rapidly glaring every direction around us.

"Let's go Son, we need to go now." Pa sounded firm as he whispered to me.

I pulled on my horse and we went back to the animals.

My father took the lead and my brother broke off, coming back towards me.

My father yelled for us to go, shouting to his horse, "heya!"

Joshua did the same and the livestock followed. We began to move and I noticed that father was taking us at a quicker pace.

After a good thirty feet or so all the animals completely halted. I could sense from the distant trees there was something all around us. I looked around, but I saw nothing. I could hear things around us though and they were getting louder and louder.

My brother was a little in front of me and he was looking to his left to the woods. His horse started to look there as well. Strangely, all of the animals at that moment turned their heads in the same direction. All looking left. Then, without warning, all the animals looked to the opposite side.

My horse Skip started to get agitated again and started to stride left then right. I quietly tried to settle down my horse. The noise got louder around us then shadows started to emerge from the distance, as if they were hiding behind trees. Then I heard a new sound, a very distinct howl. More howling and cries followed it. Wolves.

My father quickly yelled out, "move it!" He tried to pull the rifle from his side, but his horse reared on to his back legs and Father dropped his rifle.

Joshua looked terrified. His horse was out of control and was trying to run away.

My father yelled again, "Son! Stay on your horse! Do not fall!"

Father tried desperately to keep the horse and cattle at bay, but the animals hastily ran away. Just as they started to move a pack of wolves came from behind me. Skip instinctively tried to flee, strongly shifting our path, but I wanted to hold him back. Chaos was surrounding us quickly. I saw my brother and father ahead of the pack and in that moment realized I needed to move with Skip.

I was one moment too late.

The wolves had cornered us. Skip was kicking as the wolf pack nipped at his ankles and unexpectedly Skip reared on his hind legs. In the confusion I lost hold of Skip's rope and was thrown to the ground.

Landing hard on the valley floor I scurried to my feet. Skip was kicking wilding in every direction, trying to ward off the wolves. I tried to reach for the reigns and somehow get back on him, but he was flailing. The wolves began to ease off Skip when they noticed me, giving Skip just enough time to run off.

"Skip!" I yelled as he galloped away leaving me with the pack.

I spun around as the growls grew louder and closer. The wolves were surrounding me and they looked ready to attack. I did not know what to do. I began to crouch down, searching the ground for a rock or branch to defend myself. There was nothing. The wolves took a step closer as the growling persisted. Just above their snarls I could hear a commotion in the distance. Father. Joshua.

It was about to happen. I knew they would lunge. The largest of the wolves looked most aggressive and seemed to be mocking me. Crouching lower it looked ready to pounce, just as I stood fully upright. As I towered over the wolf something strange came over me. I felt no fear of them. For some reason when I stood up some of the wolves growled meekly, like a dogs being disciplined, while others stopped all together.

Out of amazement I started to mock them and stare at the wolves. I moved to my left and could see them move away from me. For some reason I stuck my arm out in front of them and they started to look down, turning their eyes away from me. They did not stare at me anymore. The wolves looked intimidated. I brought my other arm out and moved both arms around to see what would happen. When I did they moved away slowly.

From a distance I saw my brother fall from his horse.

"Joshua!" I yelled and instinctively moved my arms.

When I did I pushed the wolves out of the way, without touching them. I was scaring them.

"Out!"

I yelled at the wolves and ran towards my brother. They began to scatter.

"Out!"

I ran as fast as I could to Joshua and my Father.

Father had his gun in hand and had fired a shot into the air, trying to startle the wolves away. By the time Pa did this the wolves had already fled though, because of what I had done to them.

Luckily my brother was ok, only a few bumps and scratches. My Pa continued to fire and yelled at the wolves.

Pa rode up to us, "you ok boys?"

"Yes Pa, " I said.

"Joshua, are you ok Son?"

"Yeah Pa, I am ok."

"Come on, let's get our horses home and then take care of our animals when we get back."

"Pa, they are everywhere. Our animals."

"Don't worry, we will get them. The animals are just scared. They are not very far."

I looked up to my father and said, "Pa, take Joshua with you and get the horses. I'll watch what cattle we have with us right now."

He grabbed his rifle and tossed it to me saying, "you know how to use it, Son. Use it if you're in danger."

I watched my father and brother ride off and tried to calm the cattle and the donkey. Surprisingly, nearly all our livestock were still in the meadow, just scattered about. Our carriage however, that the donkey was pulling had become damaged from the donkey's kicking and jumping. I was not sure if the chickens inside were still ok. The cattle were fine, but some of them had been bit by the wolves. Their legs were bit up real good and were bleeding.

My father took a long while to return, but I saw him in the distance when he did. As Pa drew nearer I did not see my horse, but my brother's.

"Where is Skip?"

"Couldn't find him. He must be a little ways out there now."

I was worried about my horse. Worried if he was in danger. I told my father, "Pa, I am going to go look for him. I will take Joshua's horse with me so you can watch the animals."

My father shook his head and grimaced. Looking up he said, "ok Son. If you take long I will start looking for you, no matter what. What direction will you be going?"

"That way," I pointed towards the large mountain peak.

"Ok, hurry up ok. We need to get the animals back soon."

I tapped my brother's horse on the side and we rode fast towards the mountain peak.

We eventually found Skip in the forest that surrounded the meadow. When we approached him he was just standing there, motionless. Like he was lost. When I approached he began to panic some, still startled from the wolf attack, and I took his bridle in hand to guide him.

When we got back to Father he had wrangled the stock we had. Most were accounted for, but some had run off.

I said to my father, "Pa, it looks like some of the livestock is badly hurt."

"I know Son, we will have to wait until morning to see how they are. I hope the blood on their legs stop dripping or else we will have a big problem."

I think what he meant was that it would be a big problem for other animals. A blood trail could attract who knows what out there.

We got home very late and were welcomed by a single light from the house. Mother was still up and came to the window to meet us. She was worried about us, but father reassured her everything was okay.

In the barn we unloaded the chickens and donkey while father tended to the wounded cattle. He covered some of the deeper bites with cloth. All in all the herd was relatively unscathed. Once he was done my father came to us and said it was time to go into the house to wash up for supper. My brother and I nodded and put our horses in the barn.

As we walked in the house my mother ran to us to check our scrapes and cuts.

"Good Lord John, what happened out there?"

"We were attacked by wolves, Mary. We are ok, just a little beat up. That's all."

My mother re-checked my brother thoroughly, looking like she didn't believe him.

"Mary, the boys are fine."

"You worried me half to death."

"I am sorry Mary. We got most of the livestock back, but the other animals ran off too far. I am going to look for them early in the morning before I go to work."

My mother gave a worried look then nodded and pointed to the food.

"Well, supper is ready. Grab some food before you go to bed boys, but first wash up outside. We just moved into this house and you're already dirtying it up."

We all said, "yes Ma'am" and went out back to wash up.

I woke up the next day in my new room and looked out the window. I watched as my father rode away from our house to gather the rest of the livestock. I got up and walked into the kitchen and met my mother and sisters. My mother came to me to check on my bruises again.

"I'm ok Ma, don't worry."

My sister Mary Ann asked, "what happened to you, Jacob?"

I could see that my mother didn't want anyone else to know what had happened to us. My sisters stared at me.

"We got attacked by wolves last night."

Kate broke the silence, "Lord! Are you ok?"

"I am fine Kate, we are all fine."

After breakfast and after telling everyone about the attack my siblings began to gather their things.

"Where you going, Kate?"

"I am going to go into town. I am going to see if I can get work at one of the stores."

My sister was a very confident woman, even though during this time mostly only men worked, she was determined to find work.

"I don't need to go to school anymore, Jacob."

"Oh, well I am going to go to town to get more books. Maybe I will see you in town."

My sister nodded and closed the front door and went on her horse.

After I finished clearing the kitchen table from breakfast I was alone with my Mother.

"Your Pa wanted you to get the livestock out of the barn and check the wounded ones."

I nodded to her and walked towards the barn.

When I arrived I cracked open the door and was greeted by a rancid stench. I got a little worried so I opened the other side of the barn. I peeked around the barn, looking for something out of the ordinary, but nothing appeared wrong. I walked to my horse and he looked fine. I brought him out and put Skip in the outdoor stable then I grabbed my brother's and sister's horses. After they were out I went back into the barn and checked the animals. Some of the cows were foaming at the mouth and looked sick. I let them be and took the non-sick ones out of the barn, away from the ill. Once all the healthy were out I went back to the sickened cows inside the barn to check them. A few of them were sitting down breathing heavily.

It was then that my brother and sister came out to get their horses and head to school. I did not want to tell them what was going on in the barn until Father came home. Luckily they just took their horses and left. After they had left the valley I walked into the house and I told my mother what was happening.

"Ma, I checked the barn and there are some cows that are not looking so good. What should I do?"

My mother's eyes were wide open. "What's wrong with them, Jacob?"

"They're breathing hard and their mouths are foaming."

"Oh God, stay away from them Jacob. Let your father take care of them when he gets back. He should be back soon."

Eventually my father came home, but brought no livestock with him. My mother and I went outside to meet him.

"What happened, Pa?"

"No livestock. I went everywhere. We are just going to have to buy some more later on."

My mother then said, "John, you might wanna go check the cows in the barn. Jacob said they aren't doing so well."

My father's expression changed instantly and he began to look worried. Father quickly turned to the barn and ran off to see the animals. I wanted to go with him, but my mother grabbed my arm and said I needed to stay away from the illness.

We waited and my father came out of the barn carrying his hat. His eyes were turned down and the look on his face was of frustration.

"Well, it looks like we are going to have to put the cows down. They are rabid. We can't afford to have them around the healthy animals. You're going to have to help me with that, Son."

I nodded.

"I am going to need your help to tie them up and I am going to have to shoot them." He patted me on the shoulder. "But later. I need to go to work now. I will be back tonight. Son, here is some money." He dug in his pocket for some coins. "I need you to go to the feed store in town and get some seeds. We need to get our crops going soon."

"Yes Pa." He gave me the money and left.

After he was gone and later in the day I took my horse and rode off to town. I first stopped at the general store that sold the books. I walked in and greeted the storeowner with a tip of my hat. I headed to the books and noticed that they had brought in some new ones with new stories. I browsed through them and suddenly a young woman walked up to the side of me. She was looking at books as well. She glanced at me while I looked at her, then she caught my eye.

I nodded and said, "hello Ma'am."

She smiled and said hello back. Then she turned away and continued browsing the books.

I was still watching the young woman as she walked away from me. My heart started to beat a little faster then suddenly I dropped my book that I was looking through. The clerk glared at me. I called back my apologies and picked up the book.

The young woman looked at me again as I did this and gave a little smile. Her smile was very peaceful, with her long brown hair and hazel eyes catching mine. Fumbling to hold my book I continued browsing through the new arrivals. I kept a safe distance from the gal. I peeked around the corner of the shelves until she paid and started to leave. My eyes followed her out the door when she walked away.

I was still. It seemed like for an eternity. I was still and didn't move. Everything was quiet and the sound around me was muffled. I shook my head and everything came back to place. I shook my head one more time then grabbed the books and headed to the store clerk.

I always enjoyed my time in town. Everyone was so friendly, tipping their hats and greeting one another. I always looked forward to riding in for this.

During my ride to the feed store I had to walk by the sheriff's office. I noticed it was now open and when I passed it I looked through the window. Inside the sheriff sat at his desk. I moved along and next to the sheriff's door I could see a stack of papers that said, "wanted" on them. Underneath the heading was a picture of different men and their crimes.

"James Montoya, wanted for stealing."

"Mike Brown, wanted for the death of Jeffrey Higgins."

I was amazed by these signs. I guess because that was the first time I had ever seen wanted posters. While I was walking away a man ran into the sheriff's office. He came out quickly and had brought the sheriff with him. Together they headed to the saloon. Out of curiosity I followed behind.

The sheriff went into the noisy saloon. There was an uproar of cries and the sound of chairs being thrown around. I tried to look in through one of the saloon windows.

All of a sudden the sheriff bolted out the front of the saloon with a man that looked like he was drunk out of his mind. The sheriff dragged him back to his office. I ran to the sheriff's office and could see the sheriff put the man in a jail cell next to his desk.

The sheriff then came out of the office to meet the people who had gathered on the streets.

"It's ok. You all can go now. Everything is in well order here."

The people around the area acknowledged and went on their business.

This was my first time experiencing law enforcement. I never forgot that and thought of it endlessly as I headed for the feed store.

When I got there I opened the door and a bell sounded at the top of the door. A man came out from the back area.

"Good day, Sir. What can I do you for?"

"Good 'mornin, Sir. I am looking to buy some seed for our crops."

"What kind of seeds?" He asked.

"Corn. A good bag of corn and some squash seeds, please."

"Very well, Sir. Anything else?"

"No that is it."

The store clerk nodded and filled the bags up with seed and charged me.

"Ten cents, Sir."

I pulled out the coins and gave him more than ten cents. I was still learning how to count. The clerk smiled and gave me back twenty cents and kept ten cents.

"You gave me a little too much there, young man."

"Oh, thank you Sir."

He nodded.

I walked out the store and headed to my horse. As I put the seeds in the pouch I heard a voice call out from behind me.

"That's a nice horse you got there."

Startled, I turned around. It was the young woman from the store.

Caught off guard by her beauty I stuttered a lackluster reply, "Oh, thhhank you."

She smiled and said, "my name is Ann, Ann Miller."

She stuck her hand out and I looked at it. Hesitantly I took off my hat.

"My name is Jacob, Jacob Smith."

"Nice to meet you, Jacob."

I nodded and she asked, "how long have you been living here in the Almaden?"

I again hesitated to respond. Her mere presence captivated me in a way where everything just slowed down and came to a halt.

"I've been here since I was five."

"Oh, I see. And how old are you now?"

"I am fifffth teen." She really caught me up in my words, I couldn't seem to speak straight around her, I was so nervous.

She nodded and smiled. I was so silent after that I forgot to ask her questions. I just stood there for what felt like forever. She looked around and smiled once more.

"Well, okay." She said and started to walk away.

"Miss Miller?" I finally called after her.

She looked up to me and turned back. "Yes?"

"How long have you been here?"

"My family just moved here, not too long ago."

"Oh, I see. How, how do you like it?"

"I love it here. So many people are here. A lot of nice people."

"I know. It's nice to see people like that."

"I noticed you bought some books. Do you like to read a lot?"

I nodded and said, "well, my teacher always told me to read as much as you can. To help you speak and write."

Ann smiled again, "well, that is good Jacob. Your English sounds very good."

"Thank you, Ann."

She then looked around, over her shoulder, and turned back to me.

"Mister Smith, I need to get going now. It was nice to meet you." She shook my hand and began to walk away. "Maybe we can meet another time?"

I was frozen once again when she told me that. Shortly after I came back and said, "I come into town everyday. Maybe we can go for a walk around the town?"

Ann smiled widely, "Ok. I will be looking for you. Bye for now Jacob."

"Bye, Ann."

She walked away and I was again frozen. That was, until I started to smile. Getting on Skip I began to ride home. On my way I kept imagining Ann's smile etched upon her face as she said goodbye. She just kept popping into my head. It felt like a dream while I was riding.

When I got home I put Skip out back and grabbed the bags of seeds, new books, and walked into the house. As I did I saw my brother sitting by the table writing on his small chalkboard.

My mother came to me and asked, "is that the seed, Jacob?"

"Yes Ma."

"Ok, put it right there close to the door. You bought yourself some more books?"

"Yep, I am going to read as many as I can."

My mother smiled and said, "good Jacob. That's very good."

She looked at me closer when she said this. I saw her eyes take in my own smile. There was something in her eyes that made me think she knew what was on my mind. Ann. A new cause for me to smile. Mothers always know.

"So did you have a good time in town?"

"Ah, yeah Ma I did."

She smiled again, slyly, and looked at my brother. "Joshua, go wash up for super."

"Ok," he called back.

Joshua stood up and looked at her. His eyes were red.

"Come here Joshua, let me look at you." She checked my brother and felt his head. It was warm.

"I feel ok Ma, jeez."

She had a look of concern in her eyes and said, "you're going to bed soon, Joshua. Go, go wash up for supper."

After my brother left my mom told me to do the same.

" 'Member you have to help your Pa with the cattle when he gets home."

I nodded and sat near the table in the kitchen.

I grabbed one of my books and started reading.

My sister Kate came home before my father did. She burst excitedly through the front door to exclaim, "I got it!"

My mom walked up to her and asked, "what is that Kate?"
"I got a job at the Inn!"

Ma yelled with joy and gave her a hug.

"Good for you, Kate! Your father will be very happy!"

My sister started to hug and kiss me and my mother.
She then trotted into her bedroom where I heard her tell
my youngest sister Mary Ann the news. There were
instantly screams of happiness and giggling. Keenly
listening to these surroundings I heard my father
approaching from outside.

I stood up and began to get ready, putting my books in
my room. By the time I came back out to the family
room Father had already opened the door.

My Ma quickly said to my father, "don't! Don't come in
all dirty. Wash up outside after the cattle John!"

He tipped his hat and smiled. "Yes Ma'am."

I walked out back to meet with my father. It was almost
sundown.

"Well Son, we better get this over with before it gets
dark. We are going to have to put the cattle on the
trailer and have your sister's and brother's horses pull
it. We have to dump them near the valley so it's away
from the house."

As I was setting up the trailer I could see my father grab the rope and tie it on one of the large posts. I looked to my side and saw my sister Mary Ann looking out the window. Mother soon appeared in the window as well, only briefly, then pulled my sister away.

I grabbed the horses and tied them up to the trailer, then to the post.

"Tie them up good, Son. They will get crazy when they hear gunshots. Check the other animal pens to make sure the gates are locked also."

As I checked the pen I heard a strange cry come from one of the cows. Like a "mhew" or faint "moo" sound.

My father had pulled the first cow to his spot and I could see the cow was struggling. It knew what was about to happen. I went to help him.

"Son, tie him up at the post over there!"

I grabbed a hold of the rope that was tied to the cow then pulled. This connected both ropes together.

"I got it Pa!"

"Ok Jacob, stand behind me." He prepared his gun and aimed it at the cow.

"Pa, why are we shooting him?"

"Because his is sick. He will get the rest of the animals sick if we don't. Now stand back."

He steadied his hands on the rifle, pointing the barrel straight at the cow's neck. He pulled the trigger.

The cow gasped and took his final breath. It fell to the ground. With no thought or reason why, I suddenly walked towards the cow and touched his wound. As the blood dripped down the cow's neck I crouched down and touched my fingertips to the blood. I pulled my hand closer to my eyes and stared at the red color.

My father came up to me.

"Come on Son, get up. We have to untie this cow and drag him to the trailer."

I didn't hear him and continued looking at my fingertips, the cow, the blood.

"Son, let's go! Get a move on now!"

I looked up to my father and helped him untie the rope.

"Ok Son, let's drag him to the trailer."

We drug the body over leaving a trail of blood in our path. When we got to the trailer my father had me pull a metal pin from the side of the rig, lowering the rear gate. To get the cow's body into the bed of the trailer we hauled two heavy boards from the barn to create a ramp. The body was too heavy to lift into the bed of the trailer so we drug it up, tying a rope around the cow's mid section for leverage. It was an effort on both our parts, pushing and pulling the heavy mass, but eventually we moved it into the trailer. The rig and our clothes were covered in its blood. I started to phase out again, staring at the scarlet mess, until my father called for my attention again.

"Let's go Son, we have to get the rest of the cattle."

After tending to the rest of the sickened cows we loaded them on the trailer and got ready to head out.

"Go untie the horses, Son. I will control them on the carriage."

I untied the horses, patted them on the side, and brought them to the trailer. I clambered up to the passenger seat and sat next to my father.

"Alright, Pa."

My father yelled to the horses and whipped the reins. We headed out to the meadow.

When we arrived we unloaded the livestock bodies into the open landscape of the valley. The sun had set now and the smell of the bodies began to seep across the meadow. Once the last cow was unloaded my father re-latched the trailer. I couldn't help but stare at the mass of cows. Just yesterday they were fine and now half our herd was dead.

"Come on Jacob, let's go. It's getting late now!"

"Pa, why are we leaving the cows here?"

He looked up in the air, as if he didn't want to answer. Then he slowly turned his eyes to me.

"Jacob, it's because if we left them lying dead at the house the wolves and bears would go there. As a matter of fact Son, they're probably on their way here right now. We should get going, so we don't meet them again."

I looked back and I stared again at the dead cows. Something was bothering me with what we had done and my father noticed right away.

"Don't worry, Son. We eat meat all the time and the livestock get slaughtered anyways."

"I know Pa, it's just." I couldn't finish what I was trying to say.

"What is it Son?"

I blinked my eyes, to clear my mind. "Nothin', nothin' Pa."

Darkness fell upon us on our ride home. Our clothes were drenched in blood but despite the chill we unloaded the carriage and horses upon arriving at the house.

"Son, put the horses in the barn. I am going to herd the rest of the animals into the barn."

My father headed out the yard and I guided the horses to the barn. It still had that stench. Not the smells of manure, but something new. It reminded me of the pile of cow bodies. It must have smelled of death. I put my horse back and walked to the house.

My mother opened the door and stood there, her mouth quivering at the sign of me. The blood. The stench.

"Jacob, clean yourself outside! Look at all that blood on you."

"Ya Ma, it's from the cows."

"Well, get those clothes off and put them in this bucket. Tell your Pa to do the same." She swiftly turned around, my brother was coming. She dashed into the room and closed the door.

Outside I took my cloths off and put on a fresh pair of pants which had been hanging on the clothesline waiting for me. After stopping at the washbasin to scrub off I walked into the house. Opening the door I could see my brother was in bed and moving around a lot, like he was uncomfortable or agitated. My mother was by his side, pressing her cheek to his forehead. Something was wrong.

"Jacob, go get your father!"

I ran as fast as I could to the barn where father had just loaded the last of the animals.

"Pa, Ma wants you inside. Something is wrong with Joshua."

He sprinted to the house and I finished locking up the barn. I started to run back to the house and saw my sister's candlelight shining from her bedroom. Everyone must have woken up. Inside my whole family was gathered around Joshua, who was now shivering and sweating.

"What's wrong, Ma?" Kate was crouched beside my brother looking concerned.

"John, his head is burning up."

"Let me get a rag and a bowl of water for you."

I noticed my father's clothes were still covered in blood. My mother didn't seem to care about this mess. All she seemed to see was my brother. My father returned with a small basin of water and a rag. Mother damped the cloth in the cool water and pressed it to Joshua's head.

"He will be ok, he just needs some sleep," my mother reassured us. "I am going to stay in this room tonight with him. Jacob, you can sleep in our room for the night."

We began to clear the room. My eyes were glued to my brother as I took the blankets from my bed to join my father. I could tell he was hurting pretty bad inside. That night mother stayed with Jacob, her thoughts and body unrested as she cared for him. I don't suspect any of us got any sleep that night. I know for myself I couldn't even close my eyes. The whole night I rested my eyes on the ceiling, wondering if Joshua would be ok.

The next morning I got up with my father and we both checked on my brother. My mother was in the kitchen bright and early. She was always up before us.

"How's he feeling, Ma?"

"He is better. He is sleeping."

"Mary, I am going to ride into town and ask the doctor to take a look at him."

"Doctors are expensive John."

"Don't you worry, we can afford him. I'll do what it takes to take care of our Son."

My mother nodded as my father left. My sisters came into the kitchen just as Pa road off to town.

I remember the room was very quiet and somber all that morning. Mother served us breakfast as usual; we had eggs. Kate ate quickly then left to go to work at the Inn. My younger sister followed shortly after and rode to school. After I had finished eating and I told my mother I was going to go to town as well. Before I left she reminded me not to forget to take the animals out of the barn.

It took a few hours to complete my usual chores with this added task. Eventually I untied Skip and rode to town. I wanted to look for Ann. When I got there it seemed like I searched for her for hours. Time was moving so slowly that day.

I finally sat on a bench in front of the latest development labeled "Town Hall." This building was all white and stood apart from the other structures on the street. Resting in my thoughts I was awoken by someone calling at me.

"Hey Mister, I said for you to look around for me and I see you looking at the ground."

I looked up and saw that it was Ann. She had found me. The sun was right next to her. It shined off her face and it was very heavenly. Her eyes were glimmering as she approached. I stood up quickly and took my hat off.

"May I sit next to you?"

I nodded, "yes. Yes of course, Ann."

As she sat we both looked at each other and smiled.

"So Jacob, tell me more about your family."

"Uhh, what would you like to know, Ann?"

"Your mother, father? Were they from here?"

"Well, my Pa is from New England. He moved here and met my Ma."

Ann nodded, encouraging me to continue. "And your mother? Where is she from?"

I was not used to talking so much about myself but continued. "My Ma is from here and they got married here."

"Oh, interesting." We paused and looked around at the people.

Then I asked, "So, Ann." She turned to me, "where are your Ma and Pa from?"

She didn't look near as nervous as I did when she replied.

"Well, both my mother and father are from Boston and we traveled here. My father helps govern cities, towns, even around here. Actually, nowadays he works there." She pointed to the Town Hall. "He also runs that building over there," she pointed to the building that said Post Office.

"Govern?" I asked.

"Yes, he oversees the laws and rules of town. He is now a member of the government here in Almaden."

"Oh, like the sheriff?"

She smiled, "yes, sorta like that Jacob. My father tells the laws to the sheriff and the sheriff enforces them."

"Enforces?"

She didn't giggle at my questions, she just responded.

"It means to make sure people understand the laws."

"Oh I see. Does your ma work?"

"No she does not work. She is either at home or out in the town shopping."

"Do you work, Ann?" I couldn't believe how much I was asking her yet she was making these questions feel so natural.

"Me? Oh no, my mother doesn't want me to work. How about you, Jacob? Do you work?"

"I only do chores at home. I take care of the livestock and the barn while my father is gone."

"Gone?"

"He works. He does that mining."

Her eyes grew wide and sparkled with a new interest when I said this. "Your father works for the mining company? The Quicksilver Mining Company?"

"Uhh, I think so yeah."

"So you ever go visit him?"

"No, my pa leaves before I get up most of the time or when I am doing chores or something."

"Oh I see." The sparkle stayed in her eyes. "Do you have any brothers or sisters?"

"I have a brother and two sisters."

"Are they older than you?"

"My sisters are older than me and my brother is younger than me."

"Oh," she paused as a sound rose from the nearby saloon. We both turned our heads to hear the music.

Ann shook her head. "Boy, I wish they didn't have that saloon. So much loud noise and trouble come from there."

I nodded and looked over at the saloon. I had actually been thinking the opposite though. I was very tempted to go in and see what all the noise was about.

I asked Ann, "do you have any brothers or sisters?"

"I have three sisters and two brothers. I am the youngest out of all of them."

"Wow! What a big family you have Ann."

"Big family yes, but they all treat me like a baby. I am fourteen and they still treat me like the baby. Sometimes my brothers and sisters say bad things to me."

I wasn't sure if it was okay to ask what I said next, but I did anyways. "What kind of bad things, Ann?"

To my surprise she answered. "They said they will always have to spoon feed me and I will never marry. I don't know why they say that to me. I can take care of myself. Just because I am the youngest doesn't mean they can step all over me."

"I am sorry to hear that, Ann."

"Just be glad you're not the youngest." She sighed abruptly. "So Jacob, how are you with your brothers and sisters Jacob?"

"We get along. My little brother follows me a lot and helps me out around the house. I talk to my older sister a lot, Kate. I guess you can say we are close."

"That is so wonderful," she said.

Then I suddenly asked her, without thinking, "hey Ann. Wanna meet my sister? She works over there at the Inn."

She smiled and said ok. Together we walked to the Inn and opened the door. I immediately saw Kate from a distance. I took my hat off and I waved to her. Kate walked over to us.

"Hello Jacob," she beamed looking proud at her first day on the job. She then looked at Ann.

"And who is this wonderful looking young lady, Jacob?"

"Kate, this is Ann."

"Well, nice to meet you Ann."

"Nice to meet you also, Kate."

"Is my brother treating you with respect?" My sister winked at me.

Ann promptly replied, "Oh yes, he is quite a gentleman."

My sister looked at me and smiled.

"So how is work, Kate?" I asked my sister.

"It is good, Jacob. I love it! It is so nice to be out of school and out of the house, working here in town. I just love being here. So much so that I've actually got to get back to it."

After saying goodbye to Ann we walked out of the Inn.

"Well Ann, I need to get going and do the rest of my chores before sunset."

"Ok then. Jacob, it was nice to spend the day with you. I hope we can do it again sometime soon?"

Feeling that cloudy muffled sensation again, like butterflies in my stomach, I had trouble replying. All I could do was watch as Ann's hair was gently blown across her lips by the breeze of the wind. Time was certainly slowing down. Her beautiful eyes had met mine.
"I...I...Would like that." That was it. That was all I could say.

She smiled. "Well Mr. Smith, I will see you around."

As she walked away her long hair spun softly in the breeze. She turned her face back to me as she left, waving goodbye once more, her eyes glimmering again in the sun. I stood there for quite a while, savoring those eyes before putting my hat on and walking to Skip.

On the way home, about a mile out of town, I passed a small meadow with a river. Feeling like I wanted some more time with my thoughts, and to think of Ann, I pulled over to the river.

"There you go Skip, drink up."

I pet his neck as I climbed down and kneeled by the river myself. I splashed my face with the cool water and started to drink. Getting up I rubbed my eyes and found that my gaze was met by the reflection of a man. There was someone standing behind me. I felt his breath on my neck and I quickly turned around.

It was the tan man, the one I had seen before with the long face. He wore that distinctive black hat and his clothes were somewhat different than what the other people in the town would wear. He donned normal pants and a leather hide, like a jacket. It was him. It was that man from when I rode into town for the first time. We looked at each other eye to eye.

I was surprised that my horse did not react to the intruder earlier. I started to get on my horse to go. The man spoke.

"Wait," he said in a deep voice. "Do not leave, Jacob."

I paused and stepped back on the ground.

"How do you know my name?"

He smiled, "we have been watching you, Jacob. For many years now."

"We?"

"Yes, we have been." He walked to my horse.

"Stay away from my horse!" I yelled at him as he reached for Skip.

He looked at me and still stuck his hand out. He began petting Skip on the head.

"Do you know how you got this horse, Jacob?"

I shook my head, "my ma told me not to talk to you."

He smiled, "your mother?"

"I see you are wondering why your horse isn't acting up around me."

I looked at my horse and quickly to the tan man. He stuck his arm out to me and said, "my name is Bodaway."

I did not stick my hand out to shake his. He paused and took his hand down. Bodaway started to walk back from Skip and turned his eyes to the meadow.

"The land, it's beautiful isn't it?" He said with a sigh.

I paused and glanced around. I wondered if he was alone or not.

"Don't you ride off to the forest, Jacob? Don't you often ride to the meadows or the lake? You look around, just as I do. Don't you, Jacob?"

I nodded, but did not respond.

He smiled, "you like what you see around you. I know that about you."

"How, how do you know my name? And why is my mother telling me not to talk to you?"

"Jacob, look at my face. Look at my arm. What do you see?"

I saw markings on his arms and I noticed his skin color.

"You, you have the same color of my ma."

He smiled and his eyebrows went up. "Jacob, I gave this horse to your mother, for you to use."

I was stunned. I had never met this man before and he said such, such outspoken things.

"No! That's, that's not true. I don't believe it, that's a lie! I know my ma. She wouldn't lie to me."

Bodaway came closer to me and said, "Jacob, I know you're not understanding what I am saying, but you will in time. I will tell you everything." He looked behind my back then he said, "I must go now. If you want to know more just go to the meadow and close your eyes. After a while open them then look around. We will find you."

I started to look behind me and suddenly saw my sisters were coming towards up on horseback. I turned back and the man was gone.

My sister Kate came up to me and said, "Jacob, we must go home right away. Something is happening to Joshua. I need you to go get Pa right away!"

Something in my stomach sank and I felt panicked for my brother. "How do I get there?"

"Take the main trail past the Inn and go up the hill. You'll see a fork. Take the right fork and you'll see the mine in the distance. When you get there ask for Pa."

"Ok Kate, I will go there right now."

———————————

I got on my horse and rode off while my sister rode to the house. I passed the Inn and came to the fork of the road. I turned right and went over a hill. At the top I could see the huge mine and lots of equipment. It looked like the whole town was working here. There were so many people. I rode towards the mine entrance and saw a man covered in black dirt. The man stopped me.

"Hold it Sir, you can't go past here."

I looked at the man and said, "I need to see my Pa, it's important."

He looked around and asked, "what's your father's name, son?"

"John Smith."

A man in the distance, closest to the entrance of the mine yelled, "fire in the hole!" Everyone scattered.

The man suddenly said, "move back, Son! Now!"

As I rode back I heard a loud boom in the mine. After the shock I saw people begin to file out from the depths, their ears were filled with cotton. I guess that was to help protect them from the loud noises. I recognized one of the men coming out as my father. I rode to him.

"Pa! Pa!"

He couldn't hear me with all that cotton in his ears. I waved at him and he saw me. He took the cotton out.

"What are you doing here?"

"It's Joshua. Something is going on at home, Kate told me to get you."

"Ok Son, I am going to get the doctor and bring him over."

Pa yelled to his boss that he needed to go home because of Joshua. His boss nodded, looking concerned. My father then said to me, "go ahead and ride over to the house. Help your mother until I get there, you understand?"

I nodded, and left.

————————————

When I got home I tied up Skip and ran into the house. I saw my mother in my brother's room and my sisters around the door.

"Ma, is he ok?"

She paused for a moment, "he is not feeling good, Jacob. Go grab me a bucket of water from outside."

Everyone was scrambling throughout the house. My mother made my sisters do things as well. As soon as I got the bucket and filled it with water I saw my father from the distance coming in and with him was the doctor. They stopped their horses, dismounted, and ran quickly inside the house. I followed them, going in through the back door.

"Ma, here is the bucket."

My mother came out of the room as the doctor went in. She grabbed the bucket and went inside the room. My father called us all into the family room. We all sat there and waited. The doctor called out to my father and he asked him to grab a cup so my brother could drink some water.

It was about two hours later when the doctor finally came out. He combed his hair with his hands and put all of his instruments in his bag. The doctor walked towards us and looked down. When he got near us my father asked him, "how is he, Doctor?"

"He has a real bad fever, John. I got him to sleep, which he needs a lot of. I am sorry John, but I believe he has the scarlet fever."

My mother's eyes filled with tears and as they covered her face she ran out to the backyard. My sister Kate followed her.

"How do you know it's that, Doctor?" My father asked.

"John, he is showing the symptoms of it. He is not the only boy I've seen with it. I am taking care of a few children near town that have it also. I am sorry, John. I will stop by once a day to see how he is doing. If we do find a cure I will immediately tend to your son, but for now there is no treatment."

"What will happen to him?"

The doctor shook his head and said, "I do not know, John. I don't know. Tell Mary I said I am sorry and I will be back tomorrow."

The doctor nodded at me and my sister then left the house and rode away. My father went outside to get my mother. My sister Kate saw my father coming and she came back inside. She shut the door behind her saying, "we need to stay inside here. Let Ma and Pa be alone."

We sat there in the family room and eventually moved into the kitchen. I looked to my side and could see my sister Mary Ann hugging Kate. She had started to cry. The room was silent. No one was talking when my father suddenly came in, holding my mother. Pa was clasping her hand and hugging her.

Pa looked at us and said, "we are going to be in our room kids. Kate, make some supper for Mary Ann and Jacob."

My mother covered her face as Pa guided her into the bedroom. She did not want us to see her sad and crying. My sisters and I never saw my mother cry while we were growing up, so our reaction was not normal to this. We just stared at them while they walked to the room.

My sister Kate turned to us and asked, "do you want supper?"

My sister and I were just so sad to see our parents and our brother suffering, we did not want to eat. We were silent and Kate acknowledged it. She started to hug us and said, "let's go to bed."

As my sisters went to bed I stood in the family room. Across from me was my brother's room. I just stared at the door for what seemed like hours. I looked at his

door until the sun started to come up and only then did
I finally go to sleep in the family room.

Sadness and somber followed the next few days. After the third day of being ill my brother Joshua passed. What happened during those final moments of his life were unimaginable. To this day I cannot explain to, nor wish to, recall what happened in any amount of detail. Even as I write this journal entry I am breathing deeply, trying to recall something I've pushed far back into my mind.

When I saw the doctor come out of the room I could not hear what he was saying. At that moment, for some reason, all I could see was what was happening after he talked. The news was not good. As he told my parents my father rushed into Joshua's room while my mother cried. I saw the doctor hug my mother and I saw my sisters go to my mother's side. They were crying too. I stood motionless while I looked at everyone react to the news. The sound was still silent. It felt like my ears were plugged and I heard my heartbeat, it was beating faster than I'd ever felt it. My father came out and started to hug everyone. I looked at my father and he was crying. Again, I never saw my parents ever cry before. Never have I thought that I would see my father cry.

The doctor approached me but I could not hear a thing. I could not understand what he was telling me at the time. He looked at my family and just looked down.

Before sundown I saw the doctor help my father make a hole behind the house. My father did not want me to help. He did not say a thing when this was happening. I looked at them dig, standing near the back of the house. From there I could see my sisters and mother mourning. I was in shock and all I could do was stand there. The doctor walked in front of me and went back inside the house. I still could not hear a thing. As I looked at my father he stared down to the ground. Swiftly, he then looked straight to the door and walked past me. He did not look at me. He just went into the house and into my brother's room. When they came out I saw that my father was carrying my brother. Joshua was covered with a thick cloth. As father walked past, hugging my still brother, the doctor held my mother to keep her from grabbing Joshua. I saw... I saw my brother's body pass me.

The doctor followed, then my sisters and lastly my mother. She could barely walk, stumbling, weakened by her mourning. She followed my father towards the hole. I just stood there, looking from a distance.

I could not hear what they said when they buried my brother, I just saw their saddened expressions. I was so far away, with no expression, only a plain face revealing my disbelief.

My family surrounded my brother while the doctor buried him with dirt. I could not believe this was happening to our family. I felt upset inside, but mostly saddened. The doctor said his words to my brother and he hugged my parents, then my sisters, then walked away. Before he left he gave me a hug. I did not hug back and just stood still, I did not move. I watched my family as we stood at the grave around my brother for hours. Eventually my father grabbed my mother and sisters and walked back into the house. My father gave me a hug before they went in.

Before the night fell I went back to my brother's grave. My father had chosen an area located at one of the hills where Brother used to like to go. From there you could look out at the landscape. It was at his grave where he used to play games with us. I looked down at the small mound. I could not believe Joshua was under there.

This had happened so quickly. I felt I lost. I felt sad. I felt like this shouldn't have happened to him. I stared directly at his grave. Suddenly, I had a tear on the side of my eye. I lost my little brother that day.

Two years after my brother's death, once a day, I would walk to the valley and sit near the river to think about him. I did this every day. My mother and father had not been the same since he passed away, nor were my sisters.

Over the years Kate had gotten married and was now living on the other side of town. This left my sister Mary Ann to help my mother with chores. During the day my father still worked for the Quicksilver Mining Company. I thought of maybe getting a job at the mine, but for some reason I did not want to. The day I went there to get my father, the day we learned of Joshua's fatal illness, I had sensed that the mines were not quite a pleasant place.

Ann and I still saw each other frequently. We were in love. Some nights Ann would come over to my house for supper. My mother and father would welcome her warmly however, I knew there was something different between them. My family knew that Ann came from a rich family and I could sense that my mother felt conflicted about this. Our way of life was different than the richer folks, but Ann always wanted to come over anyways and enjoyed being around us. I do not recall my father being extremely happy for me at any time, even though Ann and I were in love. The only member of my family who did outwardly express happiness for us was my older sister, Kate. She and Ann became fast friends and loved going out together, to go to town and go shopping. Sometimes Ann would stop by the Inn just to visit my sister.

On the other side, though, Ann's father was against us being together completely. I was never invited over there, since her father knew who my parents were. Ann was not influenced by this and did not listen to her father. She always wanted to rebel from her parents. Ann tried desperately to work at the Town Hall so that she could speak with various politicians that governed the state and town. Her father did not know anything about this at the time. Ann was very active, politically and in her way of life, and did not want to be home if she could avoid it. She never did a chore in her life until our wedding and even when we were married she did little. Thankfully, after all of the years I had helped Ma at home I knew how to keep a house.

Even after those years though, even after finding happiness with Ann, I would still lament over Joshua's death. On those lonely nights Ann would comfort me. I would always wonder why and how Joshua got sick.

Why didn't we catch it sooner?

Over the years my English had become much better since I began reading books. I even impressed Ann with how much I had learned and how quickly I adapted to a new vocabulary. At times she would tell me the laws for the town and state and what it meant for everyone and I would learn them as well.

That year I also found out that my old friends Matt, Brian, and Jack were all a part of the war. It had been going on for quite some time and the boys had been gone for a while. One day I read something in the newspaper. It said that Matt was coming home. Brian and Jack however, would never make it back.

It wasn't long before I saw Matt one day while in town in a new district of Santa Clara Valley called New Almaden. Over the years our town had grown so much so that there were even larger surrounding areas to Almaden including San Jose, which was much bigger than a town, it was a city. San Jose had its own governor too, just like we did in New Almaden, and his name was George Givens.

In our part of town I had begun to notice more and more wanted posters at the sheriff's office and surrounding buildings. It seemed that there was a gang of lawbreakers in the area who had been causing some recent trouble. From the posters it looked like most of them were of Indian descent while only a few were white.

Since New Almaden was a small town, and by this time I had become a familiar face among the streets, a lot of the people and shop keeps knew me by my name. As I got to know more people they got to know me too, so much so that the town folk recommended me to apply for certain jobs. At last I was finally working in town. Mainly I did manual labor, working in yards and such, which was pretty much the same as I was doing at home. Still it was work and I was making money.

One particular day, before I headed off for one of my jobs, I met Ann at our spot in town. This was our special meeting place and was located in front of the Town Hall, near the lawn at the bench. I remember Ann that day, she ran towards me and I showed a smile to her before she gave me a big hug. My hat came off when she lunged into me. We were both happy and she was filled with joy. She kissed me on my check and we both sat down.

"How has your day been so far, Jacob?"

"It's been good. Going to go do some work over at the Jefferson Family Ranch in a bit. How has your day been, Ann?"

"It's been good. I've been in the Town Hall for a while learning everything I can."

I nodded and smiled. I looked at Ann and said, "you're the best thing I got in my life, Ann. I love you."

Ann smiled and hugged me. "I love you too, Jacob."

I suddenly heard noises coming from the bar and I turned my head to look towards it. Ann looked at me and said, "Jacob don't go in there. It's a bad place."

For some reason during my upbringing I was always fascinated as to what they were doing in there. Of course I was not afraid of going in there. I wasn't really afraid of much at all and Ann knew this about me.

"Ann, don't worry, ok. I want to see what it is all about in that saloon."

"I do worry Jacob, because I love you."

I looked down and took a deep breath, hugging Ann and said, "don't worry, ok. I'll be fine. I will see you tonight at supper, ok?"

Ann nodded and walked to the Town Hall.

As I walked to the Saloon the noises became much louder and I started to hear music coming from inside. I opened the swivel doors and it seemed as though everyone was looking at me. It was as if no one knew who I was, like a complete stranger. I stood there and looked around. I saw someone playing the piano. There was a group of people to my left talking and drinking. To one side I could see a stairway and on it were women, hardly dressed at all. Some of the women wore silk dresses with garters on their legs while others had fancy hats with long feathers attached to them. I walked up to the bar area and saw an opening so I headed there.

Back at the house sometimes I would have a few drinks when my parents weren't around. My mother forbid me from drinking at the house so I would drink away, where she wouldn't see me. Today though was my first time at a bar.

I went up to the bartender. "What can I get you, sir?" He yelled, since the music was so loud along with the general commotion going on.

"I'll have a whisky." The bartender nodded and started to pour me a drink from behind the counter.

While I was waiting I looked around a bit. Out of the corner of my eye I saw a group of men along the back of the saloon, just sitting there and not doing anything. They just sat and looked around, keeping a close eye on things.

Then all of the sudden someone tapped me on the shoulder and I turned around quickly. It was a man that I had never seen before. He had a beard and looked like he was riding a lot from his dusty clothes.

The man looked at me and said, "Jesus, you don't know who I am?"

"No I don't."

"It's me, Jacob. It's Matt!"

My eyes went wide open, and I said, "Matt! How are ya?" I shook his hand and gave him a gentlemen's hug.

"I am doing fine, how's life treating ya?"

"It's been good."

"That's great!"

My drink finally came and Matt told the bartender, "I'll have a whisky also. Give my friend here another round, would ya."

My eyebrows went up from being surprised with this other drink.

"So what do you think?" Matt asked, handing me the second whiskey.

"Think about what, Matt?"

"About this town, things have changed."

"Yeah, a lot has changed over the years."

"How's your father and mother doing?" Matt asked.

"They are doing ok, Matt."

"And your sisters and brother."

As he asked about my brother I quickly looked up and said, "my sisters are doing good, but my brother passed away a few years ago."

"Joshua?"

I nodded and drank my whisky.

"I am sorry to hear that." He paused for a while and drank. "I am sure you know about Brian and Jack?"

"Yeah, I heard."

"I knew you would. It's all over this town because they were local." Matt shook his head. "I seen them die, Jacob. War isn't a good thing."

"How did they die, Matt?"

"They got shot point blank. It was instant."

We both started to drink again.

"I see your English is a lot better. Guess reading those books helped you a lot, huh?"

"Yeah, they sure did." I glanced to the men in the corner then turned my head towards Matt. "Matt, do you know those guys?"

Matt shook his head. "Nope, don't know who they are. Guess they just came into town today."

"Did you see the wanted papers by the sheriff's office?"

"Yeah, a group of gangs are coming in soon. Looks like the sheriff is goin' to be busy for a little while. Hope you're protecting yourself and the family. Don't know what will go on in this town if they show up."

"Protecting?"

"Yeah, like having a gun on you all the time."

"Oh, I don't have a gun." Even as I said this I felt like I should be wearing one.

"Well, you best be gettin' one soon, Jacob. Especially in saloon with all this gambling and drinking going on."

"I am not worried, Matt. I sorta like it here at the saloon."

Matt shrugged and drank his whiskey. I finished my drink and patted Matt on the shoulder.

"I'll see ya around, Matt. Gotta go to work."

"I'll see ya around, Jacob."

I walked out the door and went to my horse then rode to Jefferson's place.

After my day was over I started to ride back home. It was now dark and the moon was up. The Jefferson's ranch was away from the town and north of my house. As I rode through the forest that night I saw men on horseback in the distance. Having no worries on my mind, I thought of them as just people passing by using the road. Suddenly though, they stopped and blocked the road. Skip ground to a halt.

There were four men in front of me on horses. The men had mustaches and beards, like they hadn't had a good shave in days, and they were wearing the typical outfit an outlaw would wear. Out of the shadows another man on horseback emerged from behind them. He was one of the men from the wanted posters.

He looked white and he was just staring at me. His eyes focused. After a while he looked to his right and more horses came out from the shadows. They rode behind Skip and blocked the road trail off. I was surrounded. Turning my head as they rode I saw many of the men were leaning their hands on their pistols.

"Give us your money," said the man from the posters. He put his hand on his pistol holder.

One of the men from behind me said, "come on Mister, you better do what he says or else."

"If you don't give us your money I am going to first shoot your horse then you will follow after him."

I looked around, I was not afraid of him or his group. I stared back at him and said, "I won't give you my money."

They all started to laugh and then the Wanted Man smiled. Quickly, he pulled his gun out and shot my horse. Skip fell to the ground and I, still on his back, fell off to the side. A few men then got off their horses and started to approach me. I stood my ground as the Wanted Man came up to me. He quickly approached me and looked straight at me.

He then smiled to his group and said, "look at him boys he ain't breaking a sweat of fear."

Suddenly he grabbed my neck and put the gun to my head.

"You will be afraid Mister after I..."

Just then something odd happened. There was a distorted, ghostly sound from a distance and an arrow came screaming past my ear and through the Wanted Man's head.

He went down instantly. His men pulled out their guns. Suddenly arrows started to come out from the shadows, hitting a few men. They started to scatter and shot into the darkness. Next I saw an ax fly from the shadows. It sailed across my line of sight and hit the man before me in the back. Looking around I saw that most of the men were dead, all except two. They quickly rode away while being chased by flying arrows, getting hit and wounded as they fled.

When they left it was silent. I looked around in the darkness and quickly rushed to aid Skip. He was not moving one bit. I was worried I might have lost my best friend. Suddenly, a man emerged from the shadows.

The man had dark, wrinkled skin and was dressed in feathers, barefoot. It looked as though he had markings on his face, covered partially by his long hair. Around his neck was a necklace that had feathers on it, just like what I saw when I was drowning in the lake when I was a kid. He also had a marking on his chest with the same circle and feathers right above it.

A few more men came from the shadows. They looked like the trees. The men were completely dressed in leaves and tree bark covered their chests. They had the same markings on their chests as the man, except theirs were red. They too were also barefoot.

I recognized the last man immediately. Bodaway came out from the shadows and the men looked at him while he began walking towards me. As he strode forward Bodaway was looking at my arms and legs, then he looked at the man in feathers. He spoke to the man, in some sort of tribal language, and pointed to Skip.

The man in feathers walked to my horse and looked at him for a while. He pulled some plant leaves from a small pouch and smashed the leaves up as I watched on. He put his hand on my horse's chest where the bullet went in. As he held his palm over the bloodied hole something began to come out of Skip. It was the bullet.

I looked at his hand and the bullet started to melt and ooze, falling to ground. He spread the leaves on my horse's wound and started to mumble what sounded like a chant. Suddenly, my horse stood up and I could see the wound healing. After just a brief moment it appeared to have never happened and Skip was well again.

Bodaway spoke something again in a tribal language. I could not figure out at the time what it was. After he finished the man with the feathers and the men with the bows started to walk away into the darkness.

Bodaway turned to me and spoke. "Are you ok, Jacob?"

I looked around out of amazement. "Yeah, I'm ok. How, how did that man do that?"

"Do what, Jacob?"

"Fix my horse. He was dead."

Bodaway smiled and said, "you will know soon, Jacob." He put his hand on my right shoulder. "I am sure you want answers to what you have seen, yes?"

I nodded.

"If you want to know Jacob meet me at the meadow tomorrow after sundown. There is a lot to tell you and everything will become clear to you soon. It is up to you if you want to know who you are, why we are here, and why I keep appearing to you. Be at the meadow tomorrow after sundown, understood?"

I nodded and Bodaway smiled. He then started to walk into the darkness. I grabbed my horse and he was perfectly well. I rode back home.

The next day I woke up and I remember just lying there, looking up in the ceiling thinking about what happened last night. I looked to my right at the empty area were Joshua passed away in. I knew in my mind that I should tell my mother that Bodaway approached me again, but something deep inside of me said not to, so I kept it to myself. I also kept the incident from father.

Thinking back to the attempted robbery, I did not want my money being taken away from me. I had been saving for a house and kept my money in a box in my room. Ann always told me I should put the money in the bank, but I never trusted them with it. Especially now that I know there were some lawbreakers around. I hardly spent any money at all really, just on some needed clothes and a few drinks here and there.

That day I really wanted to go to Ann's house and surprise her. Even though her family was rich and thought poorly of me, she did not care what they thought. Nor did I care. We both loved one another and that was all that mattered to us.

I got up early and washed then helped my mother with breakfast. My father was in a rush, like always, to go to work. I also had a lot of work to do here at the house before I headed over to the Jefferson's ranch. My mother was still not very talkative those days, even years after my brother's death, and would only speak here and there. She was not the same. After breakfast my mother would go to my brother's burial site and just sit next to his grave. At times, while I was working in the back, I could see my mother there. Some days a hawk could be seen flying above my mother and Joshua's grave. Neither were ever as alone as they may have felt.

After completing my work I headed to the Jefferson's ranch. On my way through town I stopped to get something to eat. I went to the store and picked up some meat and bread then went outside where I saw Ann near Town Hall. I went over to see her. She was carrying a basket with her lunch. We sat together at our spot and ate.

"How's your day been, Jacob?"

"Good," I said to Ann.

"Anything new inside there at the Town Hall?"

"Yes! A lot of new things are going on, I might even go take a trip to the city."

"Oh yeah? That's good Ann, I'm proud of you. Make sure you learn as much as you can over there."

"Oh, I will Jacob. Are we ok for supper tonight at your parents?"

"Well, yes, but I will be late. Do you still want to be there?"

"Of course, I love your family." I smiled and Ann asked, "why will you be late?"
"Well, I am going to..." I knew I couldn't tell her the truth, even though I wanted to. I just couldn't at this time so I said something else. "Well, I'm just going to the meadow to be by myself for a bit."

"Oh, I see," she replied. "Well, try not to be too late, ok?"

"I wouldn't think of it."

"I should get back in there now. I am going to find out when I am going to the city with the other folks. I will let you know what I hear."

I nodded to Ann then she gave me a kiss. She smiled over her shoulder as she walked away and inside Town Hall.

After she had gone in I began to walk to my horse, but was stopped when I saw smoke coming from behind Town Hall. It was coming from over the hill. Mostly everyone around me stopped to look at it while others mounted their horses and took off riding toward it. Out of curiosity I rode towards it as well.

The smoke was coming from the mining area. I saw it right after I got up over the hill. There were many people cantering up the hill to meet the sight, all looking and pointing. It was like nothing I had ever seen before. Near the mine something new had been built. It was a series of houses with large pipes coming out the roofs, like they were reaching high up into the sky, smoking at the top.

I could hear people around me asking, "what is that?"

There were so many workers down the hill, busy at work, and I could see them putting out silver, or cinnabar, into those big barn looking houses.

I noticed a man ride up towards us and he said to the people, "can I help you, folks?"

One man responded, "what's going on here?"

Another person followed with more questions, and then another until the first yelled, "Folks! Folks! We will be having a Town Hall meeting in a few days to inform everyone of what is developing. So, everyone get back to your homes. Get back to the town. Everything is fine here."
The curious people started to leave with uncertainty. I was one of them and we all started to leave the area.

By the time I got to the forked path at the meadow it was close to sundown. I stopped and looked down the path, contemplating whether to go or not. I looked up in the sky and looked around just waiting, and hesitating. In a split decision I pulled my horse Skip to the right, in the direction to the meadows. My horse was running faster than usual while we rode. It almost felt as if he was guiding me in somehow.

When we broke out of the forest and reached the meadow I noticed that Skip was leading us to the left, even though I tried to steer him right. He did not listen to me. Skip was directing us towards a big rock near the river and above it I could see the large mountain peak. Just as I saw this he stopped, right before the large rock. It was silent again and I looked around. I could see the light from the sun starting to fade upon the face of the mountains and hills. Not too long after we had arrived the sun settled behind mountains. Just as it did Bodaway appeared from behind the rock.

Bodaway walked towards me and I got off my horse as he approached. He greeted me and shook my hand. "So are you ready Jacob?"

I nodded in response.

Bodaway said, "the things I am going to tell you, you may not understand right now, but you will in time. I am part of a tribe called Skitcha. We have lived here before you came and before anyone else came to this land. Nowadays there are only a handful of us left." He paused to let this settle in the air.

"So what does this have to do with me, Bodaway?"

He did not hesitate to respond. "Jacob, you have Skitcha in your blood."

"I do? How?"

Bodaway looked straight at me and said, "your mother is Skitcha. She is part of our tribe."

This couldn't be true. I shook my head. "She is?"

Bodaway nodded, "you see Jacob," he patted my shoulder and we started to walk. "Your mother made a choice long ago. She chose to not live with us. Your mother did not wish to live our way of life." I wore an expression of disbelief as Bodaway spoke. "Your mother was forced to make a promise before she left the tribe. A promise to never speak of us or our ways."

Bodaway saw that I was very quiet. I had started to gaze off to the sky and to the mountain peak beyond.

He spoke again, "I notice that you look at that mountain. Do you know why you do this?"

"I don't know, Bodaway. I feel something though when I look at it."

Bodaway smiled and said, "that mountain up there is called Mount Umunhum."

"Umunhum," I repeated.

"Yes, it means 'the great humming bird'. You see, hummingbirds nest there."

"The great hummingbird?"

"Yes, the hummingbird shows skill, alertness, quickness, and bravery. Our tribe, our people Jacob, as Skitchas, are ordered to take care of this area and the mountain itself. The mountain is sacred to us, but now that new people are coming in the land they are starting to move closer and closer to us. The new folks are infringing around our land and pushing us further out."

"But, why didn't my ma tell me about this?"

"Again Jacob, she was forbidden to tell you or anyone close to her."

"I still do not know what this has to do with me Bodaway."

Bodaway continued to walk, "well Jacob, you were the chosen one. Umunhum called out your name and showed us a picture of you in our minds."

I nodded with confusion.

"I know this will take time for you to understand, Jacob. Like I said, you will understand soon enough."

"So, why do you come now to talk to me?"

"Because, there is great danger coming with the outsiders. They want everything. The land, the elements, and even the mines."

I thought in my head for a moment when he said mines. I thought about my father.

"There are many people working at the mines now. This is not something we have control of. It is why we need to protect what we do have at this time."

My mind was muddling. I was lost in his words. Until this time my parents had brought me up differently than what Bodaway was speaking of. My father would not understand what was going on. He probably wouldn't believe what Bodaway was saying to me. I wanted to ask my mother however, Bodaway told me she was forbidden to talk about it. I decided that I had to leave it alone for right now.

"And that is where you come in, Jacob. You must lead us. That's what was told to us."

"Lead you?"

"Yes, you must take command, and Umunhum said that I must train you for what is to come." Bodaway stopped and looked at me and said, "Jacob, you are our only hope. Only you can ensure that our tribe will survive, will be free. Only you can keep the great hummingbird going."

I turned my eyes from him at this point. I looked down to the ground then back at him. Bodaway locked onto my eyes. I sensed that he was telling me the truth and I knew inside of me that he was right.

"I will give you a few days to think about it, Jacob." Bodaway then grabbed something out of his bag. It was a small necklace, beaded, and had a feather on it. "Put this around your neck."

"What is this, Bodaway?"

"It is a necklace with a humming bird feather on it. Put it on right now and it will give you the visions of what you want to know."

I put on the necklace and tucked it under my shirt.

"Remember, do not tell your mother about us meeting. Do not tell her about the necklace. You understand, Jacob?"

"Yes, I understand, but will she know later on?"

Bodaway nodded. "She will know when the time comes."

Bodaway whistled. His horse came out from behind the rock and Bodaway got on and began to go. "I will see you in a few days, Jacob." He rode off and I watched him leave. Then I got on my horse and rode back home.

When I got back home and rode up to the house I could see my parents, sister, and Ann eating dinner. Ann's horse was outside pinned by the front door. I put Skip in the barn then walked to the backdoor of the house. I opened the door and the first thing I heard was my family laughing as Ann was telling funny stories. This was the first time I'd seen Mom laugh since Joshua died.

"Jacob, come have a seat and have some supper," my mother said.

I grabbed a plate and sat next to Ann. Ann was telling jokes and mocking the local politicians, how they spoke and acted.

"There is this one guy Mr. Thomas, he walks oh so very strangely." She got up and started to impersonate him. "He walks all like this with his belly sticking out and his back leaning so far back it looks like he is about to fall."

My father was laughing.

"He also has this real deep voice that sounds like a big 'ol toad." She made the voice and said, "well grrrr. I think this proclamation will not be effective! I refuse to sign!" Everyone started to laugh and then the laughter reached me.

Ann sat down and said, "oh, and there is this woman named Miss Scarlet. Oh she seems to have had a few flings with some of the men around town. She will just put her legs out to show the men, like this." Ann started acting again. "She will just pucker up and look around at the men, blinking her eyes."

My mother and sisters laughed.

"So as you see, it is very interesting at the hall."

My father said to me, "Ann told us she is going to the city in a few days."

I responded, "Uh? Oh, I know Pa. It will be exciting for her to go. She will tell us all about it."

Ann stood up again. "Well folks, I need to get going. It is getting late and I have to ride back home. Thank you Mrs. Smith."

My mother smiled and said, "you're always welcome here, Ann."

As Ann left I said, "Ann I will ride with you to make sure you make it home safe."

My mother and father smiled as I turned to go.

"I will go get my horse and met you out front."

"Ok Jacob," Ann said.

We rode together to Ann's house and passed the town, heading north. When we reached a bend in the trail we turned right and the path guided us to her home.

"Ann, have a good time at the city. Let me know how it goes."

"I will," she moved her horse next to mine and gave me a kiss and a hug. "I love you, Jacob."

"I love you too, Ann."

We both smiled and she said goodnight before riding up to her house. I turned the other way and headed back home. As I started towards town I noticed a cloud of smoke forming in the sky, far off from the path. I went to go investigate and rode in that direction.

When I got to the source of the smoke I saw what appeared to be a camp. There were groups of men around a single fire pit and there were horses near them. I pulled my horse to a safe distance in the dark cover of the trees and watched them. The faces of the men started to become clear to me and they were familiar. Almost all were white, except for one Indian. Then I remembered why they looked so familiar. I had seen most of these faces before on wanted posters.

Even though I was too far away to hear what they were talking about, it looked like they were planning something. Laughter cackled above the fire. Most of the men were smoking and drinking. They had their rifles stacked together like a teepee. I had this feeling they were going to hit the town soon. I moved as quickly as I could, loaded myself on top of Skip, and road into town.

When I got into town I rode to the sheriff's office. I walked up to the office and noticed that it was dark inside. No one was there. I thought he might be walking around town so I rode around to try to look for him. After a long time searching I never found him. I had a feeling he may have fallen asleep so I rode off and headed out of the town.
When I got home everyone was asleep. I wanted to tell my father what I had seen, but I did not want to wake him because I knew he had worked such a long day. I kept it to myself and washed up, then went to bed.

When I was asleep I had a dream. It was a dream which I have never dreamed before. I pictured every moment fully.

The dream flashed in my head and I saw the whole land of Almaden Valley. It looked like I was flying. All of a sudden I could see a ring of fire, from a far distance, with other fires scattered everywhere. In my dream I started to swoop down towards the ring of fire. Smoke started to appear and I went through the smoke. I was diving down very quickly and could feel the smoke going past my face. As I made the descent I could see people fighting. Then, without warning, I started to fall. I knew because it no longer felt like I was flying. Before I knew it I had landed on the ground. Looking up from the Earth I saw a big red hawk. It was then that I realized that I wasn't the only one flying. I had been there with that hawk. It has flown me into the ring of fire.

I looked around and it was silent. There were fires all around me and in the distance I saw people fighting.

Bodaway appeared out of the fire wall and he was pointing at me, yelling. Since it was silent I could not hear anything, like only the silence had fallen on me. Then he suddenly pointed elsewhere and I began to hear a muffled sound. I looked in the direction Bodaway was pointing and I saw a group of men running towards us. They looked Indian, but some were white and black men. They started to signal and wave.

Suddenly, from behind them, more men came in and started to move towards us. Their eyes were directed upwards and they watched as swarms of hummingbirds started to come down from the shadowy sky. They dove and dropped fire out of their beaked mouths. I looked up and could see them, their neck glowing red as the fire came out of their mouths. The fire hit the ground and patches of flames started to surround us. The men continued to go over and through the fires. Everyone started to charge, I turned and looked at Bodaway as he pointed and started to charge.

Before I knew it I was face to face with one of the men.

He jumped and lunged at me with a spear. I dodged his spear, but he tackled me down. I was struggling to get him off of me. I looked to my side and saw Bodaway outnumbered by the men. He did not escape.

I looked at the man that was attacking me, he looked like an Indian and his face looked gray like the ashes of a fire. While he had me pinned down he pulled out an axe and suddenly the axe moved towards my head.

I woke up breathing heavily and sweating. It felt far more real than a dream.

The next morning I got up and walked towards the window. Looking out I could see my father leaving to go to work. At times I would just stare out of the window in the mornings and watch this scene as my father left. Today I shook my head. It pounded with pressure. I shook my head and the pressure left. Then I got ready to leave for work myself, at the Jefferson's ranch.

In the main house my mother was getting ready to go out with my sister Mary Ann. They were going to town. Apparently she had met someone and was going to introduce him to my mother. I think they were also going to visit my sister Kate at her home as well. I grabbed some breakfast and headed to the Jefferson's ranch.

––––––––––––

Later in the day, after finishing my work at the ranch, I was riding home, but felt the urge to go see my father. Ever since I had woken up I had a feeling to do so, so I turned to the mines. When I got to the mines I slowed my horse as I approached. I saw a group of men. There had to be at least twenty men, some white, some black, and some Indian. Looking closer I saw that some of these men were from the wanted signs posted around town. I pulled Skip closer, silently, around the grounds watching the scene.

Hidden out of sight, I watched as the scene unfolded before me.

Down at the mines one of the Wanted Men, an Indian man, stepped forward and pulled out a knife. He crept behind one of the miners and within an instant stabbed him. I looked around to see if anyone else was on the road, but I was alone. No one else was going to see this.

Just then I heard gunfire. Without warning all was chaos. The miners began retaliating and a riot broke out. People scattered everywhere around the mines.

As I watched I knew what was happening. This was what those Wanted Men had sought all along, to take control of the mines or even just to completely destroy the area. I did not know why the Indian man stabbed one of the workers though. It just didn't make sense to me at the time.

Gunfire was everywhere and I saw dead people littered across the land. Fighting was still occurring and some of the Wanted Men were grabbing at what appeared to be dynamite. They started to light it and when they did people started to run out of the mines. Before the last man ran out the mine the Wanted Men threw the dynamite in. It detonated. I watched as the helpless miners became trapped within. The dynamite blew up the mouth of the mine and rocks tumbled down.

My father.

I rode down to the mines without any concern for my wellbeing. There was fire all around me. I went around one of the buildings, near one of the mines, and one of the miners grabbed me and startled my horse Skip.

"What are you doing here? You have to get away, the mines are being overruled! Go! Go now!"

I told the man, "I can't leave, my pa is in the mines!"

The man shook his head. "There is no way we can get your father out, Son. The rebels blew up the entrance and some of them went in. God only knows what they are doing inside right now."

I looked around and suddenly the ground started shaking. It looked like some dynamite might of went off inside.

"Son, get out of here now!"

I looked at the man and I started to ride back to the trail, escaping from the gunfire and dodging bullets as I fled. When I got to the trail I looked back and saw fires everywhere. Smoke began to fill the sky as the battle raged on. Over the crest of the hill I could see people from town coming towards the mines. I rode back to town to let my mother and sisters know what was happening.

On the way back to town I saw people running around scattered everywhere. Word was spreading fast of the rebel force's attack on the miners. I looked around to see if I could find my mother and sister. After searching for quite a while I finally spotted them walking near the town hall.

I rode up to them, passing a group of people who were surrounding the sheriff's office. Looking at my mother and sister I was just glad that they were safe.

"What's going on around here, Jacob?"

"Something bad is going on at the mines. It's real bad, Ma."

My mother and Mary Ann both shared the same look of worry. My mother said, "we must go over there and check on your father. Tell your sister Kate also."

"It is not safe to go to the mines right now, Ma." I tried to comfort my mother, and my sister was comforting her as well. I told my family what was happening.

"Let's go to the sheriff's office to see if there are any updates," I suggested.

As we walked to the sheriff's office we saw that just about the whole town was right there with us. The sheriff was not in however, we saw another person was there to take his place.

"People, people," he spoke, "the sheriff is over at the mines waiting for further orders. In the meantime the sheriff asked me to take his place. I am here to answer any questions you may have."

One gentleman came forward and asked, "what is going on over there at the mines? I've heard loud bangs and even gunfire."

Everyone looked at each other with concern.

The official representative said, "there has been word that a group of men have attacked the mine. Some of the men are on the Wanted List you see next to me." He motioned to the posters.

A woman came forward next and asked, "what are we supposed to do?"

"The sheriff has asked that you stay calm. He is handling the situation. The sheriff also asked that you stay at home for the rest of the day. Close the shops early please and go home to your families. Throughout the day you may see some of the Federal Army in town. They have been requested to assist in the capture of the Wanted Men."

All of the sudden my sister Mary Ann called out. "My Pa works at the mines. How do we know he is ok?"

Others started to mumble and ask the same question.

"Miss, we understand your concern and we know a lot of people work at the mines. We will find out more within the next day or so who is okay and who..."

I grabbed my mom and sister and said, "we should go see Kate, Ma. We should let her know what's going on."

When we got to Kate's house my sister briskly got off her horse and knocked on the door. Kate opened the door.

"Kate, something bad has happened."

"What is going on out there, Mary Ann?"

"Didn't you hear the big bang noises from the mines?"

"Yes, I did. They do that at times to open up the mines more."

I got off my horse and helped my mother off hers.

"Kate, something happened at the mines. There was a big riot over there," I said.

My mother did not want to hear it again so she asked to go in the house. Mary Ann went in with her while Kate and I talked outside.

"What's going on Jacob?"

I told her about me going to see Pa, and how I ran into the riot. I told Kate about the Wanted Men trapping the men in the mines and she put her hands to her mouth as she gasped.
"Oh God, Jacob. Did you go to town and tell the sheriff?"

"When I got into town everyone was running around, out of fright. Me, Mary Ann, and Ma went to the sheriff's office and there were a lot of people there. They were all asking questions. The sheriff was out of the office, but his representative said they are bringing the

Federal Army to town to control what's going on at the mines."

"What about Pa? Is he ok? Where is he?"

I looked down, and said, "I don't know. He was in the mine when all this happened. He could still be in there, Kate."

"And some of those Wanted Men are in there?"

I nodded. "The men did not look like they were from around here. The way they worked together though, it looked like they planned this for a long time."

"So, we don't know if Pa is ok?"

"No, Kate. The sheriff's representative said they'd give us any information they learn in a few days."

Kate started to cry and I held her. "Don't worry, Kate. I will find out what is happening to Pa. In the meantime can you take care of Ma here? I don't want her to be alone at home."

"Yes, she can stay here Jacob. I'll ask Mary Ann to get some of her clothes from home."

We both went inside and Kate invited Mother to stay with her. Ma nodded and Mary Ann agreed to help Ma as well.

My mother then stood up and started to walk around the house, looking worried about my father. I gave my sister Kate a hug and began to leave.

"I'll be back in a few days, Kate. Take care of Ma."

"I will Jacob."

Mary Ann and I went outside and got on our horses. "Mary Ann, take care of Ma ok? Maybe bring some of her wool work for her. To keep her mind off things."

"Ok Jacob, I will do that."

I said, "I will see you all in a few days, ok?"

My younger sister nodded and headed to the house.

I went back to the town to see if I could find out anything else about what had happened. When I got there the town was nearly empty. Everyone had done as the sheriff requested and gone home. I looked around to see if I could find Ann, but then remembered she was in San Jose for business. I looked into one of the windows of the Town Hall and could see some of the politicians scrambling around worried. One of them was Ann's father. He was saying something to one of the representatives who was dictating a telegraph.

I walked to the saloon and opened the doors. Not many people were inside, but I was hoping to find Matt. Suddenly, from the far distance, I heard a loud clatter of hooves heading down our main dirt road. A group of horses were galloping into town. I peeked my head out of the saloon and saw that it was the Federal Army. Looking down the road at them I noticed I was not the only curious resident. Many people in hiding had opened their windows to see the troops.

There were a lot of soldiers on horseback coming down the road and they were all armed. The sheriff's representative and a few politicians came out of the sheriff's office to greet the commanding officer. The sheriff's representative spoke first. "The sheriff is at the mines, located north along this trail, General."

The man was pointing to the dirt road that led to the mines while the Army General gazed down at him. The General nodded and moved to the mines. Instantly I ran to my horse and rode off trailing behind the Army, seeking a personal update on my father.

When I got close to the mines I saw that the road had been blocked. A few of the sheriff's men were at a crossroads as well as many townsmen, all waiting for an update.

I stopped my horse at the roadblock and I saw the sheriff of Almaden Valley.

"Sheriff," I yelled. He turned and looked at me. "Sheriff, my Pa is in the mines. Have you heard any new information about the riot so I can let my Ma and my sisters know?"

The sheriff shook his head. "We don't know what's going on in there right now, Son. Now go back home. It's not safe here. There is still fighting goin' on over there."

"But I need to know what's going on with my Pa!"

"Son, you will find out soon enough, ok. Now go home."

I looked at the sheriff for a while out of frustration then turned around and headed back on the trail towards town. As I was riding away I saw the army from afar coming in my direction. I stopped my horse to let them pass. When they galloped past I felt some of the soldiers staring at me, but the commander just did a quick glance and rode by.

After they passed by me I moved my horse back onto the trail and headed towards the direction of my parent's house. The sun had already begun to set.

———————————————

I knew I was getting close by the time I had reached the valley. In a trance I stared out at the valley while Skip guided us towards the house. Suddenly, I thought of something. I pulled hard on the reigns and redirected

Skip to the valley. Turning away from the pathway home I rode as fast as I could across the fields towards the big rock near the river.

When I got to the rock I stopped and yelled, "Bodaway!"

I looked around and Bodaway did not show up. I could see that Skip was tired and led him towards the river for a drink. While he drank I continued to look around and again yelled for Bodaway. Nothing except silence and crickets returned my calls.

Skip stopped drinking and I felt his muscles tense. He drew his head up from the water and looked to the right. I looked in that direction and saw a dark figure on a horse heading towards us. I was not sure who the figure was, so I prepared myself for a fight. Then, a new light shed on the man and I gained a better look at who he was.

His face was painted and he had that similar marking as Bodaway's people on his chest, the feather with the circle. He also had the marking on his forehead. It ran down to his eyes and then to his cheeks. He was armed with a spear and a long tomahawk axe. He stopped right before me and my horse. We both looked at each other. The man's daunting and mysterious eyes bore into me through the silence of the grove. He did not say a word. He just stared at me.

Finally, a birdcall interrupted our stares and spread out across the valley. The man looked up and around. He waved at me and pointed to the directions of the hills, just to the side of us. He waved again signaling me to follow him. He nodded and I cautiously nodded back.

As I followed the man I noticed we were heading in the direction of Mount Umunhum. We crossed the river and went in between a canyon formed between two towering cliffs, then over one large hill. When we were at the top of the hill I looked outwards to see what lay before us and saw my parent's house below us in the distance. We went down the hill and descended into a forest. As the man led me into the depths of these woods we came upon two hills, side by side, that appeared almost conjoined by the thicket of branches and leaves that lay between them.

As we approached this barrier of foliage the man dismounted from his horse and plowed his hands into the Earth. After some searching he lifted his hands revealing a rope hidden among the forest floor. When he pulled on the rope the barrier of branches that lay between the two towering hills lifted in the style of a gate, unveiling a worn and cleared trail. The man looked around discerningly and directed me with his hands to follow the path.

Cautiously I did as the man motioned and guided Skip onto the trail. The man closed the forest gate and followed behind me. Once the branches were lowered back in place the man curved his horse around me and led the way once more. We were on the trail for what seemed like an eternity before the man steered us right, taking us deeper into the forest.

———————————————

The sounds of the wild had been muffled by the thickness of these woods, but after some time I began to hear something. It was the sounds of song, of chants. Upon recognizing these voices I noticed that we were indeed no longer alone and people began to materialize from the woods. These figures walked beside us until we found ourselves at their village. At the center was a blazing fire.

The man guided me to this fire pit and pointed to a post where I could tie up my horse. When I got down from horse I saw that the whole tribe had surrounded me. There were both men and women, as well as a few children. At once I knew who these people were. The Skitcha tribe.

The man got off his horse and put his hand on my back. He guided me to the fire pit and helped me to a seat. I sat down and waited for what would come next. All around me I could hear the chanting again, coming from every crevice of the forest, and stared at the glow of the flames. I felt as though I was in a trance of some sort and tried to break it by looking up to the stars. As I arched my head all I could see was the face of Mount Umunhum lit by the glow of the growing fire. The flames traveled upwards with my gaze and then began to take form, separating into the shape of a man. Before me, through the flames, stepped Bodaway.

Bodaway approached me and I held his gaze, quickly standing up.

Bodaway smiled and said, "welcome, Jacob. Welcome to our village. This is the home of the Skitcha tribe."

"How did you go through the flame like that, Bodaway?"

He grinned, "soon you will know, Jacob. We have a lot to teach you."

I quickly said to Bodaway, "There was a big riot at the mines. I think my father is in danger. He was in the mines when the riot began."

"We know, Jacob. We have to be ready when they come to us next."

"You are not going to do anything, Bodaway? Can't you help my father?"

"No Jacob, not at this time. We have to prepare for what's about to come."

Out of frustration I began to say, "but, what about my pa?"

Bodaway then said, "Jacob, you need to focus on what is at hand. Don't worry about your father right now."

I just stared at him in return.

"Listen Jacob, you need to trust me. You need to believe what is right in your soul. What does your soul tell you?" Bodaway pointed in the middle of his chest.

I took a deep breath and said, "I need to stay here and train."

Bodaway put his hand on my shoulder and smiled. "You're already learning, Jacob. I want you to follow me. I will take you through the village."

As we walked Bodaway spoke.

"Our tribe is small, as you can see, but there are many more of us out of the state."

"How come they are not here, Bodaway?"

"They chose not to. Just like your mother, but if any trouble arises they would come."

As we walked I saw some children playing. They looked at me curiously.

"Your training will be difficult at first Jacob, but I know you will master it quickly."

"What is it that I have to do for training, Bodaway?"

"Well Jacob, it is more mental." Bodaway tapped his index finger to his temple. "More than anything else, your training will occur in your mind. After you mastered that you will learn from the spirits around you. Then, finally hand to hand combat."

"Spirits?"

"Yes Jacob, spirits. You may not believe this right now, but the energy that comes out of us is from the spirits. Our ancestors from the past started the paths to who we are today. They were here first and came upon this land. Before anyone else did." He paused for a moment and looked at me with warm eyes. "I see you're confused. Don't worry, it will become clear to you. When you saw me go through the flame and walk towards you, I was not alone. The spirits helped me to do that."

"I see," I whispered back, holding his gaze.

Bodaway continued to walk, "come now. I will have you meet some of our people."

We came to an area that looked like a camp. There were small houses and a group of people talking. One of the men in the group stood up and as he did the others followed. Bodaway walked up to this man.

The man was stocky and looked very strong. He had long dark hair and a marking on his arm. He was close to my height, but I was still taller than him. Bodaway spoke to him in another language, the tongue of the Skitcha tribe.

"Armija, this is Jacob."

Armija looked at me and replied back in Skitchan. Bodaway replied to him in the same language.

I stood my ground, sensing that Armija was a man to be respected in this tribe, and stared back at him. Armija stuck out his hand and I cautiously did the same. I could feel the eyes of the other tribesmen watching us. I confidently left my hand out and very sharply Armija grabbed it and started to squeeze. It was not a typical handshake and after I noticed what he was doing I started to squeeze his hand in return, without any expression of pain or discomfort.

Suddenly Armija smiled and let go. He spoke to Bodaway in Skitchan. I looked to Bodaway and he started to smile. "Armija had not believed that you were the Chosen One. Now after your hands have met, he might believe it just a little more."

Armija spoke again and Bodaway translated. "He is saying your eyes are powerful with energy. Armija knows you were strong just by looking at your eyes. Some of my people were worried about you, at first even

Armija. It is because of your skin color. You are lighter than expected, as your father is Caucasian. This tribe, you see, they know a lot about your mother." His eyes glowed with promise as he spoke.

"Armija will help you train."

Upon hearing this Armija spoke back, Bodaway translated. "He said be ready."

"I will," I repeated, holding Armija's gaze. Bodaway did not need to translate this.

Armija smiled and slapped his chest, giving out a loud thudding sound, then walked back to the group.

"How will I know the language, Bodaway?"

"You will learn it from me, Jacob." He said simply and motioned for me to follow him.

Bodaway directed me to another group of villagers further away from the other camps. It was inhabited by a different division of tribesmen. I knew this because the tents looked so distinct from the rest of the village. There were bones hanging around their tent, as well as feathers, and no one was congregating outside.

"Stay right here," Bodaway said as he entered what looked to be the main tent.

As I waited I looked around the area. From behind me I could see people had been following us. They were mainly watching me and talking amongst themselves. Bodaway came out of the tent and said it was okay to come in. I looked behind me again, to see that the people were still there watching me, then entered.

When I walked into the tent I saw just one man inside. I knew who he was immediately. Back when that gang of Wanted People attacked me, just a few days ago, he was the Skitchan man among them. He nodded to me and gestured with his palm upwardly, ushering us to sit. Beside him was a curtain. We sat down and when we did a woman came through it.

The woman was dressed in a robe and her face was covered from the hood of the robe. Barely visible, beneath the shadow of this hood, I could see that her face was dark and painted. Her skin color was so dark that it blended into the shadow of her robe, far darker than the other tribesman. She started to walk to us and was holding a bowl filled with smoke. Taking a seat beside us I stared into the bowl. Bodaway saw my curiosity then extended his hand to me, indicating to wait before doing anything.

The woman started to speak in Skitchan to the men, holding her head down, she pointed to me. The other man looked at Bodaway and he acknowledged the gaze.

Bodaway turned to my ear and said softly, "her name is Marine-Oni. She is the head shaman of this tribe and she asked for you to say your name."

"What is a shaman?"

Bodaway looked around and said, "a shaman is a spiritual healer. Now say to her your name."

I hesitated and within that instant Marine-Oni brought herself face to face with me. We were so close that we were almost nose-to-nose. She looked at my face as though she was examining me and started to smell me. I spoke at last. "My name is Jacob."

She sat back, seemingly satisfied, and continued to look at me. Marine-Oni began to speak to the men again and Bodaway translated.

"Marine-Oni said that you are like no one she has met before." As he spoke Marine-Oni continued to speak in the native tongue, Bodaway nodded in his understanding. "She also senses that you are angry and seek revenge. She said you still show anger for the loss of your brother and now are worried about your father."

Marine-Oni was still speaking, without blinking she stared intently on the smoke.

"She says you are not yet focused. You must let go of it for now. She says she will help you with that."

I asked, "am I this Chosen One, Bodaway? The one people speak of?"

Bodaway did not need to ask Marine-Oni, she replied knowingly. "She believes so Jacob, but she will not let the tribe know yet until your training is done. Marine-Oni wanted to give you something."

The woman then grabbed an empty bowl and poured a serving of the smoking liquid into it then gave the bowl to me.

Bodaway said, "she wants you to drink this right now. Marine-Oni says we will truly find out if you are the Chosen One once you do."

I cautiously drank the liquid. It was very hot and bitter on my tongue, but I did not cough or spit it out. Once drained I left the empty bowl on the table.

Marine-Oni began to talk again. Bodaway nodded to her in return and asked me to stand up. "Now Jacob, this will be a test before the training begins. We must go now." He nodded to the man and woman then guided me out of the tent.

When we got outside we found that the grouping of tribesmen who had been following us were very close to the tent, crowding the door of the shaman. As we walked away they still followed us.

"Where are we going now?"

Bodaway grabbed a torch and lit it in one of the campfires nearby. "I am going to take you to a cave, Jacob. You will stay there overnight. We call this cave the Chataw."

As we walked towards the Chataw I could see Mount Umunhum looming above us. I asked Bodaway what we would do at the cave.

"Just be strong, Jacob. I will get you in the morning."

I did not know what he meant by this and continued to follow him. Just before me was the entrance of the Chataw. When we drew nearer I noticed a door lay locked across the mouth of the cave. We stopped abruptly and Bodaway looked around at the people then spoke in Skitchan. Some clapped in response while others just looked on.

"What did you tell them?"

"I told them that your energy and spirit is among us."

I looked at the tribesmen and smiled at them then walked to the door of the Chataw. Bodaway opened it.

"Are you ready, Jacob?"

The cave was huge and very dark. I took a deep breath and looked at Bodaway. "I am ready," and I truly felt that I was.

Bodaway went into Chataw and asked me to follow. The tunnels within were enormous. I tried looking beyond the flicker of the torch as it danced upon the ancient walls, but could see nothing except shadows. We walked for a long time before I began to hear water drops falling from the roof to the base of the caverns. Walking briskly, it felt as though we were going into the heart of Mount Umunhum.

Bodaway slowed as we were met by two forks along the path, two tunnels. We turned left then continued to walk for a long while before confronted by a dead end. With nowhere to go I admired the huge cave wall before us, finding that we were in a smaller cavern of sorts. All around there appeared to be scratches in the walls. Tribal markings were everywhere. They were the markings that I had seen from the tribesmen, now plastered all around the cavern. One marking caught my eye in particular. Very distinct, it was the largest in the cavern. To view the entirety of it I had to tilt my head backwards, arching my neck for a complete view.

"Incredible isn't it, Jacob?"

"It, it is, Bodaway. Was this here since the beginning?"

"Yes, it was Jacob. Since the beginning."

I looked around some more before Bodaway spoke again.

"Jacob, are you now ready?"

I looked around once more before replying. "Yes, I am ready."

Bodaway smiled and started to walk away from me.

"Wait, where are you going?"

"I will see you in the morning, Jacob."

The room quickly grew dark as Bodaway left me in the cavern, his torch flickering in his footsteps. I suddenly thought to look one last time at the tribal markings before all light had left.

"I can't see! Bodaway! Where are you?"

It became very clear to me now, I was locked in for the night. This was my test as so it seemed.

I must of dozed off, at least for a while, before stirred by a crackling noise. I stood up, but could not see a thing. The darkness had consumed all that was around me. Not even my own hand before my face. The room was pitch dark.

Suddenly, the crackling started again. "Who is there?"

As I called out the crackling stopped. The cave fell silent, but only for a moment. I then began to hear water dropping slowly all around me. Then, out of nowhere voices started to emerge. Instinctively, I tried to feel the walls of the cave with my hands, to gain my bearings.

"Show yourself!"

My voice echoed. Even my breath echoed, but no one replied. The air in the room suddenly became thick. Trying to breath normally I felt an energy present with me, as if I were no longer alone. It was an energy that I had never felt before, coming to me like a wave. The voices started to get louder as if they were approaching. Before they fell upon me the energy suddenly came within me. As it did the voices got louder and multiplied. More and more were speaking. And then, the sound passed right through me.

I followed the sounds, turning my body around, and in amazement watched as the tribal marking became visible in the darkness. They were light, very slowly shimmering. I started to hear the loud cracklings behind me and turned to face it.

Unsteadied by the turn alone, the ground began to shake and I fell down. On the ground it felt as though everything was moving very quickly. The ground itself was moving and the voices became much louder. With it the cracking came too, more violently than before. Rolling on my back I looked at the markings on the cave walls. They had started to glow brighter and brighter.

In awe of the spectacle I noticed new noise had come to the cavern, it was an "ummmm" sound.

Suddenly, the light from the markings burst out and the glow of the source took form. Spirits walked towards me. The shapes, although dark, I knew were dressed in feathers. Nearing me something else followed them, birds. Flying behind the spirits. They soared quickly before the approaching figures and I saw that they were giant hummingbirds. Their eyes were large and glowing.

There were a total of six spirits, all comprised of light, that approached me. At least that is what I saw at first. They slowed in their pace as they neared me and tilted their heads back, all looking at one particular marking in the cave. They took one last step then stopped when the marking burst and light was expelled from the cavern. A man stepped out.

His face was pale and he had long hair. The other spirits moved aside to let him through as he exited from the marking. The spirit looked directly to me and spoke in Skitchan. Then there was silence followed by the humming of birds, flying around me.

I said, "I do not understand you."

Silence fell again in the cavern.

The man said, "Jacob, I am The Skitcha. The Skitcha people know me by this name alone. And you Jacob, are my grandson."

I must have taken a step forward towards The Skitcha because we grew closer as he said this.

"You are the chosen one. You are chosen because my blood runs through you."

"You, you are my grandfather?"

The man, The Skitcha spirit nodded. "Yes. Your mother was not to tell you about me. She wanted to keep you safe."

"Safe from what?"

"They called themselves The Hand of Transcendence, they are a group of people determined to get rid of us. They want to destroy the land that is ours."

"Who?"

"They are all kinds of people, Jacob. They walk amongst you and you would not know it. These people can be of any race or color."

I fell speechless.

My grandfather said, "you know you have a purpose in life, Jacob. You have always had that in you, in your soul. Are you starting to figure out what that is now?"

I looked up to my grandfather and said, "yes. Yes I do, Grandfather."

"Our tribe is counting on you for their survival. Your family is counting on you for their survival. And you, for your own safety, you must realize this."

"Grandfather, will I be living at the village now?"

He smiled and said, "only if you want to. The choice is up to you, Jacob. Bodaway will tell you this as well. The land we have, it has invited us to live here, but only if we respect and protect it. You can build a house of your own, should you wish."

Immediately, I thought of Ann and I started to say her name. My grandfather interrupted and smiled again. "Ann will be ok. Soon she will understand what you need to do, but that will come later."

I nodded, "so what happens next?"

"After your training you need to find the other tribe members. Now that you are with us Jacob, you can search for the rest of our people and then track The Hand of Transcendence."

"How will I do that? Wouldn't they find out who I am?"

"No, they will not. While you're scouting, especially in the town, they will not know that you're a part of our tribe." He pointed at his arm, "your skin color is different from the rest of us."

"I understand now, Grandfather."
My grandfather smiled and nodded. "Do you have any questions before the training begins?"

"How will I be able to see you again?"

He pointed to my chest, "I will always be there, Jacob. You can come here if you ever need to talk to me. Now, are you ready my grandson?"

"Yes Grandfather, I am ready."

He nodded and said, "this will be a very difficult thing for you to handle, but I know you are strong."

My grandfather spoke again in the tribal Skitcha tongue then put out his hand outwards, palm up. As he did three of the spirit men came towards me. One grabbed me and threw me to the wall of the room. I flew back instantly, crashing into the wall. Stumbling from the energy that surged through me I fell forward and landed on my chest. On the ground I looked up and could see the spirits hovering closer to me.

When I tried to get up another spirit grabbed me by my neck and looked at me face to face. He punched me in the face. I moved to the left and he grabbed my arm, biting the upper portion close to my shoulder. I grunted in pain and fought back, taking a swing at him. When I did he vanished into dust.

Suddenly the other two spirits came towards me. I grabbed one and slammed him to the ground. It turned instantly to dust. The rest of the four spirits came after me and I began to run. I ran as fast as I could, but through the darkness I could not see where I was headed and tripped. I stumbled to the ground. I turned quickly onto my back just as one of the spirits grabbed my leg. I tried to break free, but the other three spirits had caught up as well. Another grabbed my other leg and then another my head. They pinned me firmly to the ground.

Trying to wriggle free, the last spirit hovered above me and bit my leg, tearing my skin off. The other spirits began to do the same, biting at my body. The spirit that was holding my head looked down at me. Without catching my eye he lunged towards my face, teeth bared to bite.

I woke up.

Feeling like it all may have been a dream I woke up and found that I was still in the cave and my body hurt. I looked around and saw that I was far away from the cavern with the markings. Looking at my arm I saw that I was bleeding. A portion of my skin was gone and beneath it was a deep wound. My other arm appeared the same, sparse of skin and bleeding. Frantically I looked at my legs. My pants were damp with blood. I drew my hand to my shoulder and drew it away. It was vibrant red and moist from blood.

I tried to get up, but could not raise myself. Knowing I had to find a way out I looked around and started to crawl forward. I drug my body along the tunnel's stone cold ground, aching and losing blood quickly. Thinking of my family, thinking of Ann, I crawled.

Up ahead I saw a light. It was the fork of the two tunnels. I clawed towards the right tunnel. I was crawling and clawing at the ground for my life. As I drug myself the light grew brighter. From a distance I could see the big door in front of me, the one where Bodaway and I had entered earlier in the night. Desperately I crawled to the door.

I banged at the door. I banged as hard as I possibly could, but no one came. There was no response. I grabbed a rock and hit the door. The force of the sound reverberated within the cave. Still, no one came. I beat and I banged and I threw rocks until I could no more. I laid on my back and everything went dark once again.

In and out of consciousness, I faded. Eventually I woke up to find that the door of the cave had been opened. A man had appeared from the shadows and he was pulling me out. I could not hear anything and I blacked out again.

My eyes opened and I could see Bodaway walking in front of me. Two tribesmen were holding onto my arms while my legs were being dragged. Everything went dark again.

Awake, I looked around and found myself alone in a tent. In the middle of the tent was a pile of stones, smoking profusely. I tried to get up, but I could not. I was too weak from the wounds. I checked my arms and found that they had been wrapped in cloth. My pants had been stripped from me and I was wearing cloth like pants that were cut above my knees. The lower halves of my legs were wrapped with strips of cloth.

Again, I tried to force myself up, but when I attempted to do so Marine-Oni appeared. She walked through the opening of the tent and pointed at me saying, "Jacob, do not move."

She came next to me and helped me lay back down.

"You speak English, Marine-Oni?"

"Yes, I do Jacob. Some of us here in the tribe speak English."

Marine-Oni took her hood off and I saw her face for the first time in full view. She had a scar on her left cheek. Her eyes were a solid black and she was not wearing any markings on her face this time. Marine-Oni wore her long hair braided in one length with beads at the end. As I stared at her she looked as though she resembled a spirit.

"I need to go Marine-Oni, the cattle at home."

"Don't worry, Jacob. They will be ok." She gave me some water to drink.

"How did my arms and legs get like this? I thought I was in a dream."

"You were not, Jacob. You were in the Spirit World. You were bit by our ancestors."

"But, why?"

"It's part of the initiation for you, Jacob."

"Initiation?"

"To be one of us, but you have always been like us. You have just never known it. Do not worry now. I will take care of you. I am the healer for our tribe." She stood up and went to the corner of the tent and grabbed a bowl.

"What is that, Marine-Oni?"

"This is medicine. It will help you heal quickly." She then unwrapped the cloth on my legs. They were bloody, but she did not seem to mind and pulled the bowl into her lap. "Do not be afraid, Jacob."

What she took from the bowl was rubbery, like a jelly. She spread the medicine on my wounds and started to make a soft growling, or mumbling type of noise. Then I heard spirits talking, rapidly, in Skitchan.

I looked at Marine-Oni and her eyes started to turn gray. The veins in her face changed as well. Around her neck she was turning gray, like something was circulating through her instead of blood. The gray moved down to her arms and her hand and started to flash. As this happened my wound started to flash with light. She put her hands directly on top of my wound and it felt as though very tiny needles poked into my skin. I flinched ever so slightly then my wound began to smoke. Marine-Oni continued the same process with my legs and to the rest of my wounds. When she finished her eyes went back to the solid black and the spirit noises went away.

"Now I want you to rest Jacob, you will feel better tomorrow."

I nodded and then I closed my eyes, knowing in my mind that what I had witnessed was something I had never seen before.

I awoke the next day and immediately looked at my body, taking off my bandages. The bites were completely gone and fresh skin had grown across the once fleshless wounds. I stood up. My body felt fine, like nothing had happened. As I did this, without knocking, Bodaway came in the tent.

"Hello Jacob."

"Hello Bodaway."

"I need you to put these cloths on and these new shoes."

The shoes looked similar to moccasins and the clothes were identical to what the tribesmen had been wearing.

"When you are done dressing come outside."

I nodded and Bodaway went outside. When I exited the tent I saw that Bodaway was not alone. Marine-Oni and Armija were standing beside him as well as many villagers who seemed to follow me throughout the village for as long as I stayed there.

"Are you ready for your training, Jacob?" Bodaway asked and I nodded in return. He continued. "You will be with me first to learn the Skitchan language. After this lesson you will go with Armija to further your training. When he is finished with you, you will end your training with one of Marine-Oni's lessons. Follow me now, Jacob."

As I took my first step to follow Bodaway a leather ball rolled next to me. I picked it up and a small child came up to me. The child smiled and put his arms out while the other kids looked on. I smiled and threw the ball up into the air. The boy caught it and spoke in Skitchan. Grinning, I nodded to the boy as he ran off with his friends to play.

Bodaway turned and looked at me.

"That means thank you?" I guessed

Bodaway nodded and continued to walk. After a ways we eventually stopped on top of a small hill looking out over the village. Bodaway guided us to benches positioned with a wooden table underneath an oak tree.

"Have a seat, Jacob."

As I sat down Bodaway brought out from his bag a scroll. He put the scroll on the table and opened it up. When it opened I saw that the scroll was full of markings, all unique symbols, with English letters inscribed beneath them.
One mark in particular caught my eye. It was the same as the mark from the cave. The same symbol that many of the tribesmen wore on their bodies. I pointed to the mark and asked, "Bodaway, what is this?"

"It is who we are. See, the circle is on top. That represents the sun. The two marks below represent Mount Umunhum."

"Oh, I see."

"So Jacob, these are the letters of our language. Study them and I will have you spell out some words when I return."

With great pleasure, just as I did in grade school back with Miss Ross, I began to learn to read and write.

It amazingly took me only about four days to completely learn Skitchan, both verbally and written. I began eagerly by speaking with the villagers and after not too long actually found myself comfortable with challenging sentences and conversations. Some of the tribesmen even honored me with gifts such as cooking dinner or inviting me to eat with their families. I was so overwhelmed by this and so grateful. I couldn't believe that they had this much confidence in me.

One night, after I finished dinner with one of the village families, Armija approached me.

"I will be at your tent before sunrise tomorrow," he said.

The next morning I awoke startled from my sleep when I heard a horse approaching. Quickly I got dressed and walked outside. Armija looked down at me from his horse and threw a few bags in front of me.

"What's all this?"

"It's for you, for tonight. Tie it to your horse and we'll get going."

I did as he asked and was about to load myself on Skip when, to my surprise, Armija got down from his own horse. He walked towards me and drew from his pocket a black cloth. He turned me around and covered my eyes with the black cloth. I could not see a thing.

Armija guided to me to my horse. I felt Skip's body, he was standing still, and I waited. I asked Armija why I had to cover my eyes, but he did not reply. Instead he moved me up onto my horse. From atop of Skip I could hear Armija call to his own horse. Once he was saddled we took off.

Only hearing the sound of horses galloping, branches breaking under their hooves, I had no idea where we were going. After a while our horses rode onto what felt like more treacherous terrain and we finally stopped. Sitting on top of Skip I waited, wondering what was going to happen.

I heard Armija getting down from his horse and the sound of the ground beneath his feet as he approached me. Armija grabbed my leg and helped me off Skip. When the soles of my moccasin touched the bareness of the land he took off the blindfold. My vision was blurry for a little bit, but Armija did not wait, asking me to come with him. I grabbed my horse's rope and followed him.

Not long after, when my vision became much clearer, I noticed we were heading to a little opening in the path. I had fallen behind. Armija pointed to me and waved for me to come to him. I tied up Skip and approached him. He had knelt down and was pulling something out of his pouch. It was a small bowl with some kind of animal skin covering the top. He removed the skin on top and dipped his fingers in the bowl's contents.

As he did this he said to me, in hushed Skitchan, "I am now going to mark you with our secret Skitcha symbol. This will protect you along your journey."

I felt what he was drawing and knew what the marking would be. He put a circle on my forehead then underneath my eyes he put the side markings. The color was black, it felt very cold. Just as he was finishing his last stroke however, the paint became very hot.

Armija stopped and said, "I will show you how to make fire. Look closely."

Armija grabbed two sticks and walked to one of the trees nearby where he ripped off patches of lichen and bark. He started to peel it carefully and took the hairs off the bark. With great finesse Armija concentrated on this process and asked me to collect dry branches. I walked through the forest and picked up a few branches then returned.

"Bigger, Jacob. Even bigger."

Returning to the woods I continued to search for larger branches. Around me I started to form small piles for the fire, making it easier to collect. Then Armija told me to focus on him as he was about to start the fire.

Armija picked up a long branch and leaned one side to the ground, the other side laid against his own stomach. He took another, smaller branch and quickly started to rub it violently on top of the perched branch. After a while the branches started to smoke. Again, he told me to focus on his movements. I did and watched as the two pieces of wood smoked more and more. Seemingly satisfied with the progress, Armija grabbed a handful of the bark and lichen he had collected and laid it on top of the smoking timber. Suddenly it caught on fire, which startled me a little and I gave a quiet laugh.

Armija moved the fire to one of the branch piles I had made. When the flame hit the dry wood it began to grow profusely.

He asked, "do you understand how I did that, Jacob?"

I nodded in response.

"Good, because you are going to need it to survive. Your training with me starts now, Jacob. You must survive here and find your way back to the village alone."

Armija then went to his horse and pulled a thick looking staff from the saddlebag. He threw it to me.

"This staff I am giving you, it is from our ancestors. It has been passed down to us and is your weapon. Use it for your own survival."

Taking the staff I examined it. It had a unique bend to it, not straight, but slightly curved. There were markings of Skitchan etched along its body. I looked up and saw that Armija was getting back on his horse and starting to ride out.

He yelled back to me, "I will see you at the village soon, Jacob." He then yelled to his horse to go and they sprinted off into the thick darkness.

I looked around to figure out where I was. Nothing looked familiar. I had no clue where I was. All around, all that could be seen was forest. I reasoned that my best bet would be to get a good night's sleep to have a fresh start in the morning. I took the saddle off of Skip and laid it down near the fire. Luckily the flame Armija had made was still burning brightly. I made sure my horse was tied up tightly and close by.

I spent the whole day by that fire thinking of how I was going to survive. After thinking for some time the darkness of night quickly fell upon the forest. I continued to add dry branches to the fire, moving the remaining wood into piles of lumber within easy reach of the flames. Laying down I watched Skip and noticed that his ears began to move. He was hearing the sounds of the night. I patted him on the side and gazed deeply into the fire. I became lost in thought—thoughts of my family, my little brother, my father, and Ann. I wanted to see my family and Ann, but I knew I needed to be here for now. I started to feel tired so I laid back and used Skip's saddle for a pillow then fell asleep.

When I woke up the sun was shining brightly on my face. Looking up I saw that Skip was just as I had left him, near my side, but the fire had gone out. Standing up I put the saddle back on my horse and I secured the staff Armija had given me onto one of the saddle pouches. Now I had to get Skip to an area where there was green ground cover, so he could have something to eat. We also both needed water.

I hoisted myself on top of Skip and took one mesmerizing look at the night's campsite, in case I needed to retrace my steps. I thought instinctively to tear some cloth off from my outfit as a marker. I did so, ripping a strip of my garment's fabric, and tied it to a branch that would be easily visible if I became lost. Then I headed forward, careful to ride straight.

After a short while I saw a river in the distance, but still steered Skip in a straight line, to avoid getting lost. I hoped we would run into the flowing water. I looked up to the sun and noticed that is was right above me. Feeling the rays on my face I was not affected by its heat. Instead I felt that the markings on my face were protecting me.

Eventually we ran perpendicular to the river and Skip made quickly to the water source. Dipping his mouth into the river he drank. As we were stopped I realized how hot it had become. Without the breeze of the horse ride I felt exhausted and disembarked from Skip to drink the water.

When we had finished drinking, and I had loaded myself back on to Skip, I looked around to see if I could find any kind of greens to give to my horse. I looked up to the sun again, which had now moved to the right of me, just over my head. The day was moving quickly. Turning my gaze back to tree level I did not realize that we had lost our line of travel. We were no longer headed straight and no food was to be found.

Traveling again we finally came across a small meadow with some fresh greenery. When we reached the opened space both Skip and I were ravished. He began to chomp at the grass immediately. Again, I looked up to the sun and saw that it had now moved even further across the sky and was falling behind the hills. Looking around the meadow I searched for animals that I could eat. There was nothing to be found. I started to feel as though I was going to starve and looked wearily at how Skip was eating the grass.

Just then something caught my eye. A group of rabbits had run across the meadow. Tying Skip to a nearby tree I grabbed the staff and headed to the direction of the rabbits. Sneaking along the short grass I crouched behind low-lying bushes and trees, so as not to startle the creatures. With great stealth, I advanced quickly across the meadow and within moments stood just a few feet from a lone rabbit. I waited for just the right moment then jumped out in front of the rabbit and tried to hit it with the staff.

I was out of luck, it was too quick for me. Out of frustration, I threw the staff and it hit a nearby tree, making a loud noise that echoed across the meadow. I walked to retrieve the staff and as I approached it I again admired its uniquely bent shape. Thinking from my belly, I thought of a new use for the staff.

Perhaps if I could throw the staff I could knock out a rabbit.

With this new idea I walked back to my horse and began to drink more water. Letting the rabbits think I was distracted, I loaded myself onto Skip then slowly made my way back to the meadow. Making our way across this larger meadow there was no movement to be seen, but we then approached a new scene of greenery. It was a smaller meadow with a few rabbits in the distance. This time I would use my staff. For the second time I tied up Skip and crept towards the animals.

Drawing nearer they did not notice me. I was as quiet as could be. Nothing could be heard except the infrequent breeze of the wind and the soft sounds of their feet hopping against the ground. Ever so quietly, quietly. Then, there was a new noise. I was no longer alone.

Looking to my left I heard the source of the noise, a low grumble, stalking along the grass. A mountain lion was zoning in on the rabbits.

I stood still and the cat continued to creep towards the rabbits. I sensed that he knew I was there, but the mountain lion had a hunter's instinct and focused solely on the rabbits. Watching intently it crept closer and closer. Stealth, vision, its entire being concentrated on the rabbits.

I held onto my staff firmly and continued to stare at the eerie scene. The meadow fell wildly quiet except for the rabbits, who did not seem to notice they weren't alone.

Then, it happened. The cat gallantly sprinted towards its kill, leaping into the air, it extended one paw and instantly killed a rabbit. Quickly the rest of the rabbits scrambled away as the lion chased after them. The cat and its prey headed back into the forest. To avoid being seen I lingered behind a tree to continue watching the scene.

As the cat's tail disappeared behind the hoard of rabbits one lagged behind. Waiting for the precise moment, just before this last rabbit ran into the woods, I threw my staff at it. Bull's-eye. I hit the rabbit square in the head and it fell to its side. Quickly I ran towards the rabbit, making sure the mountain lion was no longer around, and scooped up my own prey. When I did I felt its warm blood drip down my arm, a sure sign that it was dead.

The sun started to descend behind the mountains and I rode out to the river. There I stopped to get a final drink before night fell. Looking around I tried to figure out what direction I had to take to get back. After a while I realized that I did not know where I was and had become lost. In that instant all that I knew was that I wanted to stay hidden away from any predators so I guided my horse back into the forest, opposite the direction of the meadow, and far away from the mountain lion encounter as possible.

I looked around trying to find some kind of shelter then came across a grouping of boulders positioned in a circle. Deciding to make camp I tied up my horse and tried to figure out how to cook the rabbit. I still had some daylight left, but I knew I had to make some fire before it fell dark. I looked around for any branches, but nothing was near the area, so I walked out a bit further to collect some wood.

After not too long I came upon an old tree that had fallen. The branches felt very dry, so I started to snap them off of the tree. I made a pile beside me then I grabbed as much as I could to bring back to camp. It took me about three go-arounds to get all of the branches to the area. To the side of the old tree I saw some very thick logs that had broken from some sort of fall. I started to drag a few to my campsite for the night.

Now I had to find some kind of timber to start the fire. I looked at the trees nearby me and the bark looked too hard to peel off, so I ventured out further. Still, there was no dry bark in sight. In frustration I turned my head upwards then heard the sound of branches breaking.

I looked in the direction where the noise had come from and cautiously walked towards it. I saw a deer and it was standing on its hind legs nibbling at a patch of lichen. Suddenly I remembered how Armija had used lichen to start the fire. Walking towards the deer I startled it and it ran off. I grabbed as much lichen as I could then, nearly frantically because of my hunger, then headed back to camp.

When I got back I tried to make a fire. I did just as Armija had taught me, leaning one stick into my belly and rubbing another against it. I started to rub the sticks together as fast as I could. No smoke was forming so I continued to rub the sticks quicker. Still, no smoke appeared.

I stopped in anguish, feeling too weak from the lack of food. I looked down in despair then up towards the stars in defeat. Then, for no reason I stood up and walked away from the pile branches. Taking a deep breath I turned and stared at the sticks, then the lichen, and then the other pile of wood. I walked back and kneeled down, took another deep breath to calm myself down, and grabbed the sticks. Again, I began to rub violently.

"Come on," I growled loudly. I was mentally fighting the weakness in my head.

Then there was smoke. At last! There was smoke and red cinders starting to fall from the sticks that I was rubbing together. The sticks began to burn so quickly that one broke under the stress of the rubbing. Quickly I added lichen to the smolder and the small pile began to smoke even more. Kneeling down I nursed the lichen, blowing air onto it, to ignite a flame. I kept blowing, despite the smoke in my eyes, but no fire formed. My body was growing weaker with every breath I blew onto the smoking lichen. With the last breath I could muster, I blew.

Something red was forming inside the lichen. I opened my eyes wider. A fire had formed at last! Yelling out of pure satisfaction, I grew the fire with the bark and branches then cooked my meal.

That night the boulders behind my camp kept the fire's heat from escaping. Although I was warm the ground was rough and what sleep I did gain was very unpleasant. I awoke before sunrise, when my fire went out and the cold overtook me. During the night I had forgotten to put more wood on the fire, despite my restless sleep. Knowing that I had a few more hours left before sunrise I tried to go back to sleep, but my shivering body did not allow me to. I looked to Skip, who had conversely had a very restful night's sleep beside me. In a thought to try to get warm I leaned into Skip. His body was warm to my touch and I rubbed his body, ensuring everything would be okay for both of us.

After sunlight filled our entire camp we began to pack up and I noticed the direction in which the sun was rising. I thought back to my night in the Chataw. The morning after I withdrew from the cave I remember where the sun had risen, just before I fell unconscious. It had been rising just behind the village. This morning now, in the woods, I thought perhaps I should face the sun when it rose. Maybe that was the way back to the village.

On the road I tried to backtrack and follow the sun. I knew before we got too far however, that we should stop for water. Surly Skip was as thirsty and hungry and I was. The only thing was, I was not sure if I was going the right direction nor did I know where the village was. I stopped and listened to the land around me, hoping to hear people, the village, or even the river. In the far distance the only thing that returned to my ears was the babble of water, the river. In my sleepless state I wondered if my mind was playing tricks on me, but it was worth checking out nonetheless.

The babble sounded like it was coming from not too far away and in following it we ended up in front of a big hill. When we arrived I realized that Skip was breathing very heavy from the ride. We had to find the water soon. I rode around the big hill and we continued on, but I began to feel a little worried. By now the sun was high above me and I had no way of finding out which direction it had risen from. I decided that my best hope of finding the village was to try to re-start my search again, between morning and noon following the sunrise.

With no water to be found I suddenly stopped, noticing that there were more hills to the left of me and groups of trees around the edges of the hills. Taking the risk I headed in that direction. This route was lengthy, weaving between the trees and uneven ground, but at last we found the river. Sadly, it was dried up.

Worried more about Skip's life than my own I tried not to panic. Leading on I knew we needed food, water, and a plan. Looking around I saw a patch of greenery in the distance. I rubbed the back of Skip's neck and led him towards what hopefully was food.

To my relief we came upon green foliage and Skip instantly began eating. While he did I did not lose sight of our next goal, water. I listened and looked around for any sign of water, but again there was nothing. Thinking it was best to leave Skip to eat I tied him up to a nearby tree limb and walked by foot to survey the area.

After gaining a better vantage point I noticed a small open area, not too far from us, with a group of trees. They were distinctly separated from the other trees around us. Thinking this was peculiar I walked towards them. Much to my delight when I got there I found a small pond. This was the area where the water had stopped flowing. I headed as fast as I could toward the pond and noticed that there was a small stream, just to my right, connecting to the main river. It was flowing, but very slowly. I could barely hear the water moving. Still, there was enough for me when I arrived to wash myself with.

I kneeled down and put my head in the water. When I did this I noticed black liquid was running off my face. The Skitcha symbol was dripping away, but it was not coming off completely. It felt as though it was attached to my skin permanently. I stood back up and quickly ran to Skip.

After regaining some strength I left Skip to drink while I
walked down the stream to scout for larger rivers.
Keeping Skip in my sight I headed down the small
stream. Down a ways, just before turning back, I heard
a larger rush of water. I grabbed Skip and we rode off
towards it. With every step the sound grew louder and
louder as we approached.

We came to a break in the forest, an opening that led us
on top of a small cliff. Below us was a bigger, forked
river. This divided the waterway in two. Observing
what lay around us I looked for a good area to make
camp for the night although, I wanted to stay as close to
the river as possible. I saw a promising spot at the
bottom of the cliff just past the fork of the river. Now all
we needed to do was find a way there.

I turned my eyes to where we were standing and I
noticed a little path on a nearby hill to the far left of the
stream. It appeared to be manmade, maybe from men
on horseback. I followed the path up to the hill and it
led us to a section of the stream that was sparse of
rocks or trees.

It was a perfect place to cross. In fact it was the only
place to jump across since the other areas near me were
very rugged, even at the edge of the pond there had
been many boulders blocking the way. This was a
challenge and I did not want to risk breaking one or
more of my horse's legs. Knowing that daylight was
about to leave us I decided to take the chance and jump
across.

I backed up my horse, patted him on the back, and
yelled, "come on boy!"

Skip started to run very fast and began his approach to
the jump. Nearing the edge of the stream I felt his
muscles tighten. He leapt.

Soaring over the stream his feet hit the other side of the river, landing on some slippery dirt. I lost my balance as we crashed to a halt, losing control I fell. Skip got nervous and started to move away. Quickly I rose to my feet and started to skid on the dirt, Skip was still pulling me. Holding onto his reigns I pulled on him hard.

"Whoa, Skip! Whoa!"

He finally stopped and was breathing heavy, he was nervous. I rubbed him on the side of his neck to calm him down. Gradually his breathing returned to normal. Now on the other side of the stream we headed to the top of the hill. The trek was great and very steep, but once we got to the top we slowly descended down to the path. Making our way down the cliff we were careful not to slip on the loose soil and zigzagged to the valley below. Once down the cliff the trail became much smoother and we made our way to the big river. There however, was another challenge. We had to cross again.

I got off Skip and started to wade across. The river was chilly, but the current was manageable. I held Skip's reins and started to guide him across. We made slow progress, but he trusted me and waded with me.

About halfway across, the river got deeper. The water was now at my chest and Skip's legs were about to go completely under the water. We pressed on. Soon the water reached my neck and I started to struggle. Still pulling Skip his body was now halfway submerged. I suddenly felt much colder.

"Come on Skip, come on boy, almost there," I encouraged.

Just when I thought we were about to be taken by the river's pull my foot caught hold of the riverbed below. The Earth was sloping upwards. We waded into the shallower edge of the river and finally completed our crossing. Fully drenched and very cold we kept on moving to make shelter.

When we reached the campsite for the night my first priority was to make a fire. I gathered wood and lichen, just as I had done the night before but, this time, my survival instincts started to appear. Starting the fire took only a minute. Once I nursed it to a healthy flame I left Skip at camp and headed for the river.

I paced around the river's edge and noticed there were fish swimming within it. I grabbed a long sturdy branch and looked at the end where it had been snapped. Peeling away strips of the wood I formed the edge into a point, a spear. Walking along the river's edge I spotted a few more fish as they swam past me. Like I did with the rabbit, I waited for just the right moment and threw my spear. I missed.

I decided that it was not just my inaccuracy, but also my shadow that had made this first attempt so unsuccessful. I started to look for a more shaded area so as not to cast my shadow for my next strike. I located an area that seemed promising. When I got there I took my shoes off and waded into the water. I stood there very still and waited.

I waited for a very long time. So long that my feet began to go numb from the cold. Growing impatient I knew I needed to stay, I needed food. Just as my body began to shiver a fish swam towards me. I waited and right when it was in front of me I threw the spear. I struck the fish and the spear began to spin around and around. The fish was flinching and I quickly ran towards it before it got away. Grabbing the spear I took my catch to my camp then returned for another. Again, I was successful. With two fish I would have enough food for the rest of the day.

Stocked well with food and firewood I felt confident as night began to fall upon me. After enjoying the last of my fish I walked to an area that was covered in tall green grass. I pulled some from the roots and brought it back to Skip. While he ate I went to the stream to drink some water.

Looking into the water I could see the moon reflecting off the surface. I stood there for a while and thought about my family. Things had moved so fast. Things were changing and appearing in my life as they never had before. I had to get back to the mines. I wanted to find out what had happened to my father. I told myself that as soon as I got back to the village I was going to search for my father. I needed to find out who that gang of bandits were. At first daylight I was determined to get to the village and head home.

Suddenly I hear Skip neighing back at camp

Gradually I opened my eyes and looked at him, dazed. I was dreaming. I was awakening from a dream. My eyes shut again.

My mother was before me. I saw her in her house, but things were being thrown from every which way, chair tables, my mother had fled screaming. In the dream I had run to the door and saw spirits hovering around the house. My mother screamed as the spirits moved towards her. They grabbed her as she tried to leave and carried her to the back area of the house.

The back door opened and the light was bright. It started to fill the house. Then there were ghostly sounds, the sounds of people dying. The spirits dragged my mother into the bright, violet light and she yelled for me, "Jacob h-e....."

The door closed and the house started to crackle. The house began to come down. It became very dark and I heard another loud crackle then everything began to shake.

My eyes opened very slowly and the first thing I saw was Skip. His ears were twitching wildly. Something was there, something was growling.

Quickly I looked to my left. There before me lurked a mountain lion.

I sat up and froze. The cat was growling. Skip was trying to break free from his rope, but it tugged at his bridle.

The lion suddenly ran towards me and lunged with his claws stretched out wide. I quickly dodged and rolled to my side, avoiding the deadly paws. I scrambled to my feet, now the cat was between me and Skip. The lion stared me down and charged again. This time the attack was quicker and I did not react fast enough.

When the lion charged it rose onto its back legs. His eyes became level with mine before he started to claw me. Backing up I could not avoid him anymore. It struck hard, swiftly digging into my shoulder. I felt as the claws carved into my skin. The attack knocked me down onto my back. I was now at the mercy of the mountain lion.

Despite the panic I rose to my feet and the cat leapt for me again. Trying to avoid the attack, I threw myself to my side. The lion caught my left side, my torso, ripping my clothes. Getting back to my feet I saw threads of my garment hanging from the cat's claws.

In a split moment the lion was concentrating on getting that piece of clothing off of his claw. Instinctively I pushed myself to get up, but when I did I fell back to the ground. I began to crawl towards Skip. When I got to him he was jumping and kicking out of fright. I knew I had to get myself upright if I was ever going to calm him down.

I closed my eyes to block the pain and began to stand. Unwillingly I cried out and pushed myself to stand. As I did I walked towards Skip, pain rushed through me with every step. I tried so very hard not to blackout. Behind me I could hear the lion growling again. I knew my window of opportunity was narrow.

Now at Skip I remembered my staff, poking out of his saddlebag. Quickly I pulled it out and as I did, within a flash, the lion was back. I took a deep breath and held tightly onto the staff. The lion was stalking me, back and forth, and his eyes were focused right at me. He held the look of a killer.

He tried to approach me and I gave out a big yell, hitting the staff against a nearby tree. The lion did not walk away. Un-phased he stood his ground waiting for the right moment to pounce.

I stood there looking at him, showing him that I was bigger and stronger than he was. I was not going to give up. I stood my ground.

The lion bolted to the left of me, ran behind me, then jumped on top of a rock. From this height he lunged at me. Reactively I swung the tribal staff and hit the cat on the side of the head.

The lion instantly fell. He lay motionless upon the cold ground, but I saw his stomach moving. The cat was still alive and breathing. Next I did something that I never believed I would have ever done. Somehow my actions came from within me, from my soul.

I touched the mountain lion's stomach and closed my eyes. I suddenly heard sprit noises and flicked my eyes open. When I did the noises faded away. I stood up, struggling, and looked again at the lion. Grabbing my staff I walked back to Skip. Looking to the sky I saw that the sun was rising just behind us.

I knew we needed to move fast. Dousing the fire with water I loaded myself onto Skip and we began to ride off. Looking back one last time I saw the mountain lion rise to its feet and slink off into the forest.

As we rode my shoulder throbbed from the deep wound left by the lion's claws. We galloped on in the direction of the sun and I tried to ignore the flow of blood running down my arm. More and more, I bled. Trying to continue, to put as much distance as I could between us and the lion. I knew I needed to take care of my wounds.

I stopped my horse and tore a piece of my clothing, my ceremonial outfit, to use as a bandage. Luckily the material was not so tough to tear and as I wrapped my shoulder I recalled what Marine-Oni had done to heal my arms and legs from the spirit attack. Inspecting myself I found that the side of my chest and belly were wounded as well, from when the lion lashed at my shirt. For this I took off my shirt completely and wrapped it around my waist, over the wound, and tied it tightly. The material stopped the bleeding, at least for now. I needed to get back to the village as quick as possible.

I rode as fast as my horse could run, through forests and constant meadows, following the same direction as the sun. I rode for what seemed to be an eternity, not knowing if I was going in the right direction or not. At some time my horse wanted to slow, but I kept him going, knowing that my wounds were worsening. With every footstep Skip took my bandages were quickly becoming a deeper hue of red.

When the sun was almost directly above me my body began to feel weaker. I began to lose the use of my wounded arm and was forced to hold onto Skip's reigns with just one hand. I knew that I was losing blood, but now I could feel its affects. I began to swoon, feeling faint. Fighting to stay conscious I saw as the light around me became dark and Skip began to ride into a deep forest. The sun was barely breaking through the thickness of the canopy. I struggled to pull myself back up to look where we were. Pulling my eyes open I saw a break in the forest. I put my head down along Skip's neck and heard his rapid breathing. My vision was leaving me faster now, I was going to black out. I knew I didn't have much longer.

Just when I didn't think I could lift my eyes any longer Skip stopped. My eyelids flickered and I saw Bodaway.

I mustered my strength, I had returned.

Greeted by Bodaway, Armija, and a group of villagers I stumbled to the ground, holding onto the ceremonial staff for support. No one helped me move. No one helped me down, despite my blood drenched clothing. I looked directly at Bodaway and stood up, leaning against the staff. My muscles were weak, but I did not want to show any pain in front of him or the villagers. When I started to walk towards Bodaway and Armija blood began to weep profusely through my clothing and down my side.

Bodaway said to the villagers, "he has returned! Jacob has returned!"

To this the rest of the villagers came out of their tents. I could not take it anymore. Armija grabbed my hand before I began to fall to the ground. He supported me to stand upright and took me to my tent.

When we arrived Marine-Oni was there with her helpers. She had been waiting for me, bearing a proud smile. Her helpers looked on as I was ushered inside. While I passed through the front door I noticed gifts were spread about, what appeared to be idols.

Armija put me down on my bed and patted me on the chest then left. Marine-Oni promptly came to my side.

I spoke softly. "Every time I see you now it is because I am wounded."

Marine-Oni smiled and said, "soon that will change, Jacob. Your training is not yet over. You need to rest now."

One of her helpers gave me some water while she served me some kind of porridge made of corn. Together they fed me while Marine-Oni tended to my wounds. It was only then that I began to fade away and fall asleep.

The next day I awoke abruptly and felt very thirsty. I stood up and fetched myself a pitcher of water, drinking the whole thing. Placing the container back down I saw that my regular clothes were sitting beside my bed. I put them on and as I did looked in the mirror to see that my wounds were completely healed. Not even a scar remained. Rested and well I wanted to see my family.

Outside I looked for Skip. He was tied up with the village horses and as I approached him Bodaway called out to me.

"Jacob! Where are you going?"

"I need to go see my family. I need to find out what happened to my pa."

Bodaway shook his head. "You shouldn't go right now, Jacob. You need to finish your training."

I grabbed Skip, and saddled up. "I understand Bodaway, but I need to get back."

I looked to my left and saw Marine-Oni coming out from her tent.

"It is important, Jacob. It is important for your tribe, your family, and the ones you love. You need to understand that."

Marine-Oni was walking to us quickly.

"Jacob," Bodaway continued, "this isn't the right thing to do right now."

Marine-Oni now stood next to Bodaway and looked him in the eye. He held her gaze. She then turned to me and said, "but you are always free to go whenever you wish."

Bodaway nodded. "You will always have a home here, Jacob."

Gratefully I left the village and rode off.
When I reached the Skitcha gate there was a man guarding it. I asked him to open the gate.

He had a worried look to his face and began to look around. In this moment I heard horses galloping behind me. Turning around I saw that Bodaway and Marine-Oni were approaching. Bodaway raised his hand to the man protecting the gate. The man acknowledged Bodaway then looked at me. His gaze had changed. This time he looked at me like I was a man. He then opened the gate and I rode off for home at last.

Sprinting through the meadow I found a familiar trail and headed to see Kate.

When I got to Kate's house I walked up to the door and knocked. There was no one home. I looked around and knocked again, nothing. Going around the back I saw no one in the back yard so I continued to check the remainder of the house. No one was there.

Leaping back onto Skip I galloped in the direction of my mother and father's home.

When I arrived at home I could hear some people talking inside. Opening the door I was met by my sisters Mary Ann and Kate, and my mother. Their eyes opened wide when I stepped in. They looked surprised to see me.

Kate spoke first. "Where have you been, Jacob?"

I replied, "I needed to get away, just for a little, but now I am back. I am sorry I took so long."

"It's been about six days since you left my house, Jacob." Kate seemed confronted by my response.

Had it really been that long? I thought.

I looked at Kate and whispered, "how is Ma doing?"

"She has been very worried about Pa, and about you."

I walked up to my mother and grabbed her hand. "I am sorry Ma, for leaving and not coming back sooner."

She nodded, but didn't say anything.

"I am going to go into town to find out what's going on at the mines. I will return soon, I promise."

I couldn't say anything else. I had worried my mother. I turned towards my sister Mary Ann and held her, comforting her. Then I walked to Kate.

"Kate, I will return. I promise. I'm going to the town before the sun sets."

"Jacob, be careful over there. The town's people have been very uptight. They are not letting me work anymore because of what has happened at the mines. Things have really changed."

"I will Kate." I went to leave then turned back. "Kate?"

"Yes, Jacob."

"Has Ann stopped by?"

"She has, yes. At both my house and Ma's, but I haven't seen her around for a few days now."

I left the house and rode to town.

The townspeople were flocking the streets and a large group were congregating in front of the sheriff's office and Town Hall. I walked to the sheriff's office to try to get some answers.

When I arrived I found a large board in front of the building listing people's names and at the top read, "Quicksilver Mining Co." As I looked at the names I noticed the people beside me were crying and mourning. I realized that this was a list of the deceased. I panicked, looking for my father's name. He was not on the list.

Next I ran to Town Hall to see if anything was going on and hopefully to find Ann. When I arrived I saw people going in and out of the building. I went in and noticed a sign near the door that read, "Town Hall Meeting Tomorrow Night."

I walked into the halls of the building. I had never been in before and once through the doors I realized how huge it was. Inside I saw congressmen walking by. The hall was busy and congested. I saw a woman sitting in front of a large desk, she must have been the clerk. I started to walk to her.

"Excuse me, Miss. I am looking for someone that works here."

"What is this person's name, Sir?"

"Her name is Ann, Ann Miller."

The woman looked around recalling if she knew Ann or not. "I don't think she is here right now, Sir."

I thanked her and looked around for Ann myself. After a while of searching I could not find her so I left for my next stop, the mines.

I quickly found that the road to the mines was blocked and guarded by the Federal Army. Soldiers were everywhere and a pair of approaching guards stopped me from passing. They were both in uniform and carried guns in one hand, the other rested on the hilt of a military issued sword.

"What's your business here, Sir?"

I tried to look beyond the soldier, trying to see over the hill.

"I want to know what is going on with my father. He was in the mines when it all happened."

The soldier grinned and looked to his partner. The soldier said, "if anything happens it will be posted near the sheriff's office."

I figured he'd say as much. "Well, why can't I go in if my pa was a worker there?"

"It is not safe right now. No one can pass this point. If you try we will arrest you."

I looked around to try to find another way around the path. The soldier was moving his fingers on his gun, staring at me as if daring me to pass. Something was telling me that I had to get in the mining area. The only question was how.

As I rode off I heard the soldier laughing to his partner.

Following the trail, I cut off from the main road and turned off onto a forked pathway. This route led me away from the guards and curved around a big hill, redirecting me to another entrance of the mines. Midway along this path I saw soldiers on horseback on top of the big hill patrolling the area. Realizing this was not an option I headed for an alternative route and led Skip up another hill. Once atop I settled us beneath an area shaded by trees and out of sight from the guard.

From this vantage point I could see the mines in full view. A lot of destruction had occurred around the mines and there were military men cleaning up the rubble. I could also see that they were working hard to get into the mines, where my father was trapped. By the looks of it they were making slow progress. Some soldiers were going in and out of the mines, taking out large rocks, but there was still a lot of work left to do.

I wanted to see more and tried to figure out a way to get in. I turned around and tied Skip to a tree in the shade.

"Stay here Skip, I'll be back."

I took my hat off and put it in a saddlebag. Then I looked around the trees for a good-sized branch, just like the ceremonial staff I used the day before. I located one and pulled as hard as I could to break it. I shaved the bark off of the thick branch with a rock, forming a spear, then secured the staff under my belt before heading towards the mines.

When I descended down the hill I spotted a few soldiers on horseback guarding the area. I quickly hid behind a nearby tree and waited for them to leave. As soon as they left their post I headed towards another hill that was covered in thick tree cover. When I reached this point I could see much more of the mines, this time at ground level. I observed the scene and strategized my next move.

Suddenly I heard some noises coming up in front of me. I quickly went behind a big bush and squatted down, looking through the crevasses to see what was going on. I heard men talking and then they came into view.

They were soldiers and they stopped right before me, talking and laughing. One of the soldiers got off of his horse and waved off the other soldier who left. The soldier before me walked further into the forest and went behind a tree. He unbuckled his belt and started to do his business.

I took my sweat rag and tied it over my nose and mouth, concealing my identity. Quietly I stood up and moved slowly towards him. The soldier turned his head and checked on his horse just as I ducked behind a tree. I stuck my head out and his head turned back. I started to sneak my way behind him.

When he started to pull his pants up and buckle his belt I ran towards him. When he turned he met me with wide eyes just as I swung the thick branch at his face knocking him out cold. I tossed the thick branch aside and turned to the horse, he was not startled. I took off my rag and headed to the horse.

"Easy boy, easy."

I grabbed the rope and brought the horse to the knocked out soldier, tying the horse beside the unconscious body. The soldier was about my height and I thought to take his uniform. I grabbed his clothes and put them on over my clothes, taking his hat as well. I hoped to blend in with the rest of the Federal Army. Confidently, I strutted out of the small forest and headed towards the mines.

When I reached the mines I kept calm and tried to act like the other soldiers. A few soldiers walked by me threw me a salute. I hesitated, then saluted back.

"Hey soldier!"

I turned and looked around to find a man standing before me. Based on the stars on his shoulder I suspected he was a high-ranking military official.

"Yeah you. Get over here."

I walked over to the man, coolly.

"Help us out with this rubble. We need to get into this building."

I looked at the building the man had indicated to. It seemed to have already been scorched by fire and damaged by a dynamite explosion. I did as the man said.

Once the rubble had been cleared I looked for my next orders from the officer.

"Well, get going solider. Go to the General for more orders," he shouted.

I started to walk in the direction of the mines and suddenly the man called back.

"Soldier! Salute your officers when they command and dismiss you."

I looked down and quickly remembered how to salute.

"You're dismissed soldier."

I turned and walked to the mines.

When I arrived to the mouth of the mines I found that
the smaller of the sub-entrances, near the main
entrance, was completely closed from the dynamite
blasts. It seemed as though the soldiers were not
worried about those miners at all. In other areas
though there were many military members going in and
out of the mines carrying stones.

I called to one, "hey soldier."

He replied casually, "yep."

"How's it goin' on in there?"

"Not so good. There has been a lot of damage inside,
but we are getting through slowly."

"Any survivors?"

"Haven't you been hearing the news? Or been helping
out over here to know?"

I shrugged. "No, I've been patrolling the area for a long
time now."

"Oh. I wish the General would switch our duties once in
awhile." He shook his head and continued. "There are
some survivors, but there have been many deaths too.
There are still more stuck deep in the mines and we are
not sure if they are alive or not."

"Could I go take a peek inside, to see how it's going?"

"Yeah, you can, but if a higher rank sees you and orders
you to help out ya best be helpin', soldier."

"I understand." I saluted and walked into the mines.

When I got in the mines were fully lit and I could see lanterns hanging from the walls. As I walked further down I started to hear clanking noises and hammering. After walking for a while I saw soldiers with pick axes and large hammers chipping away at the piles of rocks left from the blast. I was shocked to see what was before me. The damage was bad and I started to worry about my father, picturing him behind the thick wall of rocks. There was nothing I could do at this time except wait it out until they cleared the rubble. I turned around and headed back out of the mine. I wanted to avoid any higher ranking military officials as much as possible, especially the Commander himself. I headed back in the direction of the small thick forest.

Cutting behind an enormous amount of military officers I was almost to the forest when a patrol guard spotted me.

"Hey! Hey, you!"

I did not turn around since he would get a clear shot of my face. I just stood there and tried to think what to do next.

"Hey!"

I quickly glanced over my shoulder and saw that the soldier had started to walk towards me. I turned my head back to the forest and saw that it was a straight shot to the woods. I sprinted.

"Hey! Stop!"

The soldier started to run after me, but stopped shortly after a few steps. Turning back I saw that he had called upon a soldier on horseback who had now begun to pursue me. I ran even faster and somehow made it into the forest where I hid underneath some broken trees. Pulling out my sweat rag I covered my face.

The soldier on horseback entered the forest first and I saw the foot guard follow behind shortly after. I thought of the soldier that I had knocked out, he was near us. I had to move them away from this area so they would not spot the unconscious soldier. The guards were looking for me now and I kept an eye on them until they both turned their heads away. At that moment I rolled out from under the trees and started to run. I got pretty far before one of the soldiers spotted me.

"There he is!"

The soldier on horseback started to chase after me while the other man ran on foot behind him. I ran as fast as I could and did not look back. I wanted to get to my horse as quick as possible or if needed, find another place to hide.

The soldier on horseback edged closer and closer to me. I could hear the horse breathing heavily and started to run up the hill to my own horse. I looked back and saw the soldier following me. I had to run faster.

Just as I turned my head back around something caught my foot and I stumbled. Falling to my chest I quickly turned over on my back and saw that the soldier was a few feet away from me, but for some reason he didn't move any closer.

Scrambling to my feet I turned back to face the hill and saw Bodaway, Armija, and some of the Skitcha villagers on horseback. They started to stare at the soldier and I saw the other soldier, further down, frozen in his footsteps. Bodaway and Armija did not say anything to the soldier, they just stared deeply at him, intimidatingly. The soldier did not even pull his gun out. He merely turned around and left, taking the other soldier with him they headed back to the mine.

I stood up and took off my sweat rag then walked towards my horse. The tribe started to follow me.

Bodaway said, "Jacob, we know you are worried about your father. We also have some of our people in the mines that were workers there."

I turned around and asked, "how? Why were they at the mines?"

"They worked there, Jacob. That was their choice. If any one of our people are in trouble we go and help them. Even if they choose a different life."

I turned around and looked at the mine. Bodaway walked to the side of me and said, "we have a way to get in there Jacob, without the soldiers knowing."

I swiftly looked at Bodaway as he continued. "We are going into the mines through a different tunnel that they do not know about. We will see if our people are ok."

"I want to go, Bodaway. I will join you."

Bodaway nodded, "you may. And you may find out what happened to your father."

"When are we going in the mines?" I asked.

"We will go at night, but we are going in a different direction."

"Ok Bodaway. Where should I meet you at?"

"Meet us at the entrance to the village just before sundown, Jacob."

I looked at the sun, it was halfway from sundown already.

"I will meet you come sundown."

I got on my horse and rode back home.

My sister Kate was preparing supper when I arrived. Mary Ann was the first to notice when I came inside and she welcomed me to the table. My mother looked at me from a distance, but did not say anything. She returned to helping Kate with supper.

I asked Mary Ann, "how's Ma doing?"

"She is ok, Jacob. She's just been quiet and keeping busy. Have you heard anything about Pa?"

I took Mary Ann away from where my mother was and told her what I had seen. I also told her that I was going to return to the mines tonight.

"You need to not let Ma know where I am going, ok?" I added. "I don't want her to worry. Just say I went into town or something. Has Ann stopped by here?"

"No she hasn't Jacob, not for a while."

I started to worry about the safety of Ann.

"If she comes here please tell her I will be back tomorrow."

Kate saw me and my sister talking and walked over.

"Kate, we need to talk."

She nodded and told Mary Ann to finish helping Ma with supper.

Kate and I walked outside the front door, stopping near Skip. I told her what I told Mary Ann, that I was going to return to the mines that night to try to find Pa. I also told her that I would not be alone, but didn't describe who I'd be with. Then I asked her about Ann.

"You haven't seen her yet, Jacob?"

"No, I haven't seen her since we brought Ma over to your house. I've been looking for her in town, but I could not find her."

"Well, you should just come in for supper so Ma doesn't see you leave without eating. You know how she is."

I nearly laughed at this and agreed. Sitting at the table we served ourselves supper and began eating. I tried to talk with my mother.

"How was your day today, Ma?"

She paused and she said, "it was fine, Son. I've been working on my knitting."

She never called me Son. She would always call me by my first name. I knew she wasn't well because of this.

I said to her, "that's good Ma, maybe we can sell some of your blankets and sweaters in town later on for you." I started to look at my sisters and they picked up the conversation.

Kate continued, "yeah, we can ask the stores if they would like to sell them."

My mom smiled and said, "that's wonderful children."

After that response we all knew my mother was not doing very well.

Nearing the end of supper I saw the sun begin to set outside. I helped my mother and sisters clean up the meal and headed to the door. My mother looked at me and I smiled back. I looked at my sister Kate and she started to talk to my mother, distracting her as I left the house.

It didn't take me long to get to the village gate, but by the time I arrived I could hear wildlife all around me. I heard no people or horses. Waiting for Bodaway I thought of Kate and what I had shared with her. I trusted my sister and felt that she should know about our people. When I returned after the mines I set my mind to tell her about the Skitcha tribe and talk with Ma about our family's true history. While I was thinking about this I heard the gate open. Bodaway, Armija, and about ten other villagers from the tribe came through.

As they approached Bodaway motioned something to one of the men. The man trotted his horse towards me and pulled something out of his saddlebag. It was an axe with a curved handle. It was curved similar to how the ceremonial staff was and marked in Skitchan markings and feathers. The man gave me the axe.

Armija said, "use this for your protection, Jacob. In case anything happens in the mines."

Bodaway spoke next. "Remember Jacob, fight only if someone is attacking you. You still need training, understood?"

"Yes Bodaway," I replied and he nodded.

Bodaway shouted, "let's go rescue our people!"

With that we rode north, following the stream.

We followed the stream then started to go downhill, stopping when the ground flattened out. Bodaway and

Armija looked around, to make sure the coast was clear, then Bodaway signaled to Armija.

"Have some of the men check to see if anyone is around."

Armija nodded and called out to two men. The men acknowledged and rode out. We all stood there and watched for their signal.

While we waited I looked up into the sky and saw the sun fading down over the hills. It was going to be dark very soon.

Bodaway watched me. "Jacob, you will learn how to see in the dark, without light or moon light. This you will learn tonight when we are in the mines. Do what Armija tells you, understood?"

The two tribesmen emerged from over the hilltop and rode towards Bodaway.

"There are a group of men at the bottom valley, but far away Bodaway."

Bodaway looked at Armija then spoke to the men, "show us."

He pointed to the remaining tribesmen.

"Guard this area and signal us if any intruders approach." Bodaway came next to me and said, "come with us, Jacob."

We rode over the hill and just before we descended to the valley Bodaway ordered us to stop. Here we were hidden behind another hilltop and were able to survey the scene. From this point we could clearly see who we were facing.

There were about ten to fifteen men and possibly more riding to the camp. I recognized some of the members to be Wanted Men. Most were white and some were Indian.

I turned to Bodaway and asked, "do you know these men, Bodaway?"

He paused and said, "these must be the people that are coming for our land. Those two men," he indicated to the Indians, "right there, were in our tribe before."

Bodaway spoke to Armija and Armija looked at the men and nodded. He signaled to the other tribesmen that we should begin riding back to the others.

I asked Bodaway, "what's going on?"

"Nothing at this time, Jacob. We need to be patient and do what we had planned to do tonight, which is head into the mines."

"But, that looks like they are forming a large group down there."

"We will let them be for now. They will not take our land from us. I promise you."

We returned to the rest of the tribe and once there Bodaway motioned towards an indentation in the hill. One of the tribesmen approached this landmark and shuffled some branches out of eyesight, revealing a tunnel.

Bodaway looked to me and said, "this is another way to get into the mine. We have kept it hidden from outsiders. It is solely ours."

Inside, just as Bodaway had warned, the tunnel was very dark.

He spoke again, "we will now teach you how to see in the dark, Jacob."

All of the men who had been standing unmounted their horses and surrounded me.

Bodaway said, "Jacob, you must sit down. Take off your hat and close your eyes."

When I closed my eyes I could hear a small fire starting right in front of me, but I did not feel any heat at all. Softly, I heard chanting. As they picked up the cadence the chanting grew louder. With my eyes closed all I could see was darkness at first, but then I started to see flashes. Even with my eyes closed I saw flickers of light and became dizzy. Suddenly my head was involuntarily thrown backwards.

It was then that Bodaway told me to open my eyes. When I did my vision was blurry and rapidly speckled with bright flashes for a moment. Once my vision started to come back I could see gray smoke in front of me disappearing.

Bodaway ordered me to get up, "grab your weapon, Jacob."

I went to my horse and grabbed the axe from the pouch of my horse. Then, one by one we entered the tunnel.

When I got in I still had a hard time seeing. Armija noticed this challenge and walked next to me.

"You must feel, Jacob. Feel with your mind. Know that you can see."

As he said this all of a sudden the pitch darkness of the tunnel dissipated and I began to see as though it were light. The tunnel was colored dark blue and I could see the details of the walls clearly. I was so amazed that I smiled and did one quick laugh, out of excitement. I looked at Armija and I patted him on the back as a gesture of thanks. He acknowledged this and continued to walk further into the cave.

Bodaway came up to me next as we walked. "We found this new tunnel that connects with the main mines. Originally at the end there was a barricade, but we were able to pull some of the rocks out. Still, we need to pull more to get in."

"Did anyone from the tribe hear anything from the mines? Any of them working to clear the rocks?"

"We have heard nothing, Jacob." Bodaway paused briefly then we continued to walk to the barricade of rocks.

I asked Bodaway, "would our people who work at the mines still chose to work there if they could? Would the Skitcha mine from their own land?"

He looked at me and said seriously, "they are sworn not to harm our land or to tell anyone about our existence. So no, they would not do so. If they have intentions to destroy our land they would pay the consequences."

When we approached the barricade I saw piles of rock alongside the walls of the tunnel.

"We are here," Bodaway said. "Remember once we open it up be ready for anything."

Armija turned to me, "when we are inside Jacob, stay behind us."

Bodaway commanded some of the men to take the rest of the rocks from the barricade. When they did an opening was revealed.

Bodaway whispered again, "be ready."

A tribesman moved one last rock, which caused a tumble effect of the wall, creating a small opening.

Bodaway held me back. "Stay behind us Jacob, you're of too much importance."

I looked at everyone while they all pulled out their weapons. Some had axes while others had wooden staffs. They all started to walk in and I followed.

Inside it was quiet and we progressed slowly. Even from this distance away we began to see bodies of those who did not survive the blasts. Bodaway pointed and we started moving in the direction towards these deserted souls. As we approached them the smell of decay filled our nostrils. I began to cough and I covered my mouth and nose with my sweat rag. The other tribesmen were not bothered by the smell and moved forward.

When we got closer to the bodies we saw deep holes both in the ground and above us on the ceiling.

Bodaway stopped and raised his hands. Armija pushed my chest to signal to stay. They heard noises.

Bodaway signaled for two men to go with him. They started to walk near the noise and suddenly Bodaway signaled for the men to lower their weapons. One of the noises was coming from a wounded man. Bodaway knelt before the victim. Armija signaled for the rest of us to go to Bodaway. When we approached I saw that it was a man of Indian lineage lying before him. It was a Skitchan tribe member. The man started to make more sounds and one of the brother tribesmen tried to sit him up.

The man was covered in blood. His face, his mouth, everything. The man started to speak in Skitchan.

"My name is Ishmael." He coughed.

"Take your time Ishmael," Bodaway said to the man and crouched over him, holding his head.

Armija began to look around as the man continued to speak.

"They are coming," he coughed. "Bodaway, they are trying to take over everything."

"Who are these men?" Bodaway asked.

"I do not know, but they knew I came from Skitcha. They attacked me and my friend... and... warned us they will be taking over."

Ishmael pointed to where Armija was looking and spotted another man.

Ishmael continued, "he attacked first and we killed the man. We then sacrificed him, Bodaway."

Bodaway nodded and looked at the direction of the men that attacked them. He ordered a few tribesmen to examine the body. I followed them and saw that the man had been flayed and gouged, bearing deep gash wounds as though the skin was torn off his body. The men walked back to Bodaway and confirmed the sacrifice.

Ishmael started to gasp for air. Bodaway quickly looked around and ordered one of the tribesmen to give him something.

The man handed Bodaway a little pouch in which he stuck his hand. Within the pouch was some kind of liquid. I wasn't sure what color it was, since I was only able to see shades of blue color in the dark.

With the same hand Bodaway started to mark Ishmael's face and said, "Ishmael you have sacrificed yourself for the safety of our tribe. Your honor will be remembered. The flesh you have eaten from the enemy will guarantee your spirit life to watch over us and protect us from anyone that harms us."

Bodaway traced the mark of the Skitcha tribe onto Ishmael's face. "May your spirit be strong, Warrior."

Ishmael then turned to me and stared, as if he knew who I was. I watched his eyes as the man started to die, slowly. Soon his breath was no more. Bodaway closed Ishmael's eyes with his fingers then stood up.

Bodaway looked towards us and signaled to Armija. As he approached Armija said to us, "the man scarified the enemy. There are a few men with bites around him, Bodaway. The fight in this mine was very violent. There were many struggles," he pointed to the areas of the holes. "There was dynamite thrown from all directions and it looks like our people were the only ones left."

Bodaway nodded and then order two tribesmen to pick up Ishmael's body and lay it next to the other tribesmen. Once the bodies of the Skitcha people were collected Bodaway signaled for me and the other tribesmen to kneel around the deceased warriors.

"Skitcha," Bodaway began this ritual, "may you protect these men on their journey. May their spirits be strong and protect us."

Everyone around me made a loud grunt then started to get up. When I stood up I looked around and realized once again that I needed to find my father.

Armija must have noticed this thought in me and began to follow me even more closely. We walked through the cavern, over many dead bodies, more than I had ever seen in my life, but all I could think of was my father. Somehow, just as I thought I couldn't get my mind off of him, there he was.

I saw my father from a distance in a faraway corner near the other barricade. I ran towards him.

Armija called out to me, "Jacob! Wait!"

His voice echoed and the other tribesmen knew instinctively what was happening. They all turned to look at my direction.

When I got to my father he was laying on his stomach. I did not want to see him. I did not want to face him, but I knew I had to. I turned my father around and as I did saw that his body was pale. He was full of bullets. In his body and in his head. My father was gone.

I yelled out of anger.

Armija ran towards me and grabbed my shoulder. I pushed him away violently, making Armija lose his balance and stumble all the way to the other side of the tunnel. I grabbed my father and hugged him, holding in the tears and fueled my anger towards the people that did this to him.

Bodaway was at my side almost immediately and called for me, I did not respond. My emotions were everywhere and I was not thinking the right way. Bodaway sensed this and continued to call my name. Eventually I turned my eyes to him, flared with revenge.

He started to look into my eyes and he said, "Jacob, I am sorry for your father's loss. You are one of us Jacob, we are your family. I will visit your mother when we take your father home." He patted me on the back and said, "we will talk to her, Jacob."

Bodaway called to Armija, "take his arm."

Armija took my arm and turned me around. He told me, "take my arm Jacob, and release all your anger."

Taking his forearm in my palm I started to squeeze. I let out the anger I had in me. Armija showed no pain and said again, "let it out, Jacob."

I grunted from the emotion and suddenly it went away. I looked at our arms and looked at Armija. He nodded and patted my arm out of respect.

"He will be with the spirits now, Jacob. He will be watching you."

Bodaway approached me and gave me a cloth blanket. "As a sign of respect for your father you must cover him and take him home. Me and our brothers will guide you back."

I wrapped my father with the cloth and picked him up then carried him on my shoulder. As I walked back towards the outside tunnel I could see the other tribesmen doing the same with their dead.

Bodaway said, "we are done here now. Let us go."

We reached the outside of the tunnel and walked towards our horses. I laid my father on top of Skip and looked behind me to see the other tribesmen walking out.

Bodaway came up to me. "I will come with you, as will two of our people. We will take you and your father back to your family, Jacob."

I acknowledged him and was grateful.

Bodaway said to Armija, "prepare the burial, Armija. I will be there shortly."

Armija and the men put their dead on their horses and rode off.

"Jacob, I will take you to the meadow and you will lead the way to your home."

When we reached my parent's home my heart started to feel as though it was down to my legs. I started to fill with emotion once again, but Bodaway helped me to be strong. He said I needed to be strong not just for myself, but for my father and family. He was right too. I needed the strength to face my mother and sisters.

When we rode up to the house I saw Kate looking out the window. I got off my horse and was glad to have Bodaway and my tribesmen beside me. Carefully, I lifted my father's body and stood by my horse. I felt that echo muffled feeling again, just as I had felt when my brother had died. It felt like time was slowing down. Kate opened the door and saw instantly that I was carrying our father.

Screaming, crying. I saw her doing these things, but everything was muted. My head was spinning with emotions. Kate tried to pull my father out of my hands, but I had to hold on to him. I had to hold my father and I would not cry.

I will not shed a tear tonight.

Mother came out of the house with Mary Ann. Before she even made her way across the porch, or onto the dirt path, she had fallen to her knees in sorrow. Mary Ann began to cry and held my mother. Kate ran to my mother and started to comfort her. I was shocked. I couldn't feel my body. I couldn't move nor remember to breath, yet there I stood, holding my father.

Bodaway touched my shoulder, startling me. He was talking and I could not hear him. He went to my mother first.

My sisters looked frightened and I knew Bodaway was telling my sisters not to be afraid. My mother looked up at him and suddenly she leaned towards him, hitting and screaming at his chest. Bodaway hugged my mother in response. The tribesmen, upon Bodaway's signal, walked in front of me and started to talk. I shook my head to try to get the sound of their voice through my ears. I could barely hear. The sound was coming through so slowly.

"Jacob, where do you wish to bury your father?" They were asking.

I told the man, "I will bury him next to my brother in the back. Follow me."

I walked around the house to the burial site. Mary Ann, Bodaway, and mother soon followed. My older sister Kate went into the house to grab a lantern. Telling the tribesmen where the shovels were we all made our way up the hill. As one of the tribesmen started to dig I stood there holding my father. While we waited Bodaway held my mother. My sisters held each other.

Then came the signal. The hole was dug and it was time to lay my father inside. Gently, as if putting a child to rest, I lay him down in the Earth, close to my brother just as we had done years ago. We all waited to see if anyone would speak. The emotions were too high for my family and I remained silent. Bodaway began.

"Mary, his spirit watches over us and your family." He signaled to the man to cover my father with dirt. We all just stood there in the sober melancholy of loss. All that could be heard were the teardrops and sobs of my mother and sisters.

I worried for my mother. She had already been emotionally weak and now, after this loss, it was hard to imagine a full recovery. Bodaway held her during the long walk back to the house. We went inside. My sisters Mary Ann and Kate took care of my mother while I walked outside with Bodaway.

"I will be back in five days time, so your family can mourn. Now go inside and be with your family, Jacob."

I nodded and grabbed my horse. I turned back to Bodaway and said, "thank you Bodaway, for everything. Please give my thoughts to the families of the lost ones of our tribe."

Bodaway smiled respectfully and nodded. The tribesmen rode into the dark. I brought my horse in the back to unsaddle him then walked into house, still out of disbelief that I lost my father. This day I became the only son, and man, of our family.

The next few days were gruelling for me and my family. My mother would stay in her room for almost the whole day while my sister Mary Ann took care of her, checking on her almost every minute. During this time I stayed home to watch the family and tend to household chores. I still hadn't heard from or seen Ann and I grew worried.

The day eventually came when I needed to leave the house to pick up some much needed food and supplies for the house. Before leaving I visited my mother.

Walking into her room it was fairly dim, with a lone lantern hanging on the wall, making the room feel very delicate. Ma was sleeping, but I could tell she was in pain. We all knew that she had loved my father very much. I let her rest and said good bye to Mary Ann as I left. I realized this was the first time I had left the house since my father's funeral. I felt the need to visit his grave before going so I headed up the hill.

As I approached the grave I stared at the humble mound of dirt knowing who lay beneath it. Pausing at the top I closed my eyes and reflected. When I opened them I spoke to my father.

"Pa, Ma's been having a really rough time since you left. She's been very weak and does not eat much. Me and the girls are starting to worry for her. I do not know what we should do, but I wish you were here to help her. If your spirit is here, please look after her for us. I, I think you know now what I have been doing away from here. I wish you had more time for us, but I understand you had to work to keep the family going. Now I must take over to help the family, Pa." I knelt down and said, "I will watch over our family, Pa. I will promise you that and I will make you proud. I know you might not understand why I joined the tribe - I don't even know if Ma ever told you about it either, but I know she loved you very much. Me and the girls loved you also. I am going to do what my soul tells me to do in my life, Pa. I am going to follow that."

I heard someone coming towards me and I finished talking to the grave. "I must go now, Pa."

I put my hand on the soil of his grave and did the same to my brother's. "Good bye Joshua, Pa."

I stood up and turned around. It was Kate walking up the hill towards me with flowers.

"Hey Kate."

"Hello Jacob." She looked at the graves then looked at me.

"I was talking to Pa."

She nodded. "I've come to do the same."

"I will let you be with Pa and Joshua alone then."

"Thank you, Jacob."

———————————————

When I returned down the hill I prepared Skip for the ride and gave him a good scrub down. He loved getting bathed and I brushed him, knowing he would stay calm as I did so. While I brushed him I saw Kate out of the corner of my eye at the gravesites. She knelt down and put flowers on top of my brother and father's grave. I could see her start to cry and put her hands on her face. I turned around and scrubbed my horse to give my sister some time with them.

Kate was there for a long time, even after I scrubbed down my horse. I let Skip run free in the stable once he was groomed and rested my arms on the fence, watching him gallop and eat hay.

Suddenly Kate walked up to my side. "Boy, Jacob you've had Skip for a while now. He is livelier than ever."

I shrugged and smiled, "yeah, Skip is something. Let me tell ya."

We watched some more in silence at my horse running free. It felt good to be beside Kate and just be with her. Not talking about Pa or war or Ma. We just stood there together.

After Skip grew calm Kate began to speak.

"Jacob, I am not sure why that man came with you the other day, but I knew deep inside he was a good man. I could tell Ma knew him."

I grinned and said, "he will explain who he is to you soon, Kate. He is coming back in a few days. And yes, while I was gone I was with him."

"I see," said Kate. She looked at me thoughtfully and said, "Jacob, you need to do what you feel inside. Do what you know you need to, alright?"

I nodded and told her I would, giving her a big hug. I sighed, "I'm not sure how we are going to keep this place up, Kate. I know father saved some money for Ma and we're already using it up."

"I am going to help out Jacob, don't worry. Our home will be taken care of don't you worry about it. Ma will be taken care of also."

"I'm not even sure if I have any work at The Jefferson's' Ranch because I was gone for a while."

"You should stop by and see if there is any work, Jacob."

"I will before I go into town. Speaking of the town, have you seen Ann?"

"Nope, haven't seen her around town? She hasn't been around here or at my house either."

"I'm getting worried about her, Kate."

Kate started to rub my back and said, "you should go look for her then. She is a good woman."

"I will go find her tomorrow and yes, she is a good woman. I will marry her soon."

"Always remember what I told you, Jacob." She said as she walked away, pointing to her chest. I acknowledged her and smiled back, knowing what she meant.

The next day I got up early and rode off to The Jefferson Family Ranch. When I got to the main road, which was the same path I would take to go to San Jose, I noticed that the road was very quiet. Usually this area would be busy with riders and carriages, but not today. I stopped at a fork and was tempted to go to San Jose to find Ann, but knew she had visited my mother at Kate's home not too long ago. Thinking that it had not been too much time since I'd seen her I took the trail towards The Jefferson's ranch instead.

When I got to the ranch I saw people working. I rode around looking for Mr. Jefferson and spotted him in the distance. As I approached him he turned towards me after hearing the sound of Skip's hooves trotting on the ground.

I tipped my hat, "hello Mister Jefferson. I have come to apologize for not being around for a while now."

"Hello Jacob," he replied. "Well I wish I could give you some work Son, but as you can see I already have more than enough help. I'm afraid I can't afford to take on another person right now."

I desperately asked again, "is there any chance any at all that you might have room for me, Mr. Jefferson? Even part-time work? My father just passed and I need to help out my family."

He looked grim. "I am sorry Jacob, I just can't right now. I'm sorry for you loss, Son."

It stung, but I showed no expression. Instead I thanked him, tipped my hat, and rode off.

When I rode into town I saw massive amounts of people and horses lined along the street. It looked as if no one had left town for a long time. Many were at the sheriff's door again. I tied up my horse at a safe distance and walked over there as well.

When I approached the area there were people passing in tears, mourning after reading the billboard I assumed. I tried to crane my neck over the throngs of people to see what was going on. I continued to walk and the closer I got the more yelling and crying I heard. At last I squeezed through the crowd and in front of me were a line of coffins. Each was filled by a victim from the mine accident and families were lining up to identify the bodies. There was an undertaker writing things down as each family passed. I had never seen anything like this before and felt sadness rise within me. I tried to get out of the crowd and headed to Town Hall.

When I got there it was the same thing, massive amounts of people, but this time they were protesting and expressing their complaints to the politicians and local representatives. I walked towards the benches in front of the hall to see if maybe Ann was there. She was not.

I attempted to go into Town Hall to see if she was inside, but I could not even get to the lobby person. Pushed out by groups of people I stayed outside and looked for Ann. During my search I spotted someone I knew. Through a window of town hall I saw Ann's father. Looking through the glass I watched as he stepped into the next room. I did not see Ann with him. From her absence I knew she wasn't in town. If she had been, her father would be upset to see her. Because of this I knew where she would be and I ran quickly to my horse to ride off to her.

When I saw a large brick wall surrounding a grand landscape I knew I was almost at Ann's home. I rode through the front gateway and entered the grounds. Getting off Skip I walked to the door and knocked. The house was a big home so I waited a little while before there was an answer.

The door cracked open. "Yes sir?" It was the maid.

I took my hat off and said, "good afternoon Ma'am, is Ann here?"

She turned around and started to look. "One moment, Sir."

I nodded and she closed the door. I started to walk around the porch and I sat on the stairs. Suddenly, the door started to open and I stood straight up, turning to see Ann. She started to talk to me, but her mother called her in the background.

"Do not worry, Mom," she called back before smiling at me then closed the door behind her. She fell into my arms and we embraced in a long hug. Draping my head over her shoulder I saw the maid smiling at us through the window of the house.

"Jacob! Where have you been?"

"I am sorry Ann, I had to go away for a little while. I was looking for you."

"I know you were. I couldn't leave you, you see. My father has been in town all week. He would have spotted me."

"I know, I saw him alone at Town Hall. I immediately thought you would be here so I came straight to you. There are a lot of sad and angry people in the town now."

"I have heard they opened up the mine and it wasn't very pleasant."

"A lot of people died Ann."

"I know Jacob, it's very sad. I just hope the town will be the same." She paused and I knew what she was about to ask next before she even said it. "Did you find out about your father?"

"Yes, and it was not good Ann. He died."

She quickly, quietly, grabbed me and held me tight. Whispering in my ear, "oh Jacob," she rubbed my back as she hugged me into her. "I am so sorry. How is your mother?"

"She's not been herself Ann, she has not been eating much. She has been in her room on her bed a lot."

Ann started to cry and I held her tighter. "I am so sorry, Jacob." She whispered in between tears.

Suddenly the door opened, it was Ann's mother. Quickly we let go of each other as she stared at us.

"Jacob, this is my mother Audrey, Audrey Miller." Ann introduced me. This was my first time meeting either of her parents.

I walked up to her and said, "nice to meet you, Mrs. Miller."

"Jacob, I am so sorry to hear about your father. Ann told me he worked at the mines."

Surprised by her kindness I thanked her. "He was a good man, a very hard worker."

She nodded in agreement. "Ann told me a lot about your father, indeed he was a good man. I will let you two go now, nice to meet you Jacob."

"Nice to meet you, Ma'am."

After Mrs. Miller shut the door Ann turned back to me. "My mother likes you, Jacob."

I grinned, "and your father?"

"Don't worry about him, he wouldn't separate us, I promise you that." I smiled and gave her a kiss, hugging her closely. Ann said "I will come and visit you and your family soon. I just have to stay here for now. My father wants us to stay away from town until things have settled down. But, I am sure my mother will let me go see you and your family. She will take care of my father, also."

I smiled, "well I should go right now, Ann. I am supposed to pick up some food and animal feed before returning home. Don't want to miss the shops, ya know."

"It's ok, Jacob. I know you have to take care of your family. I will come and visit tomorrow."

"Ok Ann," I gave her a kiss and put my hat back on.

After loading myself onto Skip I tipped my hat and Ann waved back at me as I rode off. At last I felt relieved. Ann was okay and safe. In this moment I felt more

energized than I had all week. Heading towards home I
thought again what Kate had said to me.

I need to do what I feel inside.

The next day Ann came by to visit everyone and my mother. Ma was delighted to see her as she started to smile and laugh. Ann even got my mother up out of her bed and walked with her outside. As I was working outside I saw my sister Kate ride in on her horse from a distance. She must have been in town. I went to meet her at the stable.

"Is that Ma walking with Ann down there?"

I smiled and said it was.

Kate grinned sheepishly, "see, what did I tell you about her Jacob? She's a good woman."

Just then I spotted men on horseback riding towards our house. At first I was a little worried, but then saw that it was Bodaway and five tribesmen. I waved at Bodaway to come into the back area.

When he arrived Bodaway got off his horse and grabbed some wildflowers from his saddlebag. There appeared to be a feather tied onto the flowers. Bodaway and the group of men walked to the gravesite and put the flowers in between both my father and brother's grave. Returning from the hill Bodaway came towards me and Kate. I could see from a distance that my mother and Ann were heading to meet us. Mary Ann had come out of the house as well and walked towards us.

Bodaway came up to me and said, "I am sorry, but I haven't met your sister yet."

"Bodaway, this is my sister Kate."

Bodaway shook my sister's hand and said, "nice to meet you."

Kate nodded and everyone paused. My sister asked abruptly, "who are you Bodaway? How do you know my brother and my mother?"

"I will explain everything as soon as your mother is here."

We all looked at the direction of my mother and Ann.

Again, my sister turned to Bodaway and asked, "are you the reason why my brother has been gone?"

"Yes Kate, he was at our village."

"Why?" She was demanding of answers and did not like that there were secrets between us.

Bodaway paused and then said, "to know who he really is, Kate."

Her expression changed to one of question, "to see who he is? I don't understand."

Bodaway looked as my mother approached the group. Ann stood next to me.

"Afternoon Mary," Bodaway said.

Ma nodded back and spoke boldly in return. "Did you tell her yet, Bodaway?"

"No, I have not Mary. Out of respect and promise to our tribe. We will not speak until you allow us to."

My mother took a deep breath and looked at me, then my sisters. "And Jacob?"

Bodaway nodded deeply, "he has been with us, Mary."

To my great surprise my mother responded in Skitchan, "you were suppose to let me know before you talked to my son, Bodaway." She had found her strength again. She asked in a tone that was clearly upset.

My sisters looked at my mother in surprise and Ann grabbed my arm.

Kate said, "Ma, what did you just say?"

My mother looked at her and said, "there is much you need to know now. Both you and your sister need to hear what we have to say."

Ma turned again to Bodaway and spoke again in the tribe's tongue. "I am disappointed with you, Bodaway. You did not get my permission to talk to my son. How dare you come here now, after my husband died!"

Bodaway responded in Skitchan, "I am sorry Mary, we had to wait and you did not want us around. That was your request before leaving us." Bodaway paused for a moment then continued, "we had a sign."

"A sign?"

"Your son Mary, he is the Chosen One."

My mother's eyes opened up wider and stared at Bodaway. "That is not possible, his father is white."

Bodaway quickly interrupted my mother and said, "The Skitcha, your father told us."

My mother's expression went to shock, "my father?" Things seemed to be making more sense to her now. "No wonder I had dreams of my father."

Mary Ann, who had not understood a word of the Skitchan language, interrupted. "Ma what's going on? Why are you talking like that?"

Kate looked at me, then Ann looked at me, both with a scared look on their face. I said to my sisters, "Ma is disappointed that Bodaway has not spoken to her before talking to me."

"Jacob, no," my mother slightly gasped. She was clearly surprised I understood what she had said. Ma then turned to my sisters and said, "I will explain to you girls, let's go for walk. Ok?"

Before they started to walk she turned her head towards Bodaway. "We will back shortly, Bodaway."

In their absence Bodaway turned to Ann. "And you must be Ann."

Ann stood there, silent.

Bodaway said, "Jacob, she is beautiful. Her spirit is strong." He then looked back to Ann. "Now please Ann, don't be afraid. I know this doesn't make any sense to you, but you will also know shortly."

Ann again said nothing and only looked at Bodaway.

I said to Ann, "do not worry, Ann. I promise you will know everything soon."

I looked at Bodaway and asked, "what is my mother doing, Bodaway?"

"She is going to tell them the truth, Jacob. Your mother and sisters will have to decide if they want to live with us. They are welcomed to live our way of life, but for many it is such a different life from the one they have now. You also Jacob, will have to decide." Bodaway paused and asked me in a lowered voice, "can I talk to you for a moment alone?"

I looked at Ann and she nodded.

I signaled to Bodaway to follow me and I walked towards the stables. Leaning against the fenced corral we spoke in Skitchan.

"Jacob, I understand things are happening to you very quickly. You know what you have to do and you know that a group of men are going to come after our land very shortly. We have to prepare for them, prepare for the attack. Your mother knows what we have been doing." He paused and looked a little saddened when he continued. "We have also learned more of the attackers. We are certain that some of the men leading the riot were of Indian descent. In fact, they were from our tribe."

I looked at Bodaway and asked, "how could they be involved with those people?"

"They might have made a deal with them. There is more to this than it sounds."

"Do you think they will tell the others about the tribe and our location?"

Bodaway continued solemnly, "it could be possible, Jacob. The other people in that group could already know the location from the ex-tribe members. It all depends on what they are looking to get out of this. That is why we need to prepare, to be ready for anything. If those tribesmen told them what our land has, our resources, and about Mount Umunhum's secret they could move in very quickly."
"Bodaway, what are we going to do?"

"We must wait for now. We must find out more about these people and the tribesmen that have betrayed us. We have some of our people watching over the bandits, but soon we are going to need you to be our eyes away from the village."

"I understand."

"But Jacob, you still need to train for this. You need you to be as prepared as possible for when this unfolds. We all need you to be, for the confrontation when it happens."

I nodded and saw that my mother and sisters had started to walk back to us. Bodaway and I returned to meet them and Ann. I took her hand in mine and my mother spoke aloud to us in English.

"Bodaway, I have told my daughters the truth."

I looked at my sisters, they were quiet.

Bodaway said, "and your daughters, are they going to be living with you?"

"Just one. Mary Ann."

My sister Kate stepped forward and said, "I decided to not be a part of the tribe, Bodaway. I am sorry. I am married and am going to have a family soon. I wish to live with my husband and do not want to be involved with this other way of life. I wish for things to stay as they are right now."
Bodaway smiled, "I understand and that is your choice."

Kate asked, "will you help my mother, Bodaway?"

Ma broke in, "I am going to stay here. I made my choice long ago to part ways with the Skitcha tribe and nothing has changed my mind of that, Bodaway."

He paused, hoping she would say something more, but she remained silent.

I stepped in front of Bodaway and broke the tense air.

"Bodaway, can you have your men come by this house from time to time? To watch over my mother and sister while I train?"

He nodded. "Mary, from your son's request we will have tribesmen and women come to your house every so often. They will help with chores and protect you and your daughter."

Kate interrupted again, "what training, Jacob?" She looked at all of us and I walked towards her.

This is my sister, I thought. I need to tell her what will happen. She has my full trust and deserves to know the entire truth.

"Kate, please walk with me." I signaled Ann to stay with my mother. Before going I asked Bodaway and my mother to inform Ann of what was going to happen. They nodded in acknowledgement and I saw my mother take Ann's hand.

Kate and I ended up walking to the lake. Along the way I did not say anything to her. I could sense that she was upset about what had happened and what was kept from her. Kate was the oldest of us and was used to knowing what was going on with me and the family.

While we walked I felt her anger blow away with the wind and as it did only sadness remained in its place, as if she sensed we were about to say goodbye.

"This is the lake that I would always go as a kid."

I sat by the shore and Kate followed.

"I remember Ma and Pa taking us to this lake. You used to throw rocks in the water and Pa used to teach you how to skip the rocks on top of the surface." Kate reminisced.

I shrugged a little and Kate continued. "Yeah, you tried so hard to make the rock skip and then you would give up. Only to start throwing even bigger rocks in." We both laughed. "Oh Jacob, you were a rascal of a kid back then."

We both paused for a little bit and looked at the glassy water of the lake.

"Look over there, Kate. Remember, we used to jump off those big tree stumps when we were younger? Into the water?"

Kate squinted. "Oh yeah, boy it sure hasn't changed a bit around here, huh?"

"Nope, it hasn't." We paused for a moment.

"Kate, I know when Bodaway showed up you were upset that you didn't know what was happening. I'm sorry for not telling you first, Kate." She looked at me and listened with soft eyes. "I believe in them Kate, the tribe. They believe in me. There are things they have shown me you wouldn't believe."

Kate turned to the lake. I could tell she was divided. Half of her believing and half of her not.

"I need to be with them Kate, I need to help them. I feel like I belong there."

My sister just continued to look beyond the lake.

"They are training me for--"

Kate interrupted, "Jacob, I don't quite understand what this training is, but I am not going to disagree with you. I know in your eyes that you're doing the right thing."

She grabbed my hands and said, "you need to do what you feel inside. And, as much as I want to know what is happening with you and the tribe, all I need to know really is how you feel about it."

I nodded and squeezed her hand back.

She continued, "well, do you feel like this is the thing for you to do? Do you feel it inside?"

I nodded and she stood up. I followed her.

"Then that is all I need to know, Jacob." She smiled and gave me a hug. As I held her I thought of telling her about the upcoming war and about being chosen by The Skitcha, but there it was. She didn't need to know.

"Come on," Kate linked her arm around mine. "Let's go back to the house now. You are needed by your people."

When we got back to the house I saw one of the tribesmen helping to feed the animals and another was tending to the garden. Walking by I thanked them in our tribe's language. They signaled with their arms, acknowledging me.

My sister and I walked towards my mother and Bodaway. Mary Ann had gone into the house.

"Jacob, are you ready for your training now?"

"Yes Bodaway, I am."

"Are you prepared to stay with us until your training is done?"

I looked at my mother and felt that she was believing. She believed this was the right thing to do, and I needed this. I looked at Ann and could barely think of leaving her again. She held my gaze, certain and proud. It was a look that told me to do what felt right.

In Skitcha I replied, "Yes."

I saw my mother smiling when I said this, proudly.

"Well then Jacob, grab your horse and get ready. We will be leaving shortly."
As I walked away I could hear Bodaway begin talking to Kate. He was saying, "at your request we will not approach you in anyway or appear at your home. However, we will protect you if it is needed, or if you request it, or if Jacob requests it. You may never say a word to anyone about us, not even your husband or children. Do you understand?"

She agreed and asked, "will I be able to see Jacob ever again?"

Bodaway said, "yes, but it must still be a secret."

After loading Skip with my supplies I said my goodbyes. I walked first to my sister Kate and told her I would see her soon and asked her to take care of Mom.

"I will Jacob, be strong. I know inside you are."

I smiled and gave my sister a hug.

I walked next to my mother. She had started to cry, but tried to fight the tears.

"I am sorry, Son. I am sorry I did not tell you earlier."

"Ma, don't worry. It's not your fault. You did what you were told, Bodaway knows that."
"I am so proud of you and I am proud that you're going with Bodaway. The Skitcha is in your blood, all of them at the village, are a part of you like your family. They are your brothers and sisters. Always remember that when you're training."

My mother knew about the training and I believe that Bodaway told her what was about to come. Mom knew there would be fighting for the protection of the land. My mother grabbed me and gave me a hug.

"I will see you soon, Ma."

Then I approached Ann.

She was sad, but held that gaze of hers and started to smile. She said "I know, I know now Jacob. I am happy you are helping your tribe."

"I will be back Ann, I promise. I will never leave you."

Ann smiled and said, "I know."

"I love you, Ann."

She looked at me and said, "I love you also, Jacob."

I grabbed Ann and gave her a kiss and hug.

Ann said, "I will come and visit your Mother and sister from time to time, Jacob. I always see Kate in town too."

I nodded and smiled, turning to my horse I was about to leave then heard my name being shouted.

"Jacob!"

I turned and saw my sister Mary Ann running towards me from the house. She was carrying something.

"Here Jacob, this is for you." She gave me a picture of us of all of us, of my sisters, my brother, and my parents. I remembered when that picture was taken. A man had come to our house, just in passing, and offered to take our photo then sold it to us.

I hugged Mary Ann and smiled at her. "Thank you, Mary Ann."

Bodaway got on his horse and he approached. "Are you ready to go now, Jacob?"

I looked at Bodaway and nodded. I took one last look at my family and Ann, promising I would return, and started to ride off to the village.

The sun went down behind the mountain range before we arrived. I followed Bodaway as we rode into the village, past the hidden gate, and saw that some of the tribe paused to stare as we cantered by. Midway through the village Bodaway stopped and we found ourselves in front of a big fire. Bodaway got off his horse and signaled me to follow him. Together we started to walk toward the fire. To the right of us a group of people were preparing food. I asked Bodaway what was going on.

He turned to me and smiled, "our people are preparing dinner for you."

I looked over Bodaway's shoulder and waved at the people that were preparing the meal. Thanking them, they smiled back.

"Come Jacob, let's sit with our people around the fire." I followed Bodaway and sat down, taking off my hat.

The people of the village began to come out from their tents and congregated around the fire, catching looks at me as they passed. I looked to my right and there was a group of people crowding near me with excitement. Suddenly a little girl wearing a fancy tribal dress came through the crowd of people. I turned myself around to give her my attention.

The girl walked in front of me with her hands behind her back. She moved her hands in front of her and presented me with a small yellow flower held in a little clay pot. I smiled at the gift and lifted it from her hands. Later on I learned that this was called a California Buttercup. The girl's mother walked toward us and waited beside her. I stood up and the woman spoke to me in Skitchan.

"Hello Jacob," she nodded as a sign of respect. "My name is Halona and this is my daughter, Alyana."

"Nice to meet you, Halona." I looked down at the little girl as I started to kneel. I said to her, "nice to meet you too, Alyana."

The small girl gave me a hug. I was surprised by her generosity and hugged her back, crouching to her height.

"The flower that she gave you Jacob grows wild here on our land. If you are ever lost and hungry you can eat the roots. You can find them near streams or ponds. My daughter put her energy into this flower for you, Jacob. She did this to represent strength and love. You will notice that the flower will never die, even during the cold of winters."

Astonished by this statement I held the flower carefully and admired it. "Thank you, Alyana."
I looked beyond the fire and from a distance could see another group of people approaching. They were dressed in stunning ceremonial outfits. The females wore gems and jade stones around their necks and ankles. Around their arms and wrists they wore a string of walnuts. The woman had painted their faces and they looked beautiful. The men wore feathers and held drums, strung across their chests, as well as other unique instruments. The men's chests were painted with the symbol of the Skitcha on them. Their faces were painted also and they were muscular, fit. These were the warriors of the tribe.

I sat down next to Bodaway and looked at him. He said, "they will be doing a dance for you. It is a spiritual dance to give you strength and wisdom for your training and for the future."

The men started to drum very quietly then slowed in pace, then slower again. After a while the drums grew louder and the females began to dance around the fire.

Bodaway stood up, but told me to stay where I was. Doing as he said I watched him leave and found myself sitting alone on the log we had been using as a seat.

Suddenly, the men screamed a battle cry. The women moved in and started to dance all around me. The noise of the walnuts were so rhythmic and organized, it was tranquil. The women started to make a humming noise and looked up to the sky. They backed away and some of the men came towards me grunting and chanting. They pulled out sticks and started to shake them, then the sticks started to make noises. Wonderful sounds. These warriors were showing not just their toughness, but also their ability to work together when in battle.

The drums changed to thumps and all of the dancers started to stare up at the huge and prominent Mount Umunhum. The dancers put their arms up while the drummers drummed on. I started to look around and saw that all the people raised their arms up, praising Mount Umunhum.

The men started to chant and the drums stopped. The performers stopped dancing and quickly everyone started to clap.

One of the female dancers walked towards me and placed a necklace around my neck. She said, "this necklace is for protection and guidance, Jacob." She then kneeled and grabbed my arm, pulling her head towards the palm of my hand as a sign of respect. Afterwards she stood up and walked away.

For a moment all was quiet then a loud chant broke the peace. It came from behind the drummers. They moved in closer to me then a man emerged from their line. He was dressed all in feathers that were arranged in a complex and ornate pattern. He stopped his dance and looked directly at me. Then, he ran at me.

The drummer beat violently at their drums as he charged me. Just before he reached me however, he stopped. I did not move one bit. It was a man in a costume. He resembled a hummingbird, his headdress looking like a hummingbird's face with the long pointy beak. On his arms he wore feathers like wings.

The man looked up to the sky and yelled, "Umunhum!"

The people around me yelled the same. "Umunhum!"

Quickly the men on the drums started beating again and the hummingbird man started to dance, and sing, and chant.

He was saying, "yes, The Skitcha is around us! His spirit is around us, our ancestors are around us!"

The man started to move like he was dodging something. Hopping quickly side to side.

"Our great Skitcha gave us this bird! The Umunhum! Umunhum has quickness!"
He began to move around quickly, kicking suddenly. Then he grabbed a tomahawk demonstrating his quickness.

"Umunhum gives us skill and alertness."

He looked around as though in a state of high alertness. Then he pointed at a tree in the distance that had a cloth hanging from one of the branches. Without hesitation he threw the axe at the tree cutting the cloth in half. The axe was left stuck on the tree.

Everyone started to clap and shouted, "Umunhum gives us bravery!"

Six men started to walk to the man in the costume. The man stood straight up and, showing no fear, acted out a fight. The man fought through all the men. Every one of them fell to the ground. The hummingbird man yelled again in Skitchan.

"Thank you, Skitcha!"

The people in the background cheered and yelled, "we will keep Umunhum going. Dear Skitcha, your people are in our soul!"

The drums thumped loudly as the man kneeled down. He started to spread his arms wide, resembling wings. As he did this I could see the tribe's symbol on his chest.

The drums thumped, thumped. "Umunhum!" Again, the drums thumped, thumped, "Skitcha!"

The man looked down and the drums stopped for the last time. Everyone started to clap. The man walked to me and I stood up to greet him. The man kneeled down out of respect and I nodded to him. When he stood up I looked into his eyes and was speechless. I had never seen anything like that before. He nodded and walked away.

After the ceremony I found Bodaway and Marine-Oni with the shaman group.

"Welcome back Jacob, how are you feeling?"

"I am very speechless right now, Marine-Oni. I really have not proved anything to our people yet."

She smiled and said, "you don't need to, Jacob. They know. They know and feel your energy and soul."

"I understand, Marine-Oni."

She hugged me. "Your training will show you how to believe."

I grinned and looked around. I was aware that people continued to look at me as I spoke with my friends.

Bodaway said to me, "come, Jacob. Follow me. We will be eating soon."

I followed Bodaway towards the biggest tent in the village. I could see some of our people coming in and out of the tent, they were preparing for the feast. When we entered the tent there was a large table in the middle with chairs all around the edges. The interior was very lavish, filled with candles providing an ambiance that was both settling and peaceful. Bodaway showed me to my seat and I sat in a chair at the end of the table overlooking all the other village members.

Right when I sat down Marine-Oni came in with her shaman group. They sat next to me and Bodaway sat across the way. I started to see tribesmen bringing in pots and placing them to the side of the table. More people filled in and they all smiled at me, sitting down. Armija walked in next with a group of what I assumed to be his close friends. All of his people looked very fit, they were built to be soldiers or warriors. Armija nodded at me and sat down at the other end of the table.

Once everyone was seated Bodaway stood and spoke. "I am very excited to see that Jacob is with us, he is the Chosen One. I believe in him. He is very strong and will be tested before we are in danger. Before the trouble in town comes to our land."

One of the villagers suddenly stood up and spoke. "Bodaway, do we know when they will attack?"

"We are very close to that, in a few days time. Some of our men are watching them at their hideout, listening to their plans. We should know the date before it happens."

Another stood up, "where are they now?"

"Although we have not been around their hideout very much our men have told us they live up north."

Another man stood up from the table. "You said some of their men were from our tribe. Do you know their names, Bodaway?"

"They have made their own choices and I will not be able to share that with you. It is our tradition in our tribe to honor our word and keep from their business once they leave us, even if they do not keep to their word."

The man asked another question. "Do you think they might have family here in the village?"

"It is possible. That duty goes to Armija."

To this Armija stood up and said, "I have some of my men looking around the village and keeping an eye on things. Nothing has come up as of yet."

"They will continue to look and let me know what they find while I train Jacob."

Bodaway barely finished before another man stood up. "How do we know Jacob is the one? What if he fails his training?"

"We do not have much time. They will be coming for us and wanting to take this land of ours." Bodaway had not answered the question.

Some of the men started to talk amongst themselves. They were not satisfied.

Bodaway shouted out, "my brothers and sisters please, please. Jacob has seen The Skitcha."

This silenced everyone and every doubt in the tent.

"Jacob described to me what he saw in the Chataw." Bodaway looked at me and said, "Jacob, tell them what you have seen."

I looked around and I stood up. "I know some of you do not believe I am the One that is going to keep the tribe going." I paused, "even when I meet Bodaway, I did not believe him either. Everything was happening very quickly for me. Just a few days ago I found out that my mother was part of the tribe.

"What happened to me in the tunnels of Chataw, by Mount Umunhum, is very hard for me to explain. At least at first. But, when describing it to Bodaway he confirmed what I saw." I looked down and paused once again, taking a deep breath I continued. "I saw The Skitcha symbol carved in the tunnel. It began to glow, in pure darkness, around the edges. Then it opened like a gate to another world. I started to see people come through the glowing haze, it was our people, and there were also hummingbirds. Large ones with mouths of fire. At least that is what they looked like and they flew all around me.

"Then, a man walked towards me from out of the Skitcha symbol. He told me he was my grandfather. The Skitcha is my grandfather. He told me what I had to do."

I showed my arms to the tribesmen and said, "look here. They bit me and tore at my skin. Many of you bore witness to my wounds when I came out of the Chataw."

Some of the nonbelievers looked at my arms and their expressions changed to belief.

I looked at everyone and said, "The Skitcha has told me the name of the group that is coming for us."

Everyone looked around at each other and the tent was silent.

"They are called the Hand of Transcendence."

The eyes of the men and women around the table suddenly opened widely.

Marine-Oni stood up and said, "Jacob, that name means 'to rise.'"

"What does that mean, Marine-Oni?" I glanced to Bodaway and he was staring at Marine-Oni.

She began to describe the Hand of Transcendence to us all.

"It seems to me that they have a purpose, a vision, but it is from someone else. A vision for a leader or group of some sort. Myself and my followers will go into the Chataw tonight to speak to The Skitcha. Maybe he can give us more answers."

Bodaway then stood up. "I think The Skitcha knew about the Hand of Transcendence long ago. It must have been a sign to warn us."

Marine-Oni nodded and said, "I will go there now." Her followers acknowledged the mission and began to move in their scats.

I said to everyone, "The Skitcha, my grandfather, told me there was going to be danger soon. He told us we need to prepare for it."

I looked around, but some of the people did not acknowledge me. I began to feel somewhat disconnected all of a sudden from them. I spoke again, "if anyone here still does not believe I am the one, tell me now."

Silence.

"I passed Bodaway's training and I passed one of Armija's trainings so far. I will finish this and you will all witness the truth." As I said this I looked at Armija and said, "Armija, I want a few of your men to watch me and report to our people what my progress is during my training."

Armija nodded and I gazed at everyone, stone faced.

Bodaway broke the silence. "May the spirits guide you, Jacob!"

He brought up his clay mug to cheer.

The tribe called, "to Jacob! The Skitcha and Umunhum!"

Everyone raised their mugs and cheered. "To the strength of our tribe!"

Over the loud cheering we all started to hear people coming close to the tent from outside. It was the rest of the village listening to our tent walls.

"People," I called. "I know you prepared this food for us and I thank you for this, but I want the village to share this night and this food. Please tell them to join us."

Some of the inner tribesmen ran outside and I could hear them calling out, "everyone! Jacob wants you all to eat, come inside!"

For the rest of the night we left the tent doors open. Everyone was free to enter and exit, enjoying the food and merriment. There was music, dancing, and happiness. At one point Bodaway asked me to have some food, but I told him I wanted our people to eat first.

I started to walk around the village, enjoying the festivities, when a woman came up to me. We started to dance and I followed her lead. The village people noticed immediately that I was not the greatest dancer and everyone began laughing at my unskilled footsteps. I gave the woman a hug and thanked her for the dance.

Armija walked up to me and said, "Jacob, make sure you eat enough. You're going to need it tomorrow." He smiled and put his hand on my shoulder then walked away.

I began to wonder what the next training might be, but I was not worried one bit. I looked for Bodaway and walked towards him.

"You are not going to eat, Bodaway?"

He smiled and said, "I will wait also, Jacob. Our people haven't been this excited for a long time. You can feel their energy right now."
I smiled at him. "Thank you, Bodaway. Thank you for showing me who I really am and for bringing me to our people."

"You don't need to thank me, Jacob. The Skitcha, your grandfather, told me to do this. My duty was to get you and show you who you really are."

"I just hope I live up to what everyone believes."

Bodaway said, "if your soul believes in it, it will happen Jacob. You are strong in both mind and body. Your training will show you that and even make you much stronger. Our people feel that also. If you feel at times, that you need to give up during your training, just think of our people and feel that energy. Close your eyes Jacob, and feel the energy flowing all around us."

I opened my eyes and said to Bodaway, "is that how you can go through fire?"

He smiled. "Yes, it is the energy around us. It is the energy from our ancestor's spirits and from Mount Umunhum. We learned this from your grandfather. He discovered this and learned how to open it up. He tapped into this energy and found all that it can do. Everyday, even though he is no longer physically here, we continue learning."
"Does everyone in the village know how to do this?"

"Yes, but not all of them can do it. So far just higher tribesmen like Marine-Oni, myself, and possibly you."

"Marine-Oni knows how to do this?"

"Yes, she has been learning and teaching her followers."

"I have a feeling that Marine-Oni is going to train me. Is that right, Bodaway?"

"Yes Jacob, but how she will be training you to do this I do not know. She has kept that secret to herself. You must pass your training with Armija first however, before you can continue with Marine-Oni."

"I understand, Bodaway. I know what you need me to do."

Bodaway looked around and said, "well, I think everyone has eaten Jacob. You better have some food and try to get some sleep. Tomorrow will be a long day for you."

Agreeing, I walked to where the food was and had a plate. I don't recall what I ate, but only that I ate a lot. I kept thinking of what Armija told me and reassured myself that I would be ready for his training.

When I walked away from the food tent I could see some of Marine-Oni followers outside of the Chataw's entrance. There were torches on each side of the huge door. I wanted to walk over, but I had to go in my tent to get as much sleep as I could. When I arrived there I found more gifts, even a drawing from a child. I picked it up. It was a picture of me on top of a hill, Mount Umunhum. I smiled and brought the drawing into my tent and set it across from my bed. Before falling asleep I admired the drawing and the flower that the young girl had given me. I smiled and at last understood. I understood my destiny. Laying in my bed I felt truly happy. I was ready. I was ready for my destiny to begin.

The next morning I awoke to find a bag right in the center of my tent. There were tribal clothes hanging on the post of the tent with some shoes on the ground. Outside I heard voices. Quickly I got myself up and walked outside to find Armija talking to some of his soldiers. When I came out the soldiers rode off.

"What were you doing, Armija?"

"I was sending some of my men to replace the guards watching for the Hand of Transcendence." It sounded like his men had been observing the group all through the night.

"Well Jacob, before we begin I want to tell you something." I gave him my full attention and held his gaze. "You must obey my orders if you are to complete your training with me. Understood?"

I nodded.

"Very well. If you noticed, there is a bag and clothes in your tent. Put on the clothes and shoes. Do not open the bag until later, until I say so."

Doing as instructed I changed in the tent and picked up the bag. It was heavy, but I lifted it up over my shoulders, carrying it outside to Armija.

"Very good, Jacob." Armija called out to some of his men and they rode towards us. "Today you will not be needing your horse."

The soldiers stopped near Armija and he gave them instructions. "Help put the bag on him."

One of the men then dismounted from his horse and approached me. I noticed a couple of ropes had been tied on the bag. The man picked up the bag, with no sign of weakness, and put my arms through the ropes. This slung the bag across my back.

"Follow us Jacob," Armija commanded.

Slowly I started to walk, trying to balance myself with the weight on my back. We walked through the village and I saw that more of Armija's soldiers were joining us. I also saw one of Marine-Oni followers emerge from her tent. She also joined us.

Armija gave the signal to move on and we walked past the village. I looked up and saw that we were going the direction of Mount Umunhum. We stopped at the end of the trail and the edge of the village. Armija looked around and so did his men. We were in front a huge rock.

Armija said to me, "Jacob, this is the start of your training. You see this rock in front of you? This is a spiritual rock passed down to us from our ancestors. It is a barrier that helps to keep away any outsiders that may try to harm our land or Mount Umunhum."

"What kind of harm would the outsiders receive if they are near this rock?" I asked.

"The punishment would be very severe." He did not elaborate. "Jacob, are you ready?"
I was.

"Ok then, I want you to climb Mount Umunhum starting from right here. Start behind the rock."

I looked at everyone in shock.

"You must carry the bag on your back while you climb to the top. One of my men will be with you," Armija said. "Good luck Jacob."

Without hesitation he started to ride off and the others followed him into a small forest. Between that forest lay a hidden trail that headed straight up Mount Umunhum. I looked at the man that was staying with me, he nodded and asked if I was ready.

"It will take us two days to climb," he said to me.

I looked behind the rock and saw the first large hill before us. It was mountain sized.

Jokingly the man said, "that hill is not Mount Umunhum, Jacob. We have to go over this first to get to the real mountain."

My eyes widened and I took a deep breath. "What is your name?" I asked the man.

"My name is Dyami."

"Well Dyami, I take it you are not going to help me out here." I joked. "Not with the bag?" I smiled at him.

He smiled back and shook his head in good humor.

I took another deep breath and tried to focus my mind on accomplishing this incredible feat.

Night fell when I reached the top of the hill. I was already winded from the climb when I squatted and put my head down. Catching my breath I looked at Dyami. He was not winded at all.

"Take a look, Jacob." Dyami pointed in the distance.

I stood up and looked in the direction that Dyami indicated. Before us stood Mount Umunhum and it was beautiful. I had never been this close to it before. Only when I had been inside the Chataw, underneath Mount Umunhum, but then I could not see its mighty shape. Dyami pointed out different spectacles of the mountain. There was an edge of the peak that connected to a smaller mountain peak. When I looked up to Mount Umunhum I could see that the tip of the mountain was somewhat flat and covered in the greenery of trees.

Dyami said, "we have to walk down there, into the valley, before we climb up. This will get us closer to the mountain so we can climb it."

"Let's get going then," I said.

We started our descent down the hill. Every step we took was very risky because the slope was steep and we were very high up. I took my time as we went down.

"Remember Jacob, always look down when you take your steps. Do not look straight ahead while you move or you may slip on a rock. It is easy to lose your balance and react too late."

I nodded to Dyami as we continued downward.

We reached the bottom of the other side of the hill and were met by a dense forest. Walking through, quickly, it was soon time to make our ascent up Mount Umunhum.

Dyami said, "we must move now, Jacob. We cannot stop. I will direct you up the mountain and be right behind you."

I signaled with my arm, too out of breath to talk, that I agreed. Dyami pointed in the direction that we needed to climb and smiled cheerfully. I started to move up the mountain and felt that the ground was soft. It took only moments to relax my feet. I was glad to feel some tension leave me on this path, as I knew we were not going to stop to camp. Even though other villagers took days to climb this, Dyami and I were set to hike for two days straight. Thankfully, we did take breaks that I warmly accepted without hesitation. The further we got up the more rugged the terrain became.

Stumbling through the night, stopping here and there to rest, before I knew it the sun was again above us.

"It is midday," Dyami said, "noon. We are about halfway up the mountain now."

I was not so happy to hear this. I was growing very tired and thirsty. My legs were starting to shake from the weight of the bag. I wanted to take a break, but Dyami kept pushing me to go.

Suddenly, without thinking, I spoke. "I need to rest, Dyami."

He shook his head. "You will be tired Jacob and thirsty. You must realize this and believe that you can do this. Know within you that you can climb the mountain. Take your mind off of having water, and being tired, and know that the mountain does not consume you by its size. Know you can go over it many times."

I stopped and stared at Dyami. I turned back and looked at the mountain, straight up to the top. I turned again to Dyami and I nodded then continued on.

Later in the day we reached a rocky point of the mountain. Here Dyami pointed to the next part of our climb. It was straight up, not around. I took a deep breath and tried to clear my mind before I started to climb again.

Every step felt like an eternity. Grabbing onto huge rocks and pushing off of them, I scrambled up the route. All was going well until about halfway up the climb.

Reaching for the next rock, I suddenly slipped causing the rock above me to lodge free. It fell. I quickly grabbed another handhold and swung my body out of the way from the tumbling rock. Avoiding the falling stone I slammed myself against the face of the mountain.

"Don't look down," I heard Dyami call.

I tried to keep the pain within me and ignore it, instead trying to lift my legs to the nearest rock ledge. After a few tries I could not and I hung there, taking deep breathes.

Despite Dyami's recommendation, I looked at what lay below me. The view was magnificent. Hanging from the cliff I could see all of Almaden, San Jose, and our village. Our land was truly beautiful.

"Nice view, isn't it," Dyami joked. He patted me on the ankle, positioned below me. "We must keep moving, Jacob."

I next thought to pull myself upwards. As I contracted my arms, to lift my weight, I grunted from the pain and strain on my body. I lifted myself up so that my legs could sit on the ledge slightly above my knees. Having recovered from the initial fall I knew I still needed to climb. I used my legs to continue moving me up the rocky face. Every time I lifted I paused briefly, then repeated the process. After a short while my body began to feel worn. The feeling in my hands was fading, both from the elevation and lack of food, water, and rest. I kept moving, trying desperately to not think of what was going on in my body.

Night had fallen upon us by the time the incessant climbing finally stopped. We finished the climb by edging our way along the sheer face of the cliff's ledge then crested the crux, ending in a forest. The ground was much softer here, with hardly any rocks sticking out. We continued our journey following a zigzag trail, taking switchbacks up the next leg of the climb. For a moment I even enjoyed this, and relaxed.

Just as I did the easy part was over. Before us lay an obstacle of fallen trees. Of course, Dyami pointed and said we had to go through it. Stepping high over the fallen limbs my legs burned and to make matters worse the trees scratched at my skin. Although closer to the ground than the cliff had been, we were still climbing sharply and the fallen trees camouflaged hidden crevices in the rocks that dropped deep into the mountain's core. I struggled to find my footing on these logs, losing my balance, and started to feel dizzy.

I shook my head to rid away the feeling. It did not work. I started to feel light headed and on the verge of slipping away. Before I could let Dyami know what I was feeling, I blacked out.

I awoke very quickly. My arm caught on a rock and I felt as though I was not facing upwards. My eyes flickered open, but the sounds around me were muted. Moving slowly I realized that my caught arm had actually saved me from falling down into a rocky crevice. I repositioned myself safely and slowly turned my eyes to look for Dyami.

He was trying to talk to me and was approaching me quickly, but I could not hear him. Dyami was motioning to me and I thought I should keep going. I tried again to shake the feelings out of my head. It did not work. I remained sitting down and Dyami walked in front of me.

He grabbed my face and looked at me, we were both eye to eye. I could tell that he was checking to make sure I was okay. He kept talking to me and I shook my head again. At last, my hearing started to fade back in.

"Keep going, Jacob," Dyami said in Skitchan. He stood up and grabbed my arm helping to pull me to my feet. Again, I turned to face the mountain and continued to climb.

I didn't make it much further before my body weakened again. I stopped hiking and looked to the top of Mount Umunhum. We were still so far away. I felt pain and weakness. I felt dizzy and stumbled to my knees. My vision became blurry.

All of the sudden I started to see what appeared to be humming birds. They started to fly right by me. I rubbed my eyes and my vision started to get much clearer. I turned around to get a better look. There were hummingbirds everywhere.

Dyami pointed at the tress and I looked at the direction he was pointing. The trees were filled with many small nests, hummingbird nests. I stared in amazement.

I smiled and Dyami grabbed my shoulder, "these are the protectors. We will fight for them as they are a part of us."

For no reason, perhaps other than faith, I felt a surge of energy run through my body. I smiled and stood up. I stared up at the mountain, eager to climb.

I turned to Dyami and said, "let's go my brother."

It took us two whole days and nights to get up to top of Mount Umunhum. When we reached the top the sun was about to fall yet again.

I recall the last push to the top. I had pulled myself up and when there was no more to climb we met Armija and the shaman. They had set up a camp, with a fire, alongside the rest of the soldiers. There was barely time to enjoy this scene before everything went black again. Falling to my knees I saw Dyami stepping on the leveled ground before he ran to me. He took off the backpack and laid me on my back.

I was motionless. The shaman walked towards me as I began to fade out. She pulled a pouch from her garment and knelt beside me. The shaman grabbed my chin and lifted my head back as if I were looking towards the sky. Carefully she opened my mouth and poured the contents of the pouch into my mouth. It was some kind of water, but it had a bitter taste. I suddenly blanked out.

When I woke up I was near the fire. Feeling somewhat better I picked myself up and looked around. I saw Armija talking with the shaman and the soldiers. I began to stand up. My head felt heavy.

The shaman saw me stand and approached me. "Jacob, you must sit down for a moment. Your body is not used to this elevation. You are all right now. Please, sit and drink this."

She made me drink the rest of the liquid in the pouch. While I was drinking the liquid I saw Armija walk over and sit beside me.

"I would like to congratulate you Jacob, for climbing the mountain. This is the very view where nonbelievers will start to believe."

He signaled one of his soldiers towards us. Armija said to him, "go to the village and let our people know that Jacob has reached the top of Mount Umunhum."

The soldier nodded and ran to his horse then rode off to the village.

Armija said, "come to me when you are feeling better, Jacob." He stood up and walked to where the tents were.
Looking out across the valley the view was truly beautiful. I felt like an eagle perched in a big tree. I closed my eyes and listened to the calm breeze flowing past me. After closing my eyes for a while I opened them and looked at the fire. My head finally cleared up and I walked to Armija.

He and the shaman were sitting at the edge of the mountain.

Armija turned to me and asked, "what do you think, Jacob?"

"It's incredible Armija, I have never seen the land like this before."

He pointed and said, "that is where our village is. At night you cannot see it though because it is surrounded by a thick forest of trees. And over there," he pointed again, "are the mines. They are easier to see because the land is empty there."

I looked at Armija and asked, "Armija, how does Mount Umunhum give the special energy to certain people in our tribe?"

"It is in the heart of the mountain, Jacob. It is in the minerals. It is in our ancestors who came before us and discovered its power. At first it was forbidden to tell anyone in the tribe, only the higher people would know. The Skitcha discovered this first hand. Before he left to the spirit world he told our people what the mountain could do. He told the higher people in our tribe to study it more. Nowadays we have learned quite a bit more from the mountain's power. We know there is still a lot more to learn too. Our spirit ancestors have told us that."

"So, is this why the Hand of Transcendence wants to take over this area?"

"We believe so. That and for the precious minerals the mountain has. That is why you are here Jacob, to protect it and to learn of its powers. That way we can continue preserving our way of life and pass it and this land on to future generations."

"Can you use the power anywhere?"

"To our knowledge, only at a certain distance from Mount Umunhum. We believe from the entrance of the village is where it stops."

"Is that why the village was built there?"

"Yes Jacob. The Skitcha knew this and built the village there. We also believe that it circles around the mountain."

"Do you possess these powers also, Armija?"

"No, I do not. As I mentioned, only certain people in our tribe will possess it. Those people are Marine-Oni and her shamans."

Armija pointed to the woman and she nodded.

Armija then said, "and Bodaway can harness its powers as well."

"How is that?"

Armija pointed to the sky, "it is what the spirits give us. It's what your grandfather, gives us. Our purpose."

"Have any of our people, that are not higher rank, ever tried to harness the powers?"

"A few have, but they failed to do so since they understand their purpose in the tribe."

Hesitantly, I asked next, "do you think I will I be able to learn its powers, Armija?"

"Jacob, if the prophecy is correct, and you are indeed the Chosen One of our people, then yes. That is why you need to complete the training. Once we prove that you are the One we can train your body and mind to harness the energy that the mountain possesses." Armija put his hand on my back and said, "come over here, Jacob."

We walked to the other side of the mountain. It was my first glimpse at the far side of the valley. There were various mountain ranges headed in very far distances. I noticed clouds further back from that.

Armija said, "this is what is making the cold breeze. See those clouds over there? That is where the ocean is located."

I stared at various mountain ranges for a long time before Armija said it was time to follow him again.

He brought us back to the camp. "Jacob, I want you to now open your bag."

I walked up to the bag and started to open it. Within the bag were materials for a tent, a ceremonial outfit, a cloth blanket, weapons, and some rope.

"Jacob, I want you to set up your tent over there." He pointed at the area away from him. "It will become cold very shortly."

I had never set up a tent in my life. I looked at the other tents of my tribesmen and saw that they had used thick branches to give their tents structure. I walked to one of the tents and looked closely to see how it was build.

Armija sat near the fire with everyone and they all watched me.

I walked back to the large bag and pulled out an axe. I started to look around for some trees and saw a trail going down Mount Umunhum. I looked to my side and spotted a fallen tree. I approached it and as I did darkness surround the area immediately. My eyes started to change to the blue vision that I had when in the mines.

This was the mountain's energy, I thought.

This happened by itself, without help from the others. Now that I was able to see at night I started to chop the thick branches and drag them to the campsite.

Armija yelled to me, "you best work quickly, Jacob. The coldness may bring in rain." He pointed in the direction of the ocean and in the distance, there were even more clouds heading in our direction.

I quickly grabbed the thick branches and formed the base of the tent. Then I took some of the rope that was tied on my bag and tied the intersecting branches together, just like the other tents. I took the tent cloth from the bag and draped it over everything. I noticed a few little holes in the middle of the cloth. With the rest of the rope I put it through the holes and tied them with the branch.

When I pulled the last rope the tent propped up and stood to face the breeze. It began to billow with air and flap at its base. I noticed the other tents did not do the same. Again, I walked to one of the other tents and saw that rope had been used to tie the corners of the tent with a rock, anchoring the structure. Despite the growing wind I collected heavy stones and set them at the corners of my tent as well, trying to tie them. Just as I did the darkest of clouds moved in.

Struggling to fasten the rope to the rocks Armija sent Dyami to help me.

"I will show you Jacob, look closely."

Dyami helped me with the first rock and I completed the remaining three, grateful for the instruction. After my tent was secured Armija commended the efforts and said it was time to rest, just as the rain began to fall.

That night the weather was rough. Periodically my eyes would involuntarily fly wide open, awakened by the sound of the rain beating hard on my tent. I began to wonder if it would be able to hold or not. I listened intently, awaiting a surge of water that would surely break through. Then all at once, before I knew it, the rain went away. I was not used to this weather at all, nor this altitude. It took some effort to get back to sleep. Lying in bed I felt dizzy and spent most of the night trying to keep my eyes shut.

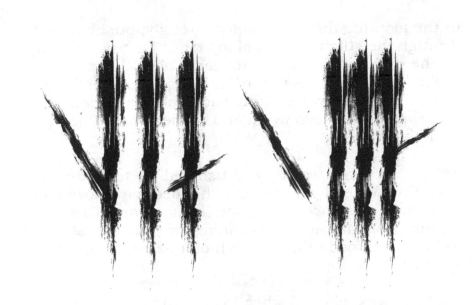

In the morning the sun beamed strongly, pushing light through the stitched walls of my tent. I got up and put on the clothes that were in the large bag. When I walked outside it was very cold, but someone had built a fire. Everyone was walking back and forth about the flame, pacing to keep warm and carried bowls filled with something.

Armija saw that I was up and ushered me towards the campfire. When I got to him he handed me a bowl and said, "take this Jacob and go to the shaman. This is the beginning of Marine-Oni's training for you. Her shaman will give you food. Eat as much of it as you can, you will need it for today."

I did as I was told and when I got to the shaman she poured some kind of corn porridge into my bowl. Looking at the mush I saw her pick up a wooden cup, remove the lid, then poured a sort of powder on top of my food. Without wishing me a good morning she smiled and handed me a wooden spoon, motioning for me to stir the powder into the porridge. I returned to the campfire as she began to serve the other soldiers.

At the fire I sat beside Armija.

"The shaman does not talk much, huh?"

"It is part of her training also, Jacob. She will talk only when she needs to."

"What is in this food, Armija?"

"It is corn and the powder that the shaman put in your food is to help you in your training. It is supposed to give you more strength."

I started to eat the porridge and the taste was very enjoyable.

Armija said, "as soon as you are done with your food you will begin your training with me."

I nodded and continued to eat. My stomach felt very empty since the climb up to the top of the mountain. I ate the porridge faster than I could blink.

When I finished I looked at Armija. "Are you ready now, Jacob?"

"Yes."

Just as he smiled in return something whistled towards me. My hands shook, still clasped around my bowl, and I saw that an arrow was sticking straight out the side. I looked to Armija, worried, and I saw a guileful look in his eyes. Looking back to the bowl it started to burn. The arrow had been lit at the tip.

I dropped the bowl and it turned into a large fire. Startled, I looked around and saw a soldier chanting behind the flame at a distance. He had been the one to shoot the arrow. I looked to Armija.

"Run Jacob. You need to dodge the arrows and take the bows from the soldiers. Once you collect the bows return them to me. Treat them as your enemy Jacob, now go!"

At that moment more arrows shot through the flames and whistled past me. I got up and started to run through the dense fog that encircled the mountaintop. Before me I could see soldiers emerging from the fog, but they were dressed differently, shrouded in leaves they resembled trees.

Suddenly, the men lit their arrows with a torch and started to shoot at me. I quickly dodged the arrows and ran to the path that led downhill. Running as fast as I could my foot caught and I stumbled. Rolling downhill I tried to control the fall, hitting rocks and branches, and at last I caught myself and stood up. Still in shock from the fall I instinctively ran behind a rock and shock my head to steady myself.

I tried to locate the men, but I could not see them approaching, nor could I hear them. Standing with my back to the rock I looked around, searching for a place to hide. Not too far from me I started to hear a noise. One of the men was coming towards me. I sprinted to distance myself from the man.

After running for quite a while I stopped and tried to find a place to hide or defend myself. Around me were thick branches that had a slight curve to them. I ran towards the branches and was relieved to find that none of the men were approaching. Or at least, none that I could see.

I began to focus on the branches in front of me and had a thought. I kicked at the nearest branch, trying to break it off, but it was too thick to break. Frantically I searched for a rock that I could use as a tool. I found one, larger than the size of my hand, and heavy. I positioned myself before the branch and I threw the rock at it. I missed and the rock made a loud thud on the ground. I worried that the soldiers might now have heard the noise, but no one appeared. I quickly picked up the rock again and threw it at the branch.

This time I aimed true and the branch broke off from the tree landing to the ground with a thud. I quickly seized the thick branch and started to run to a denser part of the forest.

The fog was still around me and at times it was very difficult to look through. When I reached the thicket of the forest I noticed that I was surrounded by rock formations and fallen trees. I hid myself behind them and waited. I waited in hopes that a soldier would walk across my path. As I stayed there the fog began to thin and the sun shone even brighter.

After some time I thought that maybe the soldiers had gone in another direction. Judging by the sun most of the day had passed and no one had walked by me yet. I began to think of food and water, but knew that now was the time to survive. I must treat the soldiers as my enemy, Armija had told me. I decided to move areas. Moving as quietly as I could I made my way to a different part of the forest hiding behind trees and rocks along the way.

As I walked I knew they were watching me. I could feel it. They were waiting for just the right opportunity to attack.

I looked to the right of me and saw a small cliff. Knowing I needed to get away from a possible strike I ran in the direction of the cliff and started to climb it. When I reached the top I had a good view of the area. Again I took cover and waited.

Suddenly, I noticed light. It was a glowing torch, like the one the soldier used to light his arrow earlier that day. I could see a group of men right below me now.

As I watched one of the men walked separately from the others. Below me the group moved onward while this lone soldier distanced himself from the pack. This was my opportunity. I was going to go after that one soldier.

Scanning the scene I quickly planned my attack. It would be swift. It must be immediate and quiet.

I began to make my descent. As quietly as I could I made my way down the cliff, stopping only briefly to take shelter out of eyesight behind trees. Slowly I inched towards him. I was nearly upon the man when he suddenly stopped moving. He knew I was near. We were at the area where earlier in the day I had broken the branch from the tree. The man pieced together my actions as he took in the scene. From behind a nearby tree I crouched down and picked up a rock, this time intending to use it in my attack.

Quickly revealing myself from behind the tree I took aim at a tree just a foot away from where the soldier was standing. I threw. The rock struck the tree and it made a loud noise.

The soldier reacted, quickly spinning in the direction where the noise had come from. In one swift motion I lunged at the soldier, catapulting myself off a large broken rock, and swinging the thick branch at the man. Falling upon him, I missed.

The man turned on the spot, saw me coming, and swung his torch at me. It caught my face, but I continued my attack through the burn. I swung again and this time struck the soldier's torch. It flew from his hand and fell to the forest floor. The soldier started to pull an axe from behind his back. I countered the man, swung again, and hit him square in the face. He fell to the ground, unconscious.

Proudly, I grabbed his bow and the quiver of arrows. Once slung over my back I put out the burning flame of the fallen torch, not wanting any of the other men to see the burn. Just one down, I backtracked to the trail to gain some bearings on the land.

It took no more than a few paces for me to realize where I was and even more, I knew where the remaining soldier had been headed.

Night fell and the feeling of being watched returned to me. Peacefully I continued to walk and discreetly looked in every direction as I went. Up ahead was a clearing. Walking through this space would put me in clear sight of the soldiers. This was not something that I wanted, but I knew it was just another obstacle along the way.

I proceeded quickly, keeping as low as I could, I sped across the clearing. It was the only way to reach the hills. As I charged the hills the feeling of being watched grew more intense, more tangible. Nearly across I could almost hear the breathing of the soldiers watching me.

I made it. Instantly I hid myself behind a big tree. I held my back tight against the trunk and let my eyes take in the land before me. I waited for what I knew was bound to come.

Above the slight breeze I heard them approach. The smallest crackle of a leaf, the softest snap of a branch. I just stood there waited, quietly and patiently. The noises grew and I knew they were close. Slowly I turned my head, rounding myself about the tree trunk, and saw a deer.

I allowed myself a sigh of relief. My legs started to feel tired and weak and I squatted before the deer, taking in this lone peaceful moment. I was growing impatient.

A whistle, a flame, and the warmth of an arrow speeding just inches from my face.

The arrow shot just in front of me and hit the tree that I was hiding behind. As it flew I saw that the flame was not a normal color of fire. This time it was white.

I quickly rolled out to the side of the tree and stood up on my feet. Luminous white arrows rained down upon me and I started to run. As I was running the men were right behind me and they continued to shoot arrows.

Dodging and ducking I fled. One shot just over me and landed right in front of my path. Trying to edge my way around the growing flame I started to tumble, but planted my other leg firmly to the ground. In the swiftness of this movement I failed to see that I had stepped onto a log. It rolled immediately beneath my weight and I was thrown to the ground. The branch I was using for a weapon fell out of my hand and rolled away from me. The bow I was carrying dropped to my other side and the arrows fell out of the quiver.

Before I could react the men were upon me. I tried frantically to get away and as I turned my head I saw another incoming round of arrows. Then, without a moment to counter the attack, one of the soldiers seized me.

Instantly I grabbed the man's neck and shoved him off. He stumbled and hit the tree next to us. I looked at the other soldier and he began to walk closer to me as he threw his torch to the ground. When it fell the torch began to glow brightly, as though some kind of power was controlling the flame's color. He then pulled two arrows from his quiver and lit them with the torch.

The man I had pushed was now slowly rising to his feet. I got up quickly and started to run away from both of the men. Arrows were chasing at my feet as I ran. I knew these soldiers were not about to give up easily.

Suddenly, pain struck as I felt one of the flying arrows graze my leg. I stumbled, but quickly righted myself just before the other man grabbed me. He tried to pull me down to the ground. I turned myself behind him and put my arms underneath his arm, my hands behind his head. He was bound and struggled, trying to break out from my grip. Looking up I saw, through the trashing, the other soldier run towards us. He was pulling his arrow and drawing his bow. He aimed then released the arrow.

Time seemed to slow as it shot through the air. I twisted, fighting the thrashing man in my arms. The arrow was a foot from us now. I turned and as I did the soldier in my hold turned with me. The arrow struck. Not me, but the now lifeless man in my arms. The arrow shook briefly, sticking straight from his chest, and I dropped the man's body to the ground.

There wasn't much time. The death of his comrade did not faze the shooter. Thinking first to flee I cannot explain why I did not follow. It must have been simply instinctual.

I charged the shooter.

The man pulled another arrow from his quiver and light it. From within me, between my strides, I began to yell. I was transforming into a warrior. I cried of battle as I charged him.

From my back I pulled two of my own arrows from the quiver. Holding one in each hand I was nearly to the shooter.

Just as he was about to release his bow I was upon him. With all my force I stuck both arrows into the soldier's chest, falling into him, we both collapsed to the ground. I rallied, preparing for a counterattack, but there was no need. The man lay still with the arrows stuck in his chest. As I lifted myself I saw that he was not breathing and his eyes were open. The man was dead, killed instantly from my attack.

Out of disbelief I saw the two bodies on either side of me. I had killed my own tribesmen, my brothers. I knelt beside each man and closed their eyes with my fingers, just as I had seen Bodaway do in the cave. Glinting from the corner of my eye I saw the white flame ablaze from the torch. Before me lay another flame, from the tip of a fallen arrow. Simultaneously they both went out.

Taking the bows from both men I began to walk away, limping faintly from my wounded leg. I made my way back to camp with both a proud and wounded heart. I had taken three bows and the lives of my brothers.

———————————

When I reached camp the shaman was the first to see me. She stood and pointed to me. The other soldiers turned and did the same. Holding their gaze I walked towards them. Armija emerged from his tent. As he did, whether it was due to exhaustion or relief in completing the task, I fell to my knees.

Armija called to his men, "bring Jacob to me."

The men helped me up and took me to the fire, sitting me down before it. The shaman came to my side and fed me water. I must have drank it all within the blink of an eye.

Armija sounded proud as he spoke. "I see you brought the bows back. That is good Jacob, very good."

"The men are dead, Armija. I knocked one out completely and I... I killed the other two."

Armija stood up and looked at me saying, "it will be ok, Jacob."

He signaled to a group of his men to find the bodies. The soldiers acknowledged and ran down to the trail to find their tribesmen.

The shaman brought me another bowl of water and while I drank she applied a white paste on my leg wound. I remember it stinging quite a bit.

"This will help you, Jacob." She said as she rubbed my leg. "This will completely heal by tomorrow."

I thanked her and she returned to her tent.

While I sat before the fire Armija paced, perhaps patrolling the mountaintop. I watched him as I was given food and began to regain some of my strength. I spoke to him as he walked.

"Your expression Armija, when I told you that two men were dead and one injured, you showed no emotion. Why is that?"

Armija turned to me and said, "you will see why in a moment, Jacob." Again, he had the look of a fox.

Bemused, I did not understand what he meant by that.

Over the cusp of the hill I saw some of the soldiers returning from the forest, carrying one of the men I had killed. Behind him followed the next body and then the man who I knocked unconscious. Armija called to the shaman and she came out of her tent. The men walked quickly towards her and the shaman signaled to the men to go into her tent. One by one they went in, each seemingly lifeless body at a time. After each body was left and the live soldiers walked out, heads held high as if they had merely dropped off supplies.

I started to hear a spirit sound around me. It was the same sound I had heard when I first met Broadway. The same sound as when the soldiers protected me from the men on horseback. The sound surrounded us and traveled towards the flame of the fire.

I followed the sound and visually saw the fire flicker away from the sound as it traveled into the shaman's tent. When this happened the sound became clearer. It was the sprits, our ancestors. They were talking in our language.

I quickly stood up out of amazement and looked closer at the shaman's tent. Through the draping of the front door I watched flashes of light creep into the tent.

All of a sudden the campfire began to flicker a spectacle of colors. Instantly the flame began changing from orange to white and then violet. The flames crackled, echoing the sounds of the spirit, amplifying the cry of the ancestors. Beneath all of this noise I heard another voice, the chanting of the shaman. The air started to become very thick and I felt as though I was breathing a lot faster than usual.

Then, without warning, a huge flash of light covered the entirety of our camp. I covered my eyes and when the light faded I watched as everything dimmed to its typical hues.

Armija stood and walked to me, glancing at the shaman's tent as he neared. The shaman came out of the tent and walked towards us.
"Armija, it is done." She called.

She turned to the tent and to my astonishment one of the men I had killed walked out. The dead had been given life. I could not believe my eyes as the next man followed, the one I had stabbed in the chest, and then the man who I had rendered unconscious. All were walking out. Renewed in their spirit and life the men walked towards the fire though their legs shook as if they were learning to walk again.

Armija ordered a few of his men to help the revived.

The soldiers held their brethren gingerly, helping them towards the fire and assisted as they drank. I could not believe my eyes.

"Armija, how, how is this possible?" I asked.

Armija spoke mollified, "this is the power that has been given to us, Jacob. The shamans are now starting to understand it more."

I watched as the revived men sat beside the fire, huddled together they began to shiver.

"What is going on with the men now?"

"They are weak," Armija said, "but, only for a moment. The energy gathered from them put them into a weakened state. It will pass."

Armija ordered the soldiers to bring the men food and warmth.

"So, our tribe can bring people to life Armija?"

"It is not as easy as it seems, Jacob. I will let the shaman explain."

Armija waved to the shaman and she walked to us willfully.

"Marine-Oni knew you would have questions after you witnessed what I have done. She has allowed for me to explain it to you, Jacob. As far as we know we cannot bring everyone back, or should I say, we do not know how many times. There are limits to this and it is a dangerous risk for any man or woman."

I asked her, "is it because of their soul?"

"Yes, some souls are weak while some are strong. As shamans we have studied the limits of this practice. From within us there is a certainty, a feeling guiding us. It is a feeling of rightness. At times The Skitcha will tell us as well."

I looked at her with understanding and wonder. "Is this why the men can take this, because they are strong in their soul and body?"

"Correct, Jacob. Some of our people in the village are strong also, but they understand their purpose in this life is on our land. At times it is necessary to die."

I was so certain as to what she meant, though craved to know more. "I understand, but I still have more questions."

I can tell she started to smile even when her mouth was covered with a cloth. "You will understand more Jacob, when you see Marine-Oni."

I nodded and she acknowledged me then started to walk to her tent.

Armija said to me, "now you know why we cannot let outsiders claim our land."

I looked at Armija and asked, "do we have enough people for this encounter with the Hand of Transcendence?"

"No, we do not at this time." Armija continued to look at the fire. "Perhaps that would change if the people who left our tribe came back to help us, but for now that is unlikely. That is why I have been sending men to find more of our people. We should know more when the men return back, if there are enough. I am hoping we have enough time for your training before they come, Jacob."

Armija took a deep breath and said it was getting late.

"You need your sleep now, Jacob. We are going to have another long day tomorrow."

I looked at Armija's face and he seemed concerned. It looked as if he was worried that I would not complete my training in time. I stood up and walked to my tent where I retired for the night, thinking only of what tomorrow might bring.

The next morning Armija woke me early and when I walked outside the sky was still dark. I could barely see the sun appearing in the east. As we walked through camp I saw other soldiers gathering their supplies for the day, spears, bows, axes. Without surprise I accepted what Armija handed to me next.

"Carry this, Jacob."

Armija gave me a bow with a quiver and a tomahawk, but it looked unique from the others in the tribe.

"What are we going to do, Armija?"

"We are going hunting today, we need food."

Another soldier and I followed Armija as we made our way out of camp. He turned back to his tribesmen when we reached the edge of the mountaintop.

Armija spoke to his men and the shaman, "we will be back in the next day. Prepare the area."

At this both the shaman and the tribesmen began to clear the camp. We then started our descent down the mountain.

We walked down a familiar route and passed the clearing where I had attacked the men the day before. Then we approached an area between the two hills, where the side of the mountain became exceptionally steep. We followed a trail that twisted beside this, making our way down the mountain until the land evened out and we could walk safely. Sun began to shine as we made our way across a flat expanse and headed into a forested wood.

Armija stopped and ordered the soldier following us to set up camp. As the soldier did Armija ushered for me alone to go with him.

I followed Armija and we walked towards a more dense area of forest. It seemed as though the walking would never cease and that the mountain kept going forever. I noticed that the trees around us looked much older now. The color of the leaves and trunks were also different than the other forests we had traveled through. We continued our path and walked directly through a thicket of forest where the trees more resembled bushes. Above these bushes, on a slight plateau of the mountain, a small valley could be seen.

Armija grabbed my shoulder and whispered, "this is sacred ground. This is where you will learn to use your bow. You do know how to hunt, correct?"

"Yes," I replied. "I learned during your last training in the woods, when I was alone."

"Very good," he smiled. "I will now teach you how to use the bow, for hunting and defense. See that field ahead of us?"

I looked to where he pointed.

"Animals will walk across there to feed in the morning and around sundown as they travel. Animals like deer and sometimes predators."

Armija guided me away from the area. He took my bow, which was slung across my chest, and demonstrated how to hold it in form. I followed as he did this, practicing with my hands. Then he handed the bow back.

He whispered, "now put the tail of the arrow onto the rope of the bow."

I noticed a slight cut on the tail of the arrow and clicked it onto the rope of the bow. Armija explained this was the nock and the feather part of the bow was called fletching.

Instructing, he continued. "Now hold on to the rope using the very end of the bow, hold them together like this." He showed me, guiding my hands. "When you hold the bow stand this way and always keep your eye over the arrow, so you can aim. Now pull back the arrow to the point where it meets the rope. Keep your eyes very close to the rope Jacob, and just have your eyes right above the arrow tail. Now watch me as I shoot the arrow."

Armija quickly pulled his own bow into form and shot an arrow directly into an old tree stump. Armija nodded at his accuracy. "Now, I want you to shoot the arrow just as I have."

I aimed for the tree stump and was about to release my pull when Armija quickly corrected me.

"Do not release the pull, Jacob. You need to get used to the tension."

I nodded and positioned my aim at the tree stump.

"Get into a comfortable position, Jacob. Take your time and shoot."

I tried to concentrate on to the target, but felt Armija's watchful eye on my form. I hesitated and suddenly lost my grip on the rope causing the bow to slip from my fingers. The nock came off the rope.

"Try again, Jacob." I saw out of the corner of my eye that Armija was smiling.

I shook my hand to get the feeling back into my finger and palm. I tried again. This time I concentrated only on myself and steadied my movements. I pulled the arrow securely in place.

Armija hushed, "pinch both the arrow and the rope much harder this time."

I nodded and took a deep breath, pinching hard. I aimed and released. The arrow flew, quivering, and was sent over the old tree stump.

"Try again, Jacob."

My next shot skipped to the ground. The next ricocheted off the stump. Each time I took aim my vision faded, honing in on my target. I shook my head out of frustration.

"Keep trying Jacob, you will get it soon," Armija encouraged.

I took a deep breath and re-centered myself. I tried again. First I pulled the rope then I aimed. My eyes narrowed and I stared at the trunk. I envisioned the arrow flying towards it, the arrow hitting the stump, I focused. I released and missed. I tried again. Closer, but miss.

I felt for my quiver and found my last arrow. I could feel Armija's hope rising. I could feel the stillness of the forest and the sacred grounds. I focused, then closed my eyes. In my mind I released the arrow and watched confidently at is struck the stump. I flashed my eyes open and released. It flew, straight, and hit directly in the middle of the stump!

I smiled out of satisfaction and relief.

Armija clapped and walked towards me. "Very good Jacob," he patted my shoulder. "You are now ready to hunt with the bow. Let us go to the area now. We will aim for food before sunset is upon us. Remember, in order to kill the animal you have to aim for the neck." Armija demonstrated by using his neck and pointing with his fingers.

I nodded and followed Armija to the small valley. We stopped right in front of the short tree bushes and kneeled behind one. Our heads were right above the shrubs and we waited.

———————————

Sundown came and we still hadn't seen one animal roam through the grounds. All around us we began to hear coyotes howling and fighting in the distance. At last we were struck with luck when a group of deer wandered before us.

Armija signaled me to prepare my bow. Very quietly he told me to take the shot only when I was ready. I nodded and moved to the left of him, behind another tree. Armija moved to the right, hiding in some very thick shrubs. I looked at the deer. They were very cautious crossing through the valley.

I positioned myself and started to slowly and quietly pull back on the bow. I took my time aiming at a deer in the middle of the grouping. Feeling that I had my shot I released. The arrow flew straight over the deer, spooking them. As the group fled I was surprised to see one fall to the ground.

I looked to Armija and he began to walk to the deer. Following him we approached the deer and I saw, sticking straight from its neck, was one of Armija's colored arrows. Armija pulled out the arrow and knelt beside the deer. He touched the animal and closed his eyes.

"Thank you Skitcha, for this animal, for our survival."

Armija opened his eyes and stood up. "Tomorrow it is up to you to hunt for our food alone. That will be the last of your training. Now, grab the deer and put it over your shoulders."

Hoisting the deer atop of me we returned to camp where we laid our kill a distance from the tents. Armija and his men then taught me how to prepare the meat. First the men used a sharpened stone to cut through the animal, separating the hide from the flesh. Within moments, with great precision, the men had completely taken the hide off of the deer. Another man then used a sharper stone, resembling a knife, to tear open the belly. Fluids began to rush out and another tribesmen caught the liquid in a bucket. As the men continued their work everything was saved. Innards, blood, fur, bone, and of course meat. Meticulously they cleansed each section of the animal with water before preparing it to be cooked above the fire.

As the meat roasted Armija reminded me that in the morning I would be hunting alone.

"I will have one of our men accompany you and help to carry your kill." The man that was going to stay with me was Dyami. Armija continued, "the other soldiers and I will pack up and walk to our last camp while you're away."

I nodded and then held his firm gaze.

"Jacob," he said intently. "Do not come back until you have at least one animal."

That night I was again encouraged to eat as much as I could to prepare for the hunt. As we ate I watched as a group of men sat a short distance from the campfire. With them they held the bucket that contained the deer's blood and another with its innards. They drew the bucket to their lips and drank, lowering it I saw that their mouths were dripping in blood.

"Armija," I asked, "are they drinking the deer's blood?"

"Yes Jacob, the blood of a kill gives you strength. Our people believe that if you drink the blood you will receive the power of that animal."

I continued to stare at the men drinking the blood and remembered my time in the Chataw.

"Armija," I spoke, "during my time in the Chataw some of the spirits bit me. They tore away parts of my body. My flesh."

Armija took a deep breath. "They did that Jacob, because it was part your initiation. It is a rite of passage in our tribe. Every higher member goes through this. It is the way through which The Skitcha shares his knowledge. Your grandfather. He tells us what we need to do."

"What happened to my grandfather, Armija?"

"He sacrificed his life for us. He knew when he needed to sacrifice himself. That is what he needed to do, Jacob."

I was confused. "How does someone know when to sacrifice themselves?"

"Signs, Jacob. At times when our higher people receive signs they share information. Certain tribesmen cannot receive the spiritual power or sometimes higher members will lose the ability to receive powers. The gift is very limited."

I tried to piece this together. "Is that what the shamans are responsible for? Reading the signs?"

"The shamans are what we call The Knowing. They receive the names of the highers, or the gifted, from our ancestors. Some people do not receive this though. Even some of our soldiers are limited now. When they go into battle for instance, some know that they will receive the spiritual power and will be revived, but not all are. Some go into battle knowing they will not be able to come back."

I paused for a moment and started to stare into the fire for a long time.

I asked Armija, "if we bite someone do we get their knowledge?"

Armija hesitated before responding. "Yes, in a way. We get their thoughts and sometimes we get other people's weakness. That may happen if we bite someone who tries to harm us. Our people know and accept this. That is why every one of our people has the chance to be with us or without.

"Because our people know when or if they can be healed they understand death in a way that others do not. They always know their options in death. You see Jacob, they have a choice.

"Sometimes they chose against it, like your grandfather. He made a choice to sacrifice himself instead of continuing to live to his natural death."

Armija waited for me to think about what he had told me.

"So, my grandfather sacrificed himself because he knew the powers were not around him anymore?"

"We do not know this. There is no record. The shaman that was with him also sacrificed himself."

"Is there anyone in our tribe who was there? Is there anyone who knew him while he was alive?"

Armija smiled. "Yes, there are elders still in our village who knew him, but they were kept in the Chataw when he scarified himself. It was a dangerous time then and even today the village elders do not fully know what happened. All we know for certain is that The Skitcha was a large component of the battle and he sacrificed himself in front of the enemy."

"Who was the enemy?" I asked, "was it the Hand of Transcendence?"

"We do not know. We believe it was some kind of people who tried to migrate here."

I looked at the fire and questions swarmed within my mind. I wanted more answers that Armija could not give me. I wanted more answers than what the elders could supply.

Armija clapped his hand on my shoulder and said, as if reading my thoughts, "answers will come soon, Jacob. The spirits will tell you what you want to know. We all have a purpose."

As we sat my mind wandered to something that I had not thought of for years. I thought of a time without worry. I dreamed back to when I was young and at the lake. I remembered having fun with family and of all the happy things that I used to do with my brother and father. Over the years things started to change. It felt sudden. It was as if overnight everything had changed.

Was this my path now? I still wanted answers, but I knew I had to let them out when the time was right.

That night I also thought of Ann. I had not seen her in so long and I missed her. I thought of her safety and tried to feel her from afar. For some reason I knew that she was okay, as if I could sense her. I knew deep inside that Ann was supporting me despite unanswered questions she might have about my choices to be with the tribe. Thinking to myself I hoped that mother would help her to find the answers that she needed.

In that moment, for the first time, I wanted to leave. I wanted to be with Ann and my family, but I knew that my training was too important. Right then and right there was just where I was supposed to be. Still, if I started to sense the slightest threat of danger, to my family or Ann, I would not hesitate to leave for them.

The next morning Dyami woke me very early. He handed me a leather pouch that was filled with water and as I got ready he packed another pouch with dried deer meat. I looked into the ashes of the campfire and saw only the smoldering bones of the feast from the night before. It was a practice of the tribe to burn any remaining flesh off of the carcass, to keep predators from attacking in the night. All around everyone was packing to leave for the last camp. Some were taking stocks of food that were preserved from the night before while others seized weapons. Soon it looked as though no one had even stayed at the site.

Armija walked up to me, carrying his own pack. "Jacob, we are going to leave now. I will see you at the main camp when you return."

Armija looked to Dyami and nodded. With that I knew it was time to go.

"We must go to the valley now Jacob," Dyami said. "Roll up your sleeping mat and supplies. Do not pack your bow, leave it accessible, and we will leave."

Packing our sleeping mats on our back, like one might sling a bow, Dyami requested I lead the way. He was testing if I knew my bearings and wanted to see if I could locate the Sacred Valley. I started off in the direction of the valley and we soon came up on it, barren of animals.

Waiting in the daylight we knew few animals would come near us so we began to look for cover. I looked for a shaded area and found one beside a large puddle of water left from recent rainfall. Dyami walked to the puddle and I followed.

Dyami crouched down and scooped mud up with his fingers then spread it across his face, arms, and legs. I did the same then followed as he led me to a nearby shrub. Dyami broke off a branch from the shrub and decorated himself in leaves, placing them through the threads of this clothes and band that was wrapped around his head. He looked as though he was a part of the forest. Dyami broke off another branch and handed it to me then helped to camouflage us into the forest. Now, nearly indistinguishable from the woods, we crouched behind a nearby bush and waited.

As we sat we watched the sun arch above us. After no time at all it was nearing dusk and nothing had happened. Keeping very silent I signaled to Dyami that I was going to move further down, he nodded and I started to move.

Since I was the only one to hunt Dyami was not permitted to advise me in my tactics or help me with my bow. Keeping visible between each other I positioned myself behind another tree, further from Dyami. Patiently I waited, focusing on the small valley before me.

The sky began to change colors as the sun curved behind the mountain and the forest came to life with the calls of birds. There was no movement around us, but I knew the animals would eventually come. As the sun began to rest below the skyline it shone a last blinding

light upon us. With my back to the trunk of the tree I
sat as quietly as I could and waited.

Across from me Dyami whistled softly. Looking up I saw
him, ever so silently, pull from his bag the pouches of
food and water. Dyami raised them both up for me to
see and signaled for me to join him. Quietly I sat up
and, keeping low to the ground, made my way to Dyami.

When I got to him he handed me a pouch filled with
berries and dried deer meat. I started to eat the berries
as Dyami sipped on the water pouch. We shared this
meal and drink together before smiling to one another.
Dyami patted me on the shoulder and I thanked him
before stealthily making my way back to my hunting
spot. Feeling energized I sat with my back to the tree
once again surveying the scene for any signs of animals.

Looking around I noticed deer tracks on the ground just
before me. They led deeper into the small valley. A few
feet away I spotted more tracks, again, leading in the
same direction. I paused for a moment and a thought
came to me.

I slowly made my way back to Dyami and whispered to
him. "Dyami, can you hand me the bag of food?"

He pulled the pouch again from his bag and I took some
berries from within. I then walked to the open valley
floor and scattered some as bait for my prey. Quietly, I
looked for a nearby hiding spot. There were shrubs all
around and rocks, sensible places to take cover under,
but an instinct within me made me think otherwise.
Looking to the taller trees I had another idea.

Keeping low I made my way to a tree trunk and began to
climb upwards. The tree was big with many branches.
As I scaled the trunk I could see much more around me.
I climbed until I was just below the tree line. There it

was high enough to stay hidden, but low enough to move quickly to the forest floor. I perched on a branch that overlooked the valley. It gave me a perfect view of the berries, Sacred Valley, and Dyami. I waved to him below and he waved back. Then, holding myself firm on the branch with my legs, I drew my bow and waited.

The sun drew deeper to the mountaintops, but the sky had yet to dim. There were no signs of any animals.

Then, I heard the distinctive snap of a branch from behind me. Looking below, out of the corner of my eye, I saw a large group of deer approaching. Looking back to Dyami I watched him signal to me, indicating to stay where I was and keep quiet. I nodded and kept still as the deer entered deeper into the valley.

The deer slowly flooded in, there were so many of them, all after my trail of berries. By the time the group flocked into the valley it was hard to see the forest floor. The deer were everywhere. I began to take aim with my bow.

I looked for my first open shot and found a good sized deer, standing with its head just above the others. I drew the bow and focused my gaze. Just as I was about to release the deer moved, making room for another deer. A large buck walked among the flock, much grander than the others.

I refocused my aim on this prominent target. Drawing my bow further back and making the force of the arrow even stronger. I knew what I needed to do.

Thank you grandfather, for this moment.

I took a deep breath and released the arrow. It sailed straight and shot through the neck of the deer. Wildly, it began to kick. Its thrashing was so violent it frightened the others and the deer scattered. Quickly, I pulled another arrow, aimed, and shot. I hit another deer square in the neck. Within a blink of an eye most of the deer had scattered leaving the buck and the smaller doe alone on the forest floor.

Swiftly, I wrapped my bow around me and headed down the tree. Dyami saw me moving and headed towards me. When I reached the ground I pulled another arrow from my quiver and loaded it into my bow. Together, we walked towards the deer.

I had prepared myself for this moment, thinking that perhaps my arrow would not have killed the buck. I did not want it to suffer. When I arrived though, the buck was lifeless. I put the arrow away and knelt beside my kill.

I whispered, "thank you, Grandfather. Please let this buck be in the spirit world with you."

I stood up and walked to the other smaller deer. This one had been trampled by the fleeing group. As I approached I watched as the deer took its last breath. When I knelt beside it I knew that it had just died. I pulled the arrow from its body. Out of respect I bowed my head and closed my eyes.

"Thank you, Grandfather. Please let this deer be in the spirit world with you."

When I opened my eyes I saw that Dyami had been kneeling as well. I put my hand on top of deer's wound and suddenly felt the deer move. It started to breath. Blinking, I looked at Dyami and he looked amazed. It was clear from his expression that he had never seen anything like this before.

The deer quickly rose to its feet and for a moment looked at me. Then, as if nothing had ever happened to it, the deer trotted away.

Dyami and I both rose to our feet and stared at each other, shocked.

"How did this happen?" I asked. "How did I do this?"

In my head I recollected the scene. I had been thinking of the deer still moving around, being free, and not in danger. When I had approached its body I pictured the doe as alive.

Suddenly Dyami said, "I must tell Armija and the shaman what we both witnessed. Let us carry the buck and head to camp, Jacob."

I nodded and we started to walk in the direction of the camp.

When we reached the main camp the sun was still hovering above the distant mountaintops. It was dusk and I notice the area was arranged differently than it was from the last campsite. There were now torches all around encircling the whole camp. We were not too far from our village. Together Dyami and I walked to the campfire and laid the buck down. Dyami gave me the pouch filled with water and we looked for Armija.

Dyami saw him approaching and spoke first. "I need to speak with the shaman at once, Armija."

He looked at us and asked, "what for, Dyami?"

I looked at Dyami and saw that he did not want to speak of the deer in plain sight. "I witnessed something I cannot explain, and it involves Jacob."

Armija looked at me and said to Dyami, "stay here."

Armija walked to the shaman's tent and waited outside for a moment before going in. When he came out he signaled Dyami to join him. Armija held the tent flap open until Dyami entered then Armija joined me at the campfire and looked at my kill.

"For many years now I have never seen a deer this big around here." He grabbed my shoulder and said, "I am very proud of you, Jacob."

I smiled out of accomplishment and looked down.

Armija said to me, "I see you have witnessed something in the Sacred Valley."

I looked at him and said, "yes Armija."

He grinned back. "Go rest in my tent Jacob, your final training will begin soon."

I did as I was told and before entering turned back to the shaman's tent. I saw her exiting and walk towards Armija. The shaman and Armija started to talk and suddenly they both looked at me. Averting their eyes I turned around and walked into the tent. Lying down on the mat I overheard Armija and the shaman's voices. I couldn't hear what they were saying, but I knew it was about what happened with the small deer. Stretching on my back I thought of the day, closed my eyes, and instantly fell asleep.

I awoke to drums beating.

Outside my tent a strange chant filled the camp and I heard voices. The tent was dark and all I could sense was noise. The voices grew louder, the drumming pounded, and then light entered the tent as the door was suddenly thrown open.

People were filing inside wearing masks that were made out of wood. I was quickly pulled out of the tent and fought to break lose. As they drug me outside I could see the torches glowing brightly in the ring. The masked figures dragged me to the center and threw me to the ground.

I stood up abruptly and noticed that night had just begun to fall. I must have dozed off for just a couple of minutes. Spinning around I watched as more people flooded into camp, all wearing masks that resembled trees. Carved of wood each mask had a pair of holes that looked like deep knots of a tree trunk and an additional open hole for a mouth. To add to the image each person wore leaves and branches, not unlike the camouflage Dyami and I wore in the forest. The new soldiers joined in the chant. Not knowing what was going on, and not recognizing anyone, I looked around to find any help.

Beside one of the torches I saw the shaman. She was wearing a different outfit, which again covered her mouth and nose.

From behind Armija approached me, his body also adorned in ceremonial attire. His eyes were outlined in black and he wore a heavy necklace made of bones and small stones, all shaped into the symbol of The Skitcha. Along with this outfit, and his already impressive physique, Armija looked intimidating.

When he reached my side he drew a small cup from behind his back. Dipping his finger into the cup he painted my face as though marking me for something. While he did this the masked tribesmen cheered and chanted.

Above the din Armija said, "ready yourself, Jacob. This is your final test."

Armija signaled a few men over and they brought weapons. They presented me with a bow, arrows, two axes, four spears, and a thick staff.

Armija then called above the tribesmen, silencing the chanting, he spoke.

"My brothers, protectors of our tribe! This is Jacob's final test in his training!"

The drums beat wildly and the people cheered.

Armija boomed, "Jacob, your training will be a battle. A fight to the death!"

I looked at Armija and then looked at the people. Knowing how serious this would be, I still felt calm. I was not shocked nor scared. I just stood and began to prepare myself.

As the tribesmen continued to cheer the shaman walked forward and spoke.

"Tonight one of you will not come back. One of you will have your life end tonight and neither me, nor any shaman, will be allowed to bring you back. This is the word of our ancestors!"

Armija looked at me and said, "if you survive this, indeed you are the Chosen One and our people will bear witness to you."

Again, the crowd cheered.

"Are you ready to meet your opponent, Jacob?"

I took a deep breath, drawing my chest forward. Within confidence I spoke loudly.

"Yes!"

As soon as I said this Armija stepped to the side and behind him I saw someone squatting on the ground. His back was facing me and I did not know who the man was.

I looked to my left and watched Armija walk out of the ring of fire.

I began to focus my attention on the man squatting down. He was very muscular by the looks of his arms and back, but I still could not see him. Waiting for something to happen the tribesmen grew silent and I could hear the man breathe deeply. Softly, the drums began to beat and the man stood up. He turned to face me.

The man was tall in stature, much taller than me, and was wearing a mask that bore tribal symbols. The detail on the mask was intricate, showing jagged teeth that were painted bright white. I thought of the spirits and I thought that perhaps the teeth were symbolic of eating the flesh of your opponent.

The man suddenly sprinted towards me and the tribesmen began chanting.

I quickly looked down at the weapons and grabbed the bow and an arrow. Instantly I drew the arrow, aimed, and released. It struck the man in the shoulder. Showing no pain the man continued to run towards me and pulled out the arrow. As he neared closer I crouched down and next pulled the axe. Just as I did this the man lunged at me. Diverting him I rolled, avoiding his attack, and getting to my feet I saw him seize an axe.

The sounds of the drums became much louder now and before me I saw the man's muscles tighten on the handle of the axe. He lunged again, trying to corner me.

I veered to the right, but as I did he responded by swinging the axe. I ducked out of the way and rolled again. Getting to my feet I turned to find him running towards me, wildly, swinging the axe. He slashed, I dodged, he swung again this time cutting off my escape route. He wielded the axe and brought it down swiftly across my chest and down to my stomach.

White, blinding, instant pain.

I fell to my knees and touched the wound. It started to surge blood. I tried to stand. The man was returning. I struggled knowing this was the perfect moment for him to attack. He ran towards me with both hands wrapped around the axe handle.

Still on the ground I seized my own axe and prepared for him to swing. I lurched forward, powerfully thrusting my blade at the man's legs. It caught, cutting deeply into his calf. He dropped to the ground, face first, and the playing field had been leveled.

In that moment I found the strength to stand then charged the man. He quickly turned over onto his back and grabbed my neck. The man picked me up off the ground and tossed me across the ring.

My body scraped across the turf as I landed and collided with a standing torch. The force of the impact shook the torch and it broke in half, falling upon me, bouncing off my shoulder and burning my skin. Instinctively I scraped off the embers and moved away from it.

The man had returned and was nearly on top of me. He pulled me by my legs and dragged me into the middle of the circle to the weapon. Letting go of me with one hand I saw him take up a spear. I rolled, avoiding his next attack, and stood to my feet. I was without a weapon, but waited until the man charged to make my next move. I waited for him, like a predator taking its prey.

He started to move towards me and I ran to the other side of the circle. Looking back the man had thrown the spear and I watched as it hit the ground right in front of me. He took up another spear and charged me at once. I leapt and hurdled myself from the man's grasp. Rounding to my feet I was still near the man and grabbed the end of his spear.

He pulled. I was no match for his strength. The man took one of his hands away from the spear to try to get a hold of me. I knew I needed a weapon. I bolted and ran for an axe.

I slid on the uneven ground as I wrapped my fingers around the handle. I steadied myself and the man came at me with his spear. He stabbed just as I ducked, seizing this moment to hack my opponent's legs. It struck and he fell to the ground.

Quickly I approached the man as he tried to recover. Re-gripping the axe I was above the man and stepped on his wounded leg to keep him down. I raised the axe with two hands and brought it down forcefully upon his head, casting my body at him in the process.

As I fell the blade of the axe struck the mask and split the face in two. The strength of the wood held tight against my blade. Tumbling onto my back I saw the mask stuck to the blade of the axe. Looking at the man, I saw him for who he really was.

There was a gash across his face, from the mask, but besides that he was covered in scars. Everywhere his body was worn. He had many missing teeth and his remaining teeth were jagged like the mask he had been wearing. His skin was dirtied. He was a warrior.

The man yelled in rage and picked up the nearest weapon, the staff.

The man rallied to his feet and swung. I tried to dodge, but my hands hit the staff. The force of the hit made me stumble and the man hit me in the stomach with the spear. Without weapons now, we were hand-to-hand. The man grabbed my hair and started to punch me in the stomach. I started to swing wildly, my hands wrapped tightly into fists, and missed. The man did the same and brought a powerful punch right into my face.

The force of this attack sent me into the air, landing me on my back. Opening my eyes the next thing I saw was the man above me then his fist. His last blow I will never remember feeling and I blacked out.

My eyes opened erratically and I immediately sat up to my knees. While I was kneeling I turned my head to the side and saw what appeared to be a swarm of hummingbirds headed towards me. Their eyes were glowing. I blacked out and fell to my side.

When I opened my eyes once again it felt like I had no control of my body. The sounds around me were faint, but I was certain there were noises. I started to look around and saw people wearing frightened expressions. The man that was attacking me was now distancing himself from my body. Again, my body stood up and suddenly a swarm of hummingbirds encircled me. I had no control of myself. My back arched and my hands rose upwards from my sides. The hummingbirds' eyes began to glow with more intensity. Swarming faster, they flew around my arms. Face to face with the birds, I started to levitate.

Rising above the arena I saw the tribesmen below. As I stared down my vision started to get bright and there was a sudden flash. I began to see more clearly and everything around me was gleaming. Just as quick as it had come it vanished and I saw everything as usual.

I was back on my knees, hunched on the ground, and saw the slash wound that had been across my chest had healed itself. There was another flash of light. Opening my eyes I was now upon the man. I was attacking him with my body. Another flash and the man was covered in blood.

Flash.

I stood to the side of the man's fallen body.

Flash.

I remember looking at my hands and began to feel them. At last I could feel my body. I was bloodied from fighting the man, but no longer wounded. I searched for the hummingbirds and saw that they were gone. I looked around me and my tribe was silent.

Again, I looked to the man's body and knelt beside him. Knowing he was dead I put my hand on his chest. Clasping my palm over his severe wound I spoke.

"Thank you my brother, your death will not be forgotten."

I stood up and the tribe flooded onto me. Quickly they were all around me and knelt to the ground, chanting. I could not figure out what they were saying at the time, even though I knew Skitchan, they were speaking too quickly for me to translate. From what I did hear however, I heard voices of thanks.

As my tribesmen knelt before me I felt that the spirits were within me. A certainty inside told me what they wanted. They were commanding me to do things.

I looked back to my people and saw Armija. He was standing and ordering his men to leave on horseback. He then walked to me and knelt down.

"We are yours to command, Chosen One."

I put my hand on Armija's shoulder and signaled him to get up. I told Armija, "I want this soldier," I pointed to the body, "to have the highest ranking burial ceremony."

Armija nodded. "As you wish."

I walked beside Armija as he began to leave, as an equal, and in a hushed voice I shared something with him. "The spirits are in me Armija, I feel them. They are telling me what I need to know and what I need to do now."

Armija nodded and said, "we will do what is needed."

I looked at my people kneeling before me and I asked them to stand. As they began to rise I was overcome by a great feeling from within. I sensed that danger was approaching, quickly. I spoke to our people.

"This is our time, tribesmen. Our time to show the intruders, the men who want to take our land, who they will be dealing with! We must protect our land at any cost!

"Yes, I have seen things. Our ancestors gave me visions of now and the future. We must stand up and fight this battle or else we will lose everything. If we fail, our children will be no more. The fate of our tribe depends on how we act now."

I looked at Armija and asked, "Armija, did we receive anymore men? Soldiers from the outside?"

"Yes," he bowed his head. "They are on their way. I just sent some of our men to tell Bodaway and Marine-Oni that you are confirmed to be the Chosen One."

I nodded and just as I was about to address the tribe again I heard gunfire coming from the village. In great haste I walked to the edge of the mountain. More shooting followed. I knew the danger was upon us.

Armija walked up to my side and looked for the source of the noise. As we looked out a tribal soldier hiked up the mountain towards us on his horse. He was wounded, I could tell from the blood running down his side. Armija approached his man and saw that he had been shot. He lowered him off the horse and the man gasped.

Armija asked, "what happened?"

Between breaths the man spoke. "They are here."

"Did Bodaway and our men bring our village people to the Chataw?"

The man nodded and said in a weaken state, "yes."

I looked up from this scene and caught eyes with the shaman. I signaled for her to come to our side. As she approached I asked her, "can this man be treated?"

She examined him and said gravely, "yes however, after this he will no longer receive more."

"Very well, quickly then," I ordered, "treat him."

Armija called for another soldier and together they took the wounded man to the shaman's tent.

I looked at Armija and said, "we must go to the village and help the other soldiers. Bodaway and Marine-Oni."

He agreed. "Shall I gather our men?"

"Armija, your men, our warriors, need to protect our land. We must quickly gather them and head to the village. We must prepare them for what I believe will be a great battle."

As Armija walked off to prepare his men I paced back and forth on the edge of the mountain. I was worried about my people down at the village. As I strategized I watched as Armija's warriors loaded their horses then donned paint on their bodies. All the soldiers began to chant, it was a battle song, and it spoke of The Skitcha and the spirits.

I walked up to Armija. "Are they ready?"

Armija nodded. I turned my head towards the group of soldiers.

I spoke to them. "My brothers! I know some of you will not return to this world tonight, you know your path in your lives. We shall fight until the bitter end to save this," I paused and opened my arms out to our land. "This is what our ancestors fought for and this is what we need to protect. We will do this tonight!"

The soldiers roared in agreement.

"Now warriors, grab your weapons! We are going to help our brothers down there," I pointed to our village. "Mount your horses my brothers, let the spirit of our ancestors protect us!"

They cried for battle again and did as I ordered. A soldier brought a horse to my side as well. It was Skip and he looked stronger than ever. I loaded myself atop of him and thanked the soldier.

The soldier yelled in return, "to the Chosen One, Jacob!"

The tribesmen continued to chant and I patted Skip as I always did. It felt like so long since I had seen him. Prepared as I would ever be, with my people beside me, I cried for battle.

"Let us ride my brothers!"

It was very late by the time we neared the village, but first we stopped at the Chataw. As we approached I saw some of the villagers going into the cave through the large opening. Soldiers stood beside the mouth of the cave guiding the people in. I called to them as we road up.

"Are all of our people in there?"

"Yes, Chosen One, all that are living. Some have died near the gate of our village." The Soldier bowed his head as he spoke.

I nodded with sadness. "Thank you brother. Please command your men to guard the Chataw. The lives of our people are at stake. Do not let anyone one in."

"As you wish, Chosen One."

Armija came up to me next. "We need to protect you, Chosen One."

I smiled to Armija, probably my last smile of the night.

"You can still call me Jacob, my brother."

Armija nodded and said, "we must protect you. That is what the spirits told us long ago."

"I know Armija, I sense that also. Please though, if I feel the need to fight with my brothers do not stop me."

Out of respect Armija nodded.

I said to him, "take the lead Armija, and leave some of your men with me."

"As you wish, Jacob."

We made our way into the village and when we arrived we found Bodaway and Marine-Oni. Armija signaled them to come to us. When they reached us Bodaway moved his horse towards me.

"Hello Chosen One," he gave me a proud smile.

"Please call me Jacob, Bodaway."

He nodded and looked in the direction of the gate.

"How is it near the gate, Bodaway?" I asked.

He shook his head and said, "they are still holding it up, however the fighting has become more intense. Marine-Oni has sent some of her followers to help the wounded, but some cannot be treated anymore."

I looked towards the gate.
Bodaway said, "I expect them to come through the gate soon, Jacob. If the shamans are killed there will be no one to treat our people."

I did not respond immediately and deepened my thoughts. More gunshots rose above our land.

I quickly signaled to Armija. "Have your soldiers form a wall over here," I pointed at the trail leading towards the gate. "If these intruders are indeed the Hand of Transcendence, which I expect them to be, they will fight hard. Have any lone solider help you. Tonight we all act as one force."

Armija acknowledged the order and prepared his men for the plan of attack. I watched as they dismounted their horses and continued on foot.

I said to Bodaway, "have your men do the same."

Bodaway yelled to his soldiers to dismount and I too unloaded myself from Skip.

I whispered to a nearby soldier, "please make sure my horse is safe, Brother."

The soldier nodded and I left Skip in his care.

"I must put the sacred markings on you, Jacob." Bodaway walked towards me with a pouch. "I am the highest rank in our tribe and it would be an honor to do so."

I nodded and Bodaway proceeded. As he marked me with our symbol he spoke.

"Jacob, there is a reason why we need to protect you. The Skitcha, your grandfather, had unlimited spiritual power. This too is in your blood and we believe the same limits of his power have been passed to you. I know your grandfather sacrificed himself, not because he was going to die and not because he couldn't be revived. The Skitcha could still be with us Jacob, but he chose to die. He did this, I believe, because of a sign he received. We need to protect you because you hold the key to the knowledge of the powers."

I nodded and said, "I understand, Bodaway."

I called Marine-Oni.

"Marine-Oni, do you have more shamans?" She nodded, tilting her head to her tent where I saw her followers preparing. "I want you to get them now. I need you Marine-Oni, to protect me if anything happens."

She acknowledged me and went to her tent to ready the shamans.

Bodaway urged the soldiers to hurry up and get ready.

Within moments there was a loud bang and in the distance I watched as light ricocheted from an explosion. It was the gate. Men flew into the air as a result of the blast and landed on the ground dead. Thick clouds of smoke fumed the area. From the murk I saw a large group of men emerge. They were walking straight towards our village. Even from afar, I saw that these men had no trace of fear in them.

Quickly they approached and soon our front line of defense was face-to-face with them. I was surprised when one of the men, one of the enemies, came forwards speaking in Skitchan.

"Please! Please, do not attack! We would like to talk!"

I looked at Bodaway and he said, "that is one of the traitors, Jacob. He may be responsible for what is to come. He may have led the Hand of Transcendence straight to us.

I looked at the traitor, a tribesman, and said to Bodaway, "go see what he wants and speak for our tribe."

Bodaway nodded and moved in front of the soldiers. Even as I paced, before the warriors, I overheard some of what was being said.

Bodaway spoke first.

"I am Bodaway, why do you come to set foot on our land? Why do you cause harm to our village?"

The traitor looked over his shoulder and another man emerged behind him. This second man signaled for the traitor to keep talking.

"We are here for your land. We will give you gold for exchange." The traitor threw the bag of gold to Bodaway.

Bodaway caught the bag and looked inside. He turned to me and I signaled for him to return the bag. Bodaway tossed it in the man's face. We were ready to fight.

"Your gold means nothing to us. You will never take this land!"

The traitor turned and walked to the man behind him. From my vantage point I could not see what he looked like.

The man walked back to Bodaway and said, "I urge you Bodaway, to take the gold. Please, take it. If you do not we will take over and destroy this village with great force."

Bodaway paused and began to speak out loud in English.

"Death will consume you, traitor!"

The man's eyes widened and he swiftly backed away. The second man came forward from the shadows. He stood before the group and shouted.

"Where is this Chosen One you all speak of?!"

It was silent.

Bodaway did not respond. The man took his gun out and pointed it at Bodaway. Bodaway stood with confidence. He was not afraid.

The man clicked the trigger back on the gun and stepped forward saying, "you better come out or I will kill him!"

I looked at Armija and signed to him that I was going to move forward. I whispered, "be ready on my signal, Armija." He nodded and I moved forward to confront the man.

In clear sight, in front of my soldiers, Bodaway still held at gunpoint, I spoke to the enemy in English.
"I am the one of which you speak. Who are you?"

The man winced at me. "My name is Ryland." He then smiled a taunting grin. It was as if he had expected nearly anyone else besides me to step forward. Ryland turned to his group and said to another man, "is he the one you've been seeing around town?"

The man did not answer immediately. Taking his time I watched him step forward from the group. I knew who he was immediately. It was my boyhood friend, Matt. Now in plain sight, he revealed who he truly was. I was shocked.

He grunted to Ryland. "Yes, it is him. That is Jacob."

Ryland turned to face me and said, "we know who you are, Jacob."

I looked at him closer.

Ryland continued, "we have your mother, Jacob, and your woman."

I knew deep inside Ann was ok, but I could not sense my mother. I stood my ground and stared at him with no expression.

Ryland began to say, "if you don't surrender they will be killed."

I looked down and brushed the painted markings on my face. This was Armija's signal. Holding Ryland's gaze I said, "you may know who I am, however, you are now on sacred ground. I can sense your fate."

Ryland laughed. "This spiritual stuff is nonsense. It's ridiculous. We will not stop until we have this land, Jacob."

I grinned and pointed to the traitor. Though I said nothing, everyone felt that this was a threat.

Matt spoke over the tension, "you all will not live to see the end of tonight."

Just then he pulled a gun from his side and without aiming shot straight at me. I quickly dodged the gunfire and pulled an axe from my keep. I threw it at my enemies, but it passed Ryland as he dogged. It collided with one of his men, standing behind him, it sliced through his body and he collapsed.

Suddenly the Hand of Transcendence charged at us. They began to shoot their guns at my men. Some fell from their horses, wounded or dead, while the remaining lunged at the shooters. They were tackled to the ground.

Guns shot wildly and I dodged another bullet. Armija came to my side and said, "stay here Jacob, we will protect you."

Through the gunfire I watched as my men, my brethren warriors, ran to my side. I need not give orders to the tribesmen tonight. They knew to protect me for it meant the survival of our people. They followed me, catching bullets in their sides, as I made my way to Bodaway.

When we crossed the path to the other side of the village I could see the fight had spread. The center of our village was under attack. Through the darkness I saw the unmistakable sparkle of dynamite. The enemy threw the bomb at my soldiers. It exploded as it landed, mining an enormous crater in the middle of our village.

Time was passing us. I quickly ran to Bodaway.

"Bodaway, we need to order some of the men back. We need to use our arrows to take down the men with the dynamite."

Bodaway acknowledged as I looked at one of our soldiers. I spoke to the man, "I want you to withdraw some of wounded men from battle. Pull them to the sides of the war, away from danger, so the shamans can revive them."

The soldier nodded and ran down to the men.

Bodaway had returned to the fight. I watched as he effortlessly threw a man clear across the path. Gunshots had no effect on him as he continued in fight. The men here tonight were bearing witness to the spiritual powers of The Skitcha, the powers within Bodaway.
Continuing to fight Bodaway also pulled some of our brothers from the war, sending them to me. When they stood before me I saw that many had become very weak and were wounded. Blood and lead oozed from the tribesmen.

Bodaway headed towards me and said, "I need to rest for a moment, Jacob. To heal."

I nodded and looked at the soldiers. "I need you all to take your bows and arrows."

The unwounded men acknowledged and went into a tent that stored the weapons. When they emerged they all bore quivers on their backs and clasped the bows tightly.

I pointed at a few men and said, "all of you, go up that hill. Shoot the intruders with dynamite. That is the source of the explosions." They all nodded. "Go! Go now!"

Half of the men sprinted up the hill and I directed the remaining half to do the same, but from a different vantage point. After they ran I saw that the shamans were leaving their tent. They ran towards me, Marine-Oni led the way.

I said to her, "we need to heal our men. Can we do that?"

She closed her eyes and said, "Yes, we can. However, there are a few men that cannot come back."

"Do you need the men here?" I asked, somberly. "Or do you have to touch them to heal them?"

Marine-Oni paused and said, "I have never tried to heal from a distance." She looked out to the battle. "I will try. We are very close to Mount Umunhum."

I touched Marine-Oni on the shoulder and said, "I know you can Marine-Oni, I believe in you."

The battle had grown intense. The violence was densely concentrated in our village and not scattered. I watched from the safety of the hill, where no one could see us between our tents, and watched my people. More and more soldiers were being pulled from the battle wounded. Only some of them were our men. Still, the violence raged on and I knew something needed to shift in our favor.

Arrows began to rain down upon the scene. It was the tribesmen I had given the order to. My brothers shot their arrows into the darkness. As they fell they were swallowed by the night.

I turned around and saw Bodaway healing himself. He looked as though he was getting better.

"Bodaway, I need you to finish them off. Your men have been fighting well. I can see only a handful of the Hand of Transcendence now, but they are still fighting with their guns. These weapons are cruel to us, Bodaway. They take down our brothers quickly." I paused, watching as he regained his strength. "Do what you can, Bodaway. I know you can still be revived afterwards."

Bodaway nodded, "I am going to help our wounded brothers first. I will rescue the fallen and bring them to Marine-Oni."

I turned to our shaman. Marine-Oni had her head down and her eyes were closed. She was trying to heal the soldiers from the hill.

Bodaway returned to the battle and Marine-Oni was in a state of trance.

For a moment I was alone. I headed to the weapon tent and searched inside. I picked up a bow and quiver, filled with arrows, and took two axes. Lastly, I seized a knife and tucked it into a small pocket on the side of my pants. Prepared for battle, I left the tent.

Before anyone could see me I hid behind a large rock close to the tent, but out of sight from my tribesmen. I was going to rescue my brothers. I waited for the right moment then ran into battle, straight towards a group of my men.

Within an instant I was beside them. "Are you ok, Brother?" I asked a Skitcha soldier who was crumpled on the ground.

The soldier nodded.

I said, "come on, let's get our men back to the hill." Before we could move I heard a man's voice speaking in English. It came from the direction of the heat of the fight.

"He's over there!"

Gunfire rang through the night and I could feel bullets soar by us. Whistles and wind. We were under attack.

The soldier beside me stood up. "I will protect you, Chosen One."

Standing he could see the enemy. The soldier drew his bow and aimed his arrow, but before he could release he was struck by a bullet. The man fell before me.

I quickly got up and started to run from the scene. The enemy was approaching quickly.

Running, I slid behind an enemy wagon. Out of sight I could hear the men following closely. With my back against the wagon I pulled two arrows from my quiver. Holding one between my teeth I steadied the other in my bow. Gunfire continued and I felt the bullets pepper the wagon.

I took a deep breath and suddenly everything felt slow. The sounds of the battle became distorted. I stood up and started to run to the outskirts of the war. Running I twisted towards my enemy, aimed my bow, and release it on one man. The force of the arrow's impact sent him flying backwards. Another man took his place in the chase. His gun lolloped as he trotted. Haphazardly he fired round after round.

Bullets landed at my feet as I evaded the man. I sprinted forward towards a fallen tree. As I ran closer I recognized that this was our campfire and before me lay the logs tribesmen would sit on. Traveling with such speed I had only a moment before I would surely collide with the log.

Within an instant I took the arrow that I had been holding in my teeth and steadied it in my bow. Next I jumped over the fallen log, which would otherwise block my path. As I leapt, falling in midair, I turned and aimed. Swiftly I shot the man in mid-chase.

I landed on my back. My feet had caught on the log, but I was ready. Leaping back to my feet I drew one of my axes. Approaching the man however, there was no need. The arrow flew true and now lay lodged in his chest.

Suddenly I heard voices. The Hand of Transcendence was nearing. I recognized Ryland's voice.

The leader yelled, "Retreat! Let's go! Head to the horses!"

The voices diminished and I quickly ran to a nearby small hill. Once on top I could see the entirety of the battle. It was unlike anything I had ever seen before.

There were men scattered everywhere. Bodies lay strewn across our land. Motionless, many of my people were dead. Of the few men that had survived I knew instantly who were tribesmen. Across the battle Skitcha traditions were performed as my soldiers bit and tore at the enemy. I continued to look for survivors and among them saw Bodaway still standing tall on his feet.

He saw me from atop of the hill and I waved to him. He acknowledged and waved back.

Close by I heard voices speaking in English.

"Let's go, move!"

I looked for the owner of the voice and saw Matt, not too far from me, running to the gate of the village. I chased after him. Leaving the hilltop I heard Bodaway scream my name.

My footsteps thudded hard to the ground and Matt
turned his head. He caught my eye as I charged him.

Matt ran past the destroyed gate and into the valley. In
the expanse of land we were alone except for a few men
on horseback fleeing. Matt was headed to his steed, but
with me at his feet he knew he would never make it. He
diverted, turning left of the trail, and headed into the
woods.

Closing in on him I held him in sight as Matt splashed
across a stream. Halfway across he slipped and landed
face first into the water.

I was upon him, reaching for his sodden body. He
betrayed me. As I approached him Matt flipped onto his
back and held out the palm of his hand.

"Jacob, wait!"

Shocked by my own movements, I stopped and stared at
him. I waited for him to speak. He did not explain, but
asked a question.

"Why are you with them, Jacob?"

I lingered to reply.
"Because, those are my people Matt. Why are you with
those men? The Hand of Transcendence?"

He looked down for a moment, still laying in the stream,
and said, "they helped me, Jacob. They took care of me
and for that I must do what they tell me to do. I am in
their debt."

"Destroying people's land and killing? That is the debt you owe? You are putting more violence into this world, contributing to their cause, this must all be very gratifying for you, Matt!"

"I must do what I am told." He took a deep breath. He looked enraged.

I saw him start to go for his gun. Quickly I loaded an arrow into my bow.

He shot.

I threw myself to the side, dodging the bullets, and shot the arrow. Matt did not have a second chance to counter my attack before my arrow struck his arm. He dropped the gun.

I dropped my bow and shed my quiver, leveraging the fight. I ran to Matt, who was standing on his feet, and tackled him. The force of the strike threw us both to the other side of the stream.
Twisting from my grasp Matt rolled on top of me and pulled a knife. I tried to break from his grip, but was sliced down the side. Ignoring the pain I grabbed his arm and wrist then slammed his hand into a rock. The force of impact caused him to drop the knife. Matt countered, without weapon, and took my throat in his hand. He squeezed, choking me.

Wriggling I could not break his hold, but something caught my eye as his strength overcame me. My arrow stood upright from his arm. I pulled the arrow out, but it caught on his shirt. The arrowhead dug deeper into Matt's arm, tearing his flesh, and he released his grip on my throat.

Screaming in pain Matt kicked me in the chest as he recoiled, rolling me down the bank of the river. I landed on my back, submerged in the shallow water.

Startled and foggy, I threw my head to the surface and gasped for air. Scrambling to my feet I headed to the bank where Matt was holding his bleeding arm. I charged him, seizing his shirt, and slammed him into the slope of the riverbank. Now on top of him we were eye to eye.

"Matt, you have been my friend ever since we were kids. I need you to tell me where the Hand of Transcendence gathers. If you tell me I will let you go, but I do not want to see you here anymore."

His expression, so stern, twisted dramatically to hysterics. He laughed.

"Jacob! Oh, Jacob. We are everywhere! You just don't know it! People in town, the city, this whole state! You just don't see it. There are many of us Jacob, and you're just seeing the start of it."

He laughed again and I shook my head out of disbelief. The deceit. The betrayal was unconceivable. One of my own friends. My oldest friend. I used to think I was one of his people. I could not trust this.

How could he?

He spoke again, "soon enough Jacob, your tribe will be no more!"

How could he?

I looked into his eyes one final time before speaking the last words he would ever hear.

"Good bye, Matt."

I swung my axe with the force granted to me by The Skitcha. It struck firmly, hitting Matt directly in the forehead. I closed my eyes and pulled the axe from his skull then turned around.

Slowly I started to walk away and cross the river, still dragging my bow and quiver in hand.

How could he?

Above the babble of the river, there was a sound. It was familiar, like the fizzle of a dying flame. I turned to Matt's body.

Down the slope of the riverbank rolled a stick of light dynamite.

I sprinted down the rocks in the river. I scrambled hearing the soft thud of the dynamite as it rolled. My feet scratched the sand of the opposing bank. The rolling continued. I stretched my step up the bank when, all of a sudden, I was too late.

The blast knocked me from the riverbed, catapulting my body into the slope of the rock bank. For just a moment there was peace then an unwelcome ringing in my ears followed by pain.

Dazed I shook my head. All I could hear was ringing. My vision was blurred. I blinked and blinked until the scene started to clear. Before me the river was muted in dull, thinning smoke. Through the opaque screen I saw a large hole before me. The blast had destroyed nearly half the hillside. The ground was littered with sand, river stones, and something else. Red rocks were everywhere glistening in silver.

The banks were covered in the fading dust of the smoke and a ways down river I spotted my bow and quiver. As I lifted myself from the banks I heard the branch of a tree break. Danger still lurked and I could feel it within me.

Running downstream I grabbed my bow then sprinted up the riverbank. Atop the slope I looked in the direction of the sound. The moon was bright and illuminated the sparse forest. Suddenly I saw a man. It was Ryland.

I charged at Ryland and the sound of my feet made him turn his eyes in my direction. He saw me and ran.

There were lights up ahead and Ryland fled towards a group of small homes. Before I could follow him into the house however, I heard a horse gallop from behind me. I turned to see a man on horseback heading straight towards me. In his hand he held onto a length of rope curved in a loop. It was a noose.

The rider flew by me and wrapped the noose around my neck. Instantly the rope tightened and swept me off my feet. Dragging behind the horse I dropped my bow.

Flailing behind the rider dirt flew into my eyes as the noose tightened. I could not breath.

"I got 'em!"

Gasping, I heard the rider laughing in triumph. He did not slow.

Skimming the rock surface of the road I began to lose feeling in my face as blood surged through my body. I twisted onto my stomach in an attempt to raise my face above the ground for air. It was no use. On my back rocks kicked up from the horse and cut into my face. I closed my eyes and remembered that I was armed. Holding onto the rope with one hand, to maintain my air supply, I prodded my pockets and withdrew my second axe. Holding firmly to the handle I opened my eyes. With my other hand I fumbled at the knot of the noose, slipping my fingers through the narrow space between my neck and the rope. In one movement I raised my axe, swung at the rope, and was set free.

The rider continued galloping as I was thrown behind him, not noticing what had happened, and rode to Ryland.

Tumbling I steadied myself and removed the rope from my neck. Fleeing for cover I returned to my element, darkness. This is where I had the upper hand on my enemy.

Thank you Skitcha, for allowing me to see in the night.

I started to run back to where I had been caught, to locate my bow and quiver. I was nearly there when gunfire erupted behind me. The rider had realized that I had cut myself loose. Frantically I searched the ground. Then, there it was. My bow.

A few feet from me and I could hear the galloping of the rider grow louder. I knew the horseman was drawing nearer. Sprinting I grabbed my bow and loaded an arrow. I threw myself onto my back, the horse reared in surprise, now atop of me. I raised my bow and released.

The arrow shot the man in the arm while he simultaneously fired his gun at me. A bullet grazed my shoulder as I threw myself to my feet and continued to run. The rider had poor aim while he shot at me, a deadly target, and unlucky for him my next arrow hit its mark. The rider slumped when I drove an arrow directly into his chest.

For a split second I allowed myself a deep breath before the chase continued.

Ryland called to another two men on horseback. They began to charge as I headed into the thick forest.

Once inside, still ahead of the riders, I immediately headed for a tree. It did not take long to find one sturdy enough to climb. I slung my bow across my back and heard the horsemen riding in close. I climbed and soon became invisible to them. Stalking my enemy from above I lay quiet with my bow at the ready, loaded with an arrow.

"Where the heck is he?" Called one rider to the other.

"Come out! We got you out numbered!" Replied the second.

They continued to search the forest on horseback. Slowly inching along the forest floor, they searched for me.

I did not have a plan. I did not know what to do, except believe. I closed my eyes and felt the spirits flood me. They began to guide me and gave me strength.

I let my eyes fly open just as I released my first arrow. It hit one of the riders. As it did I slung the bow across my back, alongside the quiver, and leapt from the tree. I now had my axe at the ready.

I landed to the side of the struck man and pulled him down to the ground. It took only one quick slice to the chest for the man to become overwhelmed by blood as it rained across the forest floor.

Not stopping my hunt, I saw the other man right before me. He was still and had his back to me. Swiftly I walked around the horse and saw the man in the moonlight. There was an arrow in his head.

I relaxed my grip on the axe and allowed myself another deep breath. In that moment I hoped for either Bodaway or Armija or even a tribesmen to show themselves however, no one did.

I looked in the distance of the village and the night was still. Turning my head in the opposite direction I saw Ryland and his men near the house. I stood up and moved quickly away from the slain men and edged my way around Ryland's troops. My plan was to circle the land in front of the house.

As I moved I stayed well behind the tree line where I could keep a close eye on Ryland. He was very near now. Quietly I stalked him. Keeping alongside him in the shadows I circled his troops, hiding behind rocks and trees until I was just a foot from him.

Taking cover behind a boulder Ryland could not see me. I savored this moment knowing that my next move would be of revenge for my fallen tribesmen and my father.

Again, I looked in the direction of the village. I could see Ryland's men galloping back to battle. I had a feeling they were searching for my wounded men, to finish off my tribe. I did not worry though as I sensed within me that the Skitcha people would be ok.

This was my chance to put an end to this.

I took another deep breath and loaded my bow. I repositioned myself on the boulder and peeked over the edge of the stone. There were still a few more men in sight and Ryland was directing them. I let him finish and then watched the men leave the house.

Pulling my bow tight I rounded the rock and walked towards Ryland. Steadying the arrow directly at his head I spoke to him, his back turned to me.

"Do not move a muscle or I will shoot this arrow in you."

Ryland put his hands up and turned to face me. He was smiling.

"Go, Jacob. Go ahead and kill me. My death will not end this war. The others will come and replace me. They will continue to finish you and your tribe off."

He then pointed to the direction of Mount Umunhum and said, "that mountain and the area around it is going to be ours, Jacob. There will be nothing that can stop us from doing that."

I pulled the bow tighter.

"We know what's in that mountain, Jacob." Ryland continued. "Besides, your whole stupid spirit thing," he mocked, "we know there are rocks that glimmer inside the mountain. Special rocks, Jacob. Valuable elements."

He paused again and his eyes glistened.

"Oh, I know." He smiled eerily.

My face became stone as fury raged within me.

With another smirk, Ryland whistled.

Windows opened from the houses. Torches were lit. Men appeared with rifles and pistols. All were aimed at me.

Ryland grinned, elated by his surprise attack. "Drop your weapon, Jacob." He lowered his hands.

I wanted to shoot him then and there, in front of his people, but something within me told me now was not the time. I dropped my bow and quiver.

Ryland told me to turn around. Obediently, I did. He told me to raise my hands, revealing the axe, and he seized it from me. He walked around me and we looked at each other, face to face. With all of his men around us, guns pointed, Ryland took this moment to show a twisted smile revealing few teeth. His entire look was smug.

And then, I listened to The Skitcha Spirit.

I lunged for his neck with my teeth. He barely had time to react as I tore the flesh from him. I bit harder, deepening the wound, and with my teeth I found a vein. I pulled. Blood cascaded between us.

I grabbed his body and used him as a barrier against the armed men. Wrapping my arm around his neck I reached into my pant pocket and withdrew the knife I had kept hidden throughout the night. Without hesitation I led the knife into Ryland's stomach. I pushed deeper and deeper until I could push no more. For good measure, I left it in. He was dead.

Ryland fell slowly down my body and landed on his back in the dirt.

Surging with energy I was overcome. My breathing intensified and my vision cleared. I heard my ancestors talking through the air and I looked up at the armed men. They could hear it also.

Suddenly the men started to shoot. I was hit repeatedly with bullets. The pain was numbing. I felt every bullet enter and stick within my body. I fell to my knees.

The spirits, my ancestors, were chanting. With every beat of my heart the pumping grew louder and faster. And then, I was taken away just as I had been when I encountered the hummingbirds.

Flash.

My vision went dark.

Flash.

I opened my eyes as wide as I could to find that I was holding my hands before me, over my wounds. The bullets were being pulled from my body. The wounds were healing.

I blanked out.

When I opened my eyes. I was standing and saw Ryland's men before me. There were fewer this time. I suspect some had run away, probably from the flash. Here I was again, now, breathing before them.

The men mercilessly raised their weapons and fired another round at me.

Instantly hit, I fell to the ground.

This time there was no flash, only the dampening of sound around me. I knew the Hand of Transcendence was headed to the village. I could feel the bullets entering me, but all I could do was lay there and look at the stars.

Thank you Skitcha, for bringing me to my people. Let

them be protected tonight and for time to come. Skitcha, thank you.

Eventually, although I could not hear it, the shooting stopped. My eyes were flickering as the shapes of men leaned over my body.

Peacefully, everything faded to black one last time.

About The Author

An American Storyteller
Born in and native to San Jose, California, Julian was
raised in a town called "Willow Glen." His art of
storytelling began during his childhood through the
visual arts. The first story he made was a picture
stylebook called The Rabbit that Knew Kung-Fu.

Julian focused his college studies on art, history,
philosophy, art history, and design. Heavily experienced
in the arts, his style focuses mostly on surrealism.

Later, Julian had a major interest in movies, especially
in the thriller/horror genre. As a kid (as early as five) he
would watch horror movies with his older cousins. After
being engrossed with movies Julian founded Silent Eye
Productions. He was inspired and completed an
independent film called Hicks Road. After the movie was
privately released through various film festivals it
received rave reviews. However, his decision not to show

his film to the public has been a mystery. When his beloved wife, Roxanne, came into his life she realized that Julian had something special with his movie and said to him "you should make a book about this; tell the whole story you've imagined" and thus gave birth to the beginning of this story—Hicks Road: Jacob's Story. That was his spark, the key that opened him to a world of storytelling on a greater scale.

The book is based on the actual mountain called Mount Umunhum, which has a road called "Hicks Road." Many locals from generation to generation have heard stories about this road and the urban legends that involve it. When he was a kid Julian himself experienced this legend firsthand. Until this day teens and enthusiasts drive to the road during the night to see it for themselves...

When he isn't writing Julian is a lover of wine, art, food, gardening, the outdoors, socializing, watching movies, and reading (of course with some wine). You can follow him at the button underneath his profile picture and you can also go to his production company's website at http://www.silenteyeproductions.com for social media and updated news, stories, and historical information.

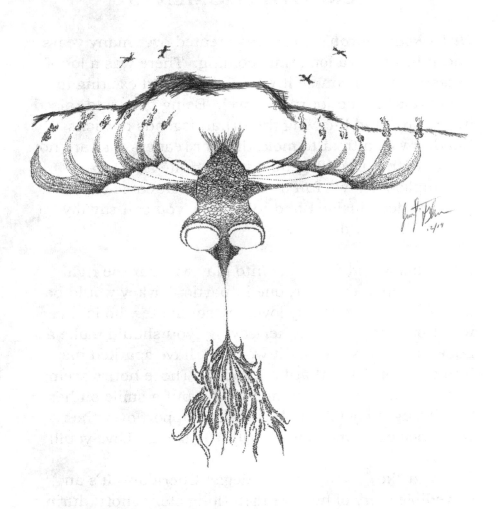

ACKNOWLEDGMENTS

Hicks Road: Jacob's Story was created over many years and it has been a long time coming. There was a lot of pressure but of course it was very fun and exciting to make this "found journal" novel. Being born and raised in the area and knowing the urban legends of Hicks Road, it was a treat to mold that for readers that are not aware of the urban legends; it was quite a feat to accomplish but yet fun seeing all of that come together.
   I knew deep inside I had to do this, you can say my goal in life—my destiny.

All of this would not come into play without the right "keys" to open the door, one in particular key would be the key to my heart, my love, my soulmate who is my wife Roxanne. Without her saying "you should make a book about this" I think it wouldn't have sparked me into the storyteller that I am today. Those hours seeing her read my manuscript and how it put a smile on her face brought joy to me. Her major support over the years helped tremendously with the book. Love you!!!

The next "key" is my editor, Megan Sheridan. It's an incredible story of how we met—long story short, during interviews for an editor Megan was the last person I met. I told her the story and she looked up and with so much excitement she said "I used to live around the area myself and I know about the urban legend"! I knew right off the bat she was the one to take up this challenge of editing the manuscript. To see someone very passionate with this story other than me is an incredible feeling. I would not be able to put out this book without her and her editing skills. I give you many thanks Megan!!!

Last but not least the final "key", my friends, family and supporters be it social media/ contacts over the years I thank you all from the bottom of my heart. The wait is over, the secrecy you have all endured over the years is now over. Or is it...

Julian P. Flores – 2017

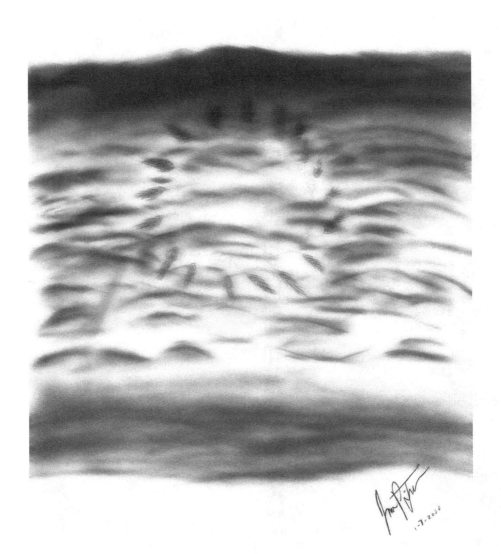

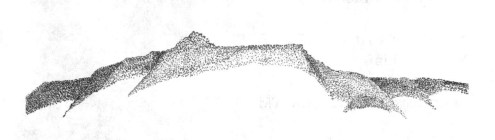

Hicks Road: Jacob's Story

by Julian P. Flores

editor/ co-writer
MM Sheridan

Silent Eye Productions TM

ISBN-13: 978-0-9981351-2-0

SILENT EYE PRODUCTIONS™